DEVIL
SHARKS

Also by Chris Jameson

SHARK ISLAND

DEVIL
SHARKS

CHRIS JAMESON

St. Martin's Paperbacks

This is a work of fiction. All of the characters, organizations, and events portrayed in this novel are either products of the author's imagination or are used fictitiously.

DEVIL SHARKS

Copyright © 2018 by Daring Greatly Corporation.

For information address St. Martin's Press, 175 Fifth Avenue, New York, NY 10010.

ISBN: 978-1-250-13956-6

Our books may be purchased in bulk for promotional, educational, or business use. Please contact your local bookseller or the Macmillan Corporate and Premium Sales Department at 1-800-221-7945, ext. 5442, or by e-mail at MacmillanSpecialMarkets@macmillan.com.

Printed in the United States of America

St. Martin's Paperbacks edition / July 2018

St. Martin's Paperbacks are published by St. Martin's Press, 175 Fifth Avenue, New York, NY 10010.

10 9 8 7 6 5 4 3 2 1

CHAPTER 1

Efrim thought if he kept very still, Machii might not kill him. He lay belowdecks, wrists bound behind him and ankles tugged together with the same zebra-stripe duct tape he had over his mouth. The duct tape might kill him, even if Machii and his guys decided not to. Dried blood plugged one nostril, so Efrin could only breathe through the other—the left—in a desperate, steady wheeze.

His head pounded, still ringing from the fists and boots and the gun butt that had struck his skull. Blood had leaked from his right ear, his lips were split, and his tongue had found three broken teeth. From the neck down, he knew he was worse off. Left forearm broken. No telling how many ribs. His balls felt like they'd been kicked all the way up into his stomach.

But you're alive, he thought, forcing his heart to slow, forcing his breathing to steady. That wheezing sound from his one open nostril kept him alive. A cloth bag, someone's stinking laundry bag, had been yanked over his head, and he knew if he squirmed and twisted and dragged his head on the floor of the wheelhouse he might get it off, but what would that earn him? A few seconds' glimpse of the interior of the wheelhouse and then more broken ribs, maybe another boot to his broken nose that would close his other nostril, ending his life.

You're alive.

Forcing himself to breathe, to be quiet and still, Efrim tried to think. How long had they been out on the boat? How far might they be from the Big Island now? Where the hell were they taking him? He'd been unconscious for a bit—too many knocks on the skull—but couldn't be sure exactly how long. Too many questions . . . and all of them just a distraction from the big one, the only one that mattered. Yes, he was still alive. But why? Why the hell hadn't they just cut his throat or put a bullet in his brain?

And what about Isko? Efrim had heard them beating on his friends, heard Isko cry out, but nothing after that. Guilt weighed on him. The others had been greedy little shits, just like Efrim himself. They'd all known what they were getting into. But Isko had only gotten involved because he and Efrim had been friends forever, and now that loyalty had led him here.

The sway of the boat and the hum of its engine as they cut across the water helped to calm him, let him think. Did he have something Machii wanted, some bit of information? Or maybe . . . shit, maybe they'd admired his work. Maybe they'd take him into their operation, make him earn back the money he'd cost them. Shit, was that even possible?

He tasted copper. Blood. Wanted to spit it out, but the zebra duct tape blocked his mouth so he had to swallow, and only then did he realize how much harder it had become to breathe. How much thinner the wheeze coming from his one open nostril sounded. His chest began to hurt and he tried to quicken and deepen each breath, but panic ignited in his brain. Blood or mucus or some combination had started pooling, closing off his last breathing passage, and blackness crept in at the edges of his mind.

Efrim shoved his tongue out. Up and down, working the edges of the zebra duct tape. Strongest muscle in the body, they said, and he jammed it against the tape, wheezing, panicking.

One of Machii's men cursed in Tagalog and kicked him in the side. Cracked ribs broke and he felt something stabbing inside him, but then his tongue poked out the top of his mouth, forcing the duct tape away from his upper lip, and he dragged in a breath of sweet Pacific Ocean air that had been filtered through a dirty laundry bag. Pain singing in his broken ribs, Efrim sighed and let his body relax and he said nothing, just kept working at the zebra duct tape to guarantee he'd continue to breathe.

He'd barely noticed that the boat had slowed. Now as he gratefully inhaled, he felt the floor rocking harder beneath him and listened to the engine and realized the skipper had throttled down, nearly to a stop. His pulse quickened and his thoughts spun. What were the magic words, here? What could he say to convince Machii?

Hands grabbed his ankles, dragged him across the wheelhouse floor. He'd barely managed the first syllable of his pleading when those hands hauled him over the threshold of the hatch and out onto the deck. His ribs bumped up over the four-inch threshold and he screamed as things tore inside him.

"Shut him up," a voice said, clipped words, an audible snarl.

Machii.

"Please . . . ," he groaned. Did he dare say the man's name, reveal he knew exactly who'd taken him, and why? Maybe he'd better not. But as he curled into a fetal ball, trying to make himself the smallest target, hoping to protect the shattered ribs that were daggers now inside him, he couldn't stop the words from coming. "Machii, please, I can help."

The zebra duct tape had come almost completely free of his lips.

Someone crouched beside him, he heard the shuffle of their shoes and a grunt, and then a strong hand clamped over his face as if to shush him.

"Don't talk," someone said quietly. "Better for you."

He wanted to ask about Isko but kept his mouth shut.

Other hands took hold of him, hauled him up from the deck, forced him to stand. He grunted quietly, hissed between his teeth, leaned on the unbroken leg. Efrim wanted to whisper further pleas, but if silence would be better for him then he would do his best. He stood on one foot on the deck, letting the hands clutching at his bloodied clothing hold him in place. The boat swayed, the engine idled, and he listened to men grunt and murmur to one another as something was dumped overboard. Half a dozen somethings, hitting the water with heavy splashes, and tears spilled from his eyes, both because he knew those heavy somethings had been his friends and because he was not among them.

Machii. He wanted to speak up again, to make his case, to ask what the hell was going on.

When strong hands clutched his head, he wanted to cry out, but still he bit his tongue. Then he felt warm breath, even through the fabric of the laundry bag, and Machii spoke to him.

"You wonder why you're still in the land of the living."

Efrim would have nodded, but Machii held his head firmly.

"I'll tell you. I liked you, Ef. I knew you were dumb as a rock, but I liked you. What I did not understand was precisely how dumb you really were. You made me regret liking you. You hurt my feelings, Ef."

"Machii—"

"Do it."

For half a second, Efrim didn't know what Machii wanted him to do. But Machii hadn't been talking to him. Hands lifted him. Broken bones ground together, but he struggled anyway as they raised him off the deck. Fear washed over him. He thrashed, screaming for them to stop, shouting for Machii as if the man were his friend instead of a brutal, merciless, soulless killer. Even then, it still hadn't clicked for Efrim . . . not until he felt himself hoisted, felt the strength of the men carrying him as they cocked their arms.

They hurled him into nothing. Efrim screamed inside the dirty laundry bag, his nostrils still clogged with his blood. The bag flew off as he fell and he had a glimpse of the boat's hull and then he hit the water, plunging deep, the shock of it driving all the air from his lungs in one drowning bellow. He snapped his mouth shut, eyes bulging, adjusting, more light underwater than there had been inside that bag. If only he'd taken a breath and held it, he might have a moment.

Dumb. Efrim knew the level of his own stupidity. It had put him here. Yet the shock of the water snapped his thoughts into some order of clarity and he twisted around, chest already burning for air, and spotted the broken and bloody corpses of his friends surrounding him.

One of those corpses opened its eyes.

Isko. Not dead after all. The water had shocked him backed to consciousness, and now as Efrim stared in astonishment Isko glanced about underwater, then turned and started to swim past the bodies of their dead friends.

Go, brother. Go! Efrim thought.

Pain screaming in his broken limbs, he kicked toward the surface, knowing Machii would still kill him but thinking he could buy Isko a moment or two and wanting only, in that moment, not to drown. Anything but that. Anything but the suffocating pressure that crushed his chest and made his brain cry out for him to open his mouth, to inhale, to *breathe*.

Something dark flashed by in the water. Nothing mattered but breathing, and yet somehow a deeper fear was triggered in the most primal part of his brain. From the corner of his eye he saw a corpse jerk, tugged, bleeding into the water.

Efrim reached the surface, gasping for breath, sucking in sweet blessed air.

Something bumped his thigh, nudged him hard, and then he felt razor teeth clamp down and rip his flesh, felt himself dragged and twisted, and he screamed as he went under for a second time.

Eyes open, in a cloud of his own blood, mind numb, he saw the sharks feeding on the bodies floating around him. Saw the cold, dull, black eyes of the one knifing toward him. The one who would end him.

Swim, Isko, he thought.

Swim.

CHAPTER 2

The airplane jostled Alex Simmons awake. His heart jumped and he gripped the armrest, braced for something ugly. The Walter Mosley novel on his lap slipped to the floor with a thump and he knew he'd lost his page. The plane juddered again, the overhead bins rattling, and he heard the whine of the engines as the plane began to slow, in the midst of its descent.

"You're adorable when you're scared out of your mind," Sami said.

Alex wiped a bit of sleep drool from his mouth as he sat up straighter in his seat. "Not scared. Just sleeping."

"Uh-huh. Tell that to the armrest you just man-handled."

He cocked his head and glanced sidelong at his wife. "I'll tell you what's gonna get manhandled."

Sami arched an eyebrow and pursed her lips. "Mmm-hmm. Okay. We get into a room all our own and I'll show you what it's like to be 'womanhandled.' Till then, you just do some breathing exercises."

Alex exhaled loudly, a smile on his face. He'd planned to watch movies and read through most of the ten-hour flight from Chicago to Honolulu, but instead he'd slept off and on throughout the journey, which was for the best considering the electrical current of anxiety that ran through him anytime he boarded a plane. All his life he'd had this fear, and it infuriated him. He'd faced up to bullies as a kid and been beaten in parking lots. He'd driven too damn fast and survived a crash off a bridge into frigid water that should have broken or drowned him. He'd served a tour in Iraq and come home with a bullet hole in his shoulder and a host of images seared into his brain that he'd never share with his wife or his daughter. Hell, he'd married a woman so sharp, so funny, so beautiful, that she still intimidated him most days, and their six-year-old daughter Tasha was shaping up to be everything her momma was and more.

But put him on a fucking airplane and even the little happy pill that was supposed to smooth out the static buzzkill of his flying fear couldn't do the job.

Alex reached over, slid his hand behind Sami's neck, and bent to kiss her with lips still slicked with his naptime drool. She laughed and ewwed and wiped her mouth with the back of her hand, but when he went to kiss her again she sank against him with the same sultry surrender that always made him feel like himself again. Sami's husband. He'd had a lot of roles in his life, but that and Tasha's daddy were his favorites by far.

"You all right?" she asked quietly.

The landing gear started to grind and whine as it deployed. Alex jumped a little and then nodded. Landing gear, that was a good sign. He studied Sami, the tight coils of her close-cropped hair, the copper gleam of her eyes, the smile lines at the corners of her mouth. In her lap she held a biography of a queen he'd never heard of, and that seemed right to him. Sami would teach their daughter to enter every room like a queen, to claim her authority. Alex had a lot of what his own mother had called backbone. He had plenty of swagger to him, and he still stepped up, fists clenched, if a situation warranted. But day by day over the past eight years with Sami, he'd been teaching himself to step back when she wanted to step up.

"Perfect," he said. "I'm perfect."

Sami smirked. Any other time she'd have teased him about claiming perfection, but she must have figured she'd teased him enough for one flight. Anxiety still buzzed inside him, but Alex exhaled again and felt some of the tension go out of him. He bent to pick up the book he'd dropped, flipped through until he found the last page he could remember having read, and folded it down. He made a show of dog-earing the page. Sami thought anyone who didn't use a bookmark had to be a monster.

"You ready for this?" she asked. "Seeing Harry again?"

"I'm not focused on Harry."

"It's his reunion."

"Nah. Don't say that. It's my reunion. Harry's just paying for it."

Sami arched that eyebrow again. "*Alexander.* You can't pretend our host is invisible, no matter how much you may want to. He paid for our plane tickets. We're staying in his home tonight. We'll be on his boat all week."

Alex pointed a finger at her. "True. It's just a shame he has to be there with us."

"You said you'd play nice. The guy was your friend once upon a time."

He nodded slowly, remembering those days. Harry Curtis hadn't just been a friend; he'd been one of Alex's closest friends. There had been eight of them then, a disparate group of students at Brown University who'd arrived in Providence, Rhode Island, as freshmen hoping they would finally fit in. Brown was an Ivy League school, after all, a whole campus full of kids who had been competitors in high school, kids who weren't kids anymore, kids who were serious about where life was going to take them next. Only life on College Hill hadn't been like that at all. Students' at Brown might've been smarter than average when it came to schoolwork, but the alcohol still flowed freely and the school had its fair share of vomiting, ignorance, and campus rape.

The eight of them had found one another sophomore year, mostly because of Harry Curtis, who played soccer but didn't spend all his time with the team. Who

liked to host parties and get people laughing and dancing, but who never seemed to get so drunk himself
that he'd shirk those duties. Who double majored in
philosophy and business because he knew manipula-
tion was the key to corporate success. That last bit had
amused them all through their college careers, right up
until it became clear how serious Harry felt about it.
How little conscience he had. How profoundly he believed that anyone who engaged in business took on
the risk of ending up well-and-truly-fucked by a merciless bastard who would take advantage of any flaw, any
misstep. Harry Curtis aspired to become that merciless
bastard.

As far as Alex knew, he'd fulfilled those aspirations.

In college, though, they'd loved Harry in spite of
himself. Luisa had even slept with him once, on a
weekend they were all up in Vermont together, hiking
the snowy woods and skiing and drinking peppermint
schnapps, Cat playing guitar by the chalet's fireplace
at night, Alex curled up on the sofa with Alliyah, which
meant it had to be February of their junior year,
because that mistake hadn't lasted longer than February. The shortest month, thank God. They'd stayed
friends, just like Harry and Luisa had stayed friends.
Just like they'd all stayed friends.

Until Derek Li had thrown himself off the library
roof because he'd gotten a C on his biochemistry mid-
term, fucking his whole semester. Derek, who'd been
the kindest of them, somehow both the quietest and the
funniest of them. Derek, with his passion for 1980s pop

and movies everyone else hated. Derek, who'd been the best of them.

"Who does that?" Harry had said. They'd been sitting under a shade tree on the Main Green, the seven of them who remained now that Derek had left them. Alex and Harry and Nils. Luisa and Cat and Alliyah and Nalani.

"I wish I'd known," Cat had said, wiping at her tears. "I wish he'd talked to me."

Alex had felt numb. Sick. He'd cradled his head in his hands. "The poor bastard, thinking this was the answer."

Harry had scoffed. Alex had twisted to stare at him, sure it must have been a cough or something. But the others were looking, too, and Harry's facial expression seemed clear enough.

"Fuck that guy," he'd said, climbing to his feet, glancing around at them all with disdain. "He quit. You play to win, that means you've got to deal with it on those occasions when you lose. Derek wasn't playing to win. He didn't know what he was even working for. Guys like that, they're always gonna lose."

"You piece of shit," Alliyah had breathed. "He's dead. It's not a game."

Harry rolled his eyes and turned to walk away. He'd gotten half a dozen steps before Alex had reached him, spun him around, knocked him on his ass. Nalani and Nils stopped him from taking it further.

An apology had come days later, Harry saying he'd just been angry at Derek for giving up, for not reaching out to one of them, just like Luisa had said. They'd all accepted his apology, but the damage was done. Between Derek's suicide and Harry's words, nothing had ever been the same after that. When graduation had arrived, it had felt to all of them like a relief.

Nothing could have surprised Alex more than the email he'd received three months ago, the invitation from Harry Curtis to come and celebrate their tenth reunion in Hawaii, a week aboard a luxury sailing yacht, with Harry covering all expenses. They'd all been invited, the remaining group and their spouses or significant others. No kids, though. That was Harry's one request, to leave the kids at home so they could all relax.

Alex had a dozen reasons not to go. Marketing companies didn't like to see their art directors go on ten-day vacations, even when they had that vacation time coming to them. And Tasha . . . their little girl was only six. Sami's mother had offered to stay at the house, make sure Tasha was fed, did her homework, went to school, but still it didn't sit right with him.

Sami wasn't having any of that. The lure of the tropics cried out to her—and if Alex allowed himself to get past his old resentment, it tempted him just as much, as did the prospect of reconnecting with the old friends he actually liked, but whom he'd only seen sporadically over the past decade.

When the plane landed, he grabbed the carry-on and stood in the aisle waiting for people to deplane. The ten-hour flight from Chicago had made him claustrophobic, but once he and Sami were out into the terminal both that and his anxiety vanished completely. At baggage claim, waiting for their luggage to appear on the carousel, they could feel the warmth that waited for them outside. The afternoon sun shone through the windows. He spotted a handful of people who wore Hawaiian shirts without any apparent ignorance or irony, and that pleased him.

Only when they started away from the baggage claim area, suitcases in tow, did they see the enormous black-suited driver, his face covered in traditional tattoos, and his massive hands clutching a printed sheet that read: ALEX AND SAMANTHA SIMMONS.

Sami strolled right up to him, a huge grin splitting her face. "I think you're looking for us."

The giant had a smile that matched hers. "Welcome and aloha, Mrs. Simmons."

He tucked the sign away and started to gather their bags, talking incessantly about the island, the weather, how pleased he was to make their acquaintance. His name was Kahale, and by the time they'd reached the car Harry had sent, the driver had shared the names of his sisters, his favorite surfing story, and the early history of the Hawaiian islands. Alex wanted to be irritated, to silently grumble about the man's incessant chatter, but Kahale was so damn charming, and they were in Hawaii.

The trip of a lifetime, Sami had said, after she'd told him they'd be fools not to go.

As they drove across the island and he caught sight of the ocean, realized they were on a little dot in the middle of the Pacific, thousands of miles from any continent, Alex Simmons couldn't get the smile off his face. All that old resentment didn't seem to matter so much in that moment. Maybe all Harry wanted was a chance to reconnect. A fresh start. And Sami was right—they'd been friends once. Great friends.

After all the trouble and expense Harry had gone to, the least Alex could do was give him a chance.

Kahale had started talking about the ancient Samoans who had first settled in Polynesia, and the wayfarers who had first settled in Hawaii, navigating their way across the sea in outrigger canoes by following birds a little farther every year, risking their lives for the thrill of discovery alone. Their week aboard Harry's sailboat would be nothing like that, and yet still Alex felt a tremor of excitement.

The trip of a lifetime.

Maybe Harry really had changed.

As she climbed out of the car in the circular driveway, Sami couldn't wipe the smile off her face. The afternoon sun felt deliciously warm on her bare arms and her face, a gift from heaven after the seeming eternity of the flight. Back home in Chicago it would be cold and dark, the wind frigid off the lake. Here the wind brought the crisp smell of flowers and the tang of salt from the ocean. With a soft laugh, she threw back her head and drank in the sunshine.

"You gonna strip down, too? Offer yourself to the sun god?" Alex asked.

"We're in Hawaii, baby," she said. "If I'm offering myself to anyone, it'll be the volcano god."

Kahale laughed heartily, just the way she imagined he would. The big man hoisted their bags out of the trunk as if they weighed nothing, then led the way. Alex tried to protest, offering to take the bags himself. Outside of a restaurant, her husband didn't like anyone serving him—bellmen, red caps, even taxi drivers. Being waited on made him uncomfortable, made him feel apart from other people. Sami, however, wanted an entire team of Tolkien elves to pamper her and bring her fruity drinks with umbrellas in them, and stat.

When no elves appeared, she contented herself with following Alex and Kahale up the front walk, which wound through a lovely flower garden. Alex succeeded in wresting one of the carry-ons from their giant new friend. Sami thought about the hospital she'd left behind, knew that other doctors would curse her for her absence, and didn't care. This doc was on vacation.

"Holy shit, there he is!" a voice cried happily, and a string of profanity followed.

As Sami walked toward the front steps of the sprawling estate, the house nestled amidst palms and other trees, splashed with color and Polynesian and Hawaiian design flairs, she began to slow. The guy with his arms spread, walking down the steps from the veranda like King Kamehameha himself, could only be Harry Curtis. Tan and healthy, with a blinding white smile, Harry looked like a young Tom Cruise . . . but only if Cruise had started to let himself slip into a world of too many margaritas and possibly too much coke. He had the shoulders and arms of a guy who spent plenty of time lifting weights, and the beginning of a paunch that belied the rest, like that nascent belly had snuck up on him one night while he was sleeping and he still hadn't quite noticed it.

Don't judge, she told herself.

"Alex Simmons, you handsome motherfucker," Harry said, sweeping Alex into a bear hug. He stepped back to look at Alex the same way Sami's grandmother had always done to her. "Man, you have no idea how great it is to see you. I love it. This is gonna be the greatest week of our lives."

Harry kissed Alex's cheek, causing Alex to flinch backward and wipe off that kiss. Harry pushed him away and they both started laughing. Sami exhaled, unaware she'd been holding her breath. They'd come halfway across the world for this, or so it seemed. She had inconvenienced a lot of colleagues, doctors who had to cover for her—not to mention her mother and daughter—in order to make it happen. An opportunity like this . . . if they hadn't gone, she knew that she and Alex would have regretted it. But more than that, they both needed this, Alex especially. He'd gotten lost in his work the past few years. She and Tasha loved having him home, but he hardly ever did anything but work and hang out with them, and this chance to reunite with his old friends, to reignite some of the passion and positivity of his twenties, was not to be missed.

Alex complimented Harry on the house, thanked him for his generosity, and turned to introduce her.

"Damn, Mrs. Simmons . . . ," Harry said, eyeing her in a way she was sure he thought of as a compliment. Then he held up his hands in apology. "Sorry, *Dr.* Simmons. You are even more beautiful in the flesh."

He took her hands, gazed at her with sudden sincerity, as if the cheerful bluster had been a mask. "Welcome to my home. Sincerely, Samantha, I'm so happy you and Alex are here." Those eyes told her that Harry Curtis might be smarter than he seemed, more self-aware. They told her, too, that there was pain in him, alongside the bullshit and the Tom Cruise smile.

"It's our pleasure," she said. "Please. Call me Sami."

"Sami it is." Harry squeezed her hands, turned, and escorted her back to Alex, whom he clapped on the back. "Truly. The greatest week ever."

They started up the stairs together. Kahale stood on the veranda, in front of the frosted glass of the double front door, still holding their luggage.

"Mr. Curtis," the driver said, the smile Sami had loved on sight now absent. "The next group arrives in twenty minutes. I should get moving."

"Yeah, you should," Harry replied dismissively, brow creasing. "What the fuck are you still doing here?"

Kahale froze, seemingly at a loss for how to respond. Then he nodded toward the house, his hands too full to gesture. "The bags, sir."

Harry opened the door and pushed it open, ushering Kahale into the foyer. "Go on, then. Put that shit down and get gone. You never did get those leis for everyone. If they're for sale at the airport, make sure the others get them the second they see you."

"Absolutely. I'll make it happen."

"Good man. That's what I love about you," Harry said, his smile returning. He turned to his guests. "This guy's the best, right? This island has the greatest people on earth."

Kahale set the bags down gently, lined them up, and edged around them to get out the door. On the veranda, he turned to look back inside. *"Mahalo."*

"Mahalo to you, Kahale. Thank you so much," Sami said.

Alex added his own thanks, but by then Kahale had closed the door behind him and Harry had already begun to announce the first stop on their tour of his estate. Even from the foyer, as Sami and Alex followed him deeper into the house, she could see the vast, open great room and the open sliders along the back wall, the perfectly landscaped lawn, the broad stretch of sand, and the Pacific Ocean beyond. Sami wondered how much the house had cost, and knew that Harry Curtis was the kind of guy who would have told her if she'd asked, pretending that anyone could afford such a place.

Mahalo.

She'd seen the mask drop away from Harry Curtis's face, seen the sincerity there and the humanity. But as he led them through the house—this place where he lived just three months out of each year, totally alone, with his Tom Cruise smile and his too-tan paunch—

she wondered if maybe that glimpse of humanity had been the real mask.

Alex had been reluctant to come here, even with all of the peace and beauty Hawaii promised. Sami had persuaded him.

For the first time, she began to wonder if that might have been a bad idea.

CHAPTER 3

Isko Flores woke in enough pain to convince him that, somehow, he was still alive. He opened his eyes to slits. The sun burned the horizon and for a moment he wasn't sure if what he witnessed was dusk or dawn. Surely he couldn't have been unconscious for a night and a day, so he reasoned it must be sunrise. The light hurt his head and he lifted a hand to shield his eyes.

He shifted on the beach, the surf rolling up the shore toward him, and as he moved his lower body he felt the throb of heat in his left thigh. Heat and pain, deep and profound enough to make him catch his breath. Isko did not want to look at his leg. The heat subsided and now that leg felt cold and sluggish, as if the leg itself had vanished and all that remained was a ghost of it, pure pain in the shape of the leg he'd once had.

Isko forced himself to look. His face twisted in grief and tears welled in his eyes, not for the leg—no, the leg was still there. His tears were for his wife Tala and their little daughter Dalisay. His girl had the brightest eyes, shiny like copper, and a smile that always made him feel as if all his sins might someday be forgiven. Three years old, and all the world was a gift to her. How would she and her mother survive without the money Isko earned? What would Tala do to look after the girl?

The questions flowed like his tears and he wished he could stop them both—*had* to stop them both. His wife and daughter thought him the strength of the family. Tala always told Dalisay that Papa was the tall tree who put down the roots beneath them and whose branches kept them safe from harm. It had never been true, not really, but his ego made him allow this myth-making. He wanted his daughter to see him that way. He wanted—

God, he wanted to see her again. Dalisay. His little Daisy-girl.

Isko forced himself to look at his left thigh. The thin fabric of his trousers had been torn away there; ripped tatters hung from his leg. The exposed flesh had a half circle of ragged punctures, the bite of a shark. Another second or a more determined shark and the entire leg might have been torn off. Instead, there were those tooth marks, blood crusted on most of them but still pulsing and seeping from the worst and deepest of them. Sharks sometimes mistook people for their most natural prey, bumped and bit before finding the texture unfamiliar. It had to be what had happened to him, and yet . . .

He lifted his head, vision swimming, head muzzy from the blood loss. His skull throbbed and blackness crept at the edges of his vision. He closed his mouth and took deep breaths through his nose, steadying himself. Isko glanced out at the water but saw no trace of the boat that had brought them, nor any sign of the others. Machii had thrown them all into the water—Isko had opened his eyes underwater and seen Efrin; he was sure of it. A quick glimpse before the sharks attacked, but despite the blur of his memories, he remembered the terror in Efrin's eyes.

Efrin. His friend.

Isko scanned the water again, then glanced up and down the sand.

Efrin. His dead friend.

"Little Daisy," he whispered, and forced himself to sit up.

The scream that burst from within surprised even him. Pain cut deep into his thigh with such ferocity that it made what he'd felt upon waking seem like pleasure. He took deep, sucking breaths, but the pain kept flowing and his eyes rolled back in his head and he felt himself toppling sideways.

When his eyes flickered open again, his first instinct was to glance at the sun. It hadn't moved much, still just above the horizon, so he hadn't been out long. On his side, he rolled slowly, tilting farther onto his stomach, wary of that pain. Craning his head back, he could see part of the bite wound at the back of his leg, much worse than the front. The flesh had been torn. The sand and the pressure from how he'd been collapsed on the shore had let the blood crust and temporarily seal the wound, but he'd opened it again and now blood had begun to pool under him. A wave crashed, rolled up beneath him as the tide came in, and washed some of it away, but there would be more blood. He'd keep bleeding until he had none left to give, and then he'd die, and Tala and Dalisay would never know what had become of him.

Drawing small breaths through gritted teeth, trying to stay conscious, he worked himself into a sitting position again. Though the left leg of his pants hung in strips, the idea of trying to tear them off—jostling that leg—made his stomach turn. Instead, he pulled off his T-shirt, which had mostly dried overnight. He brushed the sand from the shirt and then began to tear it apart. Despite the pain, he managed to rip the fabric into strips and bind his left thigh. Blood spotted the cloth immediately, but he'd tied the leg tightly and hoped it would slow the bleeding. If he could stitch it up somehow, he might survive. If not, he would have to hope that God might take an interest in a fisherman who'd agreed to work for the wrong men.

With another deep breath, Isko glanced around again. He blinked. The sun had risen a bit higher now and for the first time he noticed a glint of metal among the palms far off to his left. He'd washed up in the most beautiful, desolate place on earth, but maybe not as desolate as he'd thought.

The glint of metal got him on his feet. It took long minutes and he nearly passed out three times, hissing through his teeth. The blood soaked the strips of

T-shirt around his thigh, but he started limping along the sand toward that glint of metal, more certain with every step that it was precisely what he'd thought it was.

The corner of a roof.

Hope flickered in his chest, not quite a spark. An image of little Dalisay came to him. He could almost hear her sweet laughter, almost picture her running to him along the sand, ready to jump into his arms.

The sand shifted as he limped. His right foot slid, threw him off-balance, and he tried to catch himself with his left. The pain buckled his leg and he crashed to the sand, blacking out as his blood seeped through his makeshift tourniquet.

The sun kept rising and the tide rolled in, but Isko did not move for a long time.

CHAPTER 4

Morning came too soon. There had been drinking the night before, as one after another of the guests arrived, but Harry—who had put away more than any of them—turned out to have been quite serious about their departure time. Shortly after dawn, he had gone through the house banging on bedroom doors, instructing them to rise and shine. Now they were in the back of a limousine and Sami had a glass of fresh pineapple juice in her hand. She'd rolled the windows down and the island breeze whipped her hair around her head while Alex groaned, slumped in the seat beside her, hungover but relaxed.

They were sharing the limousine with Nils Falk and his husband, Patrick, as well as Luisa Kershaw, who was married but flying solo on this trip. Sami and Alex sat at the back of the car, facing Nils and Patrick, with Luisa perched on the bench along the driver's side. The others had gone in a second car, though all of them were running behind Harry by an hour. He'd made sure they were all awake and knew where to find the breakfast room—and what time the cars would arrive to transport them to the marina—and then he'd left them there in his home, most of them quiet after the wonderful welcome they'd all had the night before.

"It's nice to see him so excited," Luisa said to nobody in particular.

Nils glanced up at her, eyes icy blue. "Harry?"

"Who else? I don't remember him ever being so enthusiastic about anything."

Nils smiled. "Anything?"

Luisa sprang from her seat and whapped him on the leg. "Don't be fresh."

"Hey," Patrick said. "That's my line."

Sami watched them bicker. Nils and Patrick seemed nice enough, though she had only spoken to them briefly the night before. Thin and handsome, hair in artful disarray, Nils edited crime novels for one of the handful of major publishing companies in New York, and had apparently written a series of mysteries set in his native Norway that had found great success there but almost no traction in the United States. Nils loved to talk and seemed to seek out common ground, wanting to know if others shared his passions for certain foods or particular actors or musicians. He'd been on an Irish Punk kick lately, according to the previous evening's excitement, but he'd not said a word about it this morning.

His husband, Patrick, Sami reasoned, seemed to be

the source of his fascination with Irish Punk. First-generation Irish, Patrick spoke with a bit of a brogue he'd picked up from his parents. Several years younger than the rest of them, he'd established a career as an attorney and agent for professional athletes, mostly football players, which meant he spent a lot of time texting and checking email on his phone, and yet he seemed always to be smiling at Nils and holding his hand. Sami had started to think of Patrick as *the multitasker,* more in admiration than annoyance. Black Irish, he had dark hair and eyes, a little bit of Spanish blood passed down through generations.

Luisa and Nils had remained close over the years, which was how they'd all ended up in this car together. A petite woman with wild red hair and a spray of freckles across the bridge of her nose, she seemed almost as enthusiastic as Nils, at least when she wasn't making snarky comments. She had an edge to her that Sami had liked instantly, but that had been last night, and Sami had been three drinks into the evening before Luisa had arrived in a whirlwind of kisses and hugs, and then literally jumped into Harry's arms, so that he'd been forced to catch her. The snark of Luisa Kershaw came along with a lot of eye rolling and sighing, and Sami had been surprised the night before to discover she wasn't an actress, although she still wasn't clear about exactly what Luisa did. Something in the fashion industry.

"Alex!" Luisa cried, leaning forward from the bench seat along the passenger seat of the driver's side of the limo. She reached out and clapped her hands three times. "Come on, you sexy beast. It's only day one. The party's just getting started!"

Sami smiled, the words *day one* echoing in her head. If Luisa kept this energy up all week, it would be exhausting.

Alex shot Luisa the middle finger, which seemed to delight her, eliciting a peal of laughter. The woman actually bounced on her seat, and for the first time Sami wondered if there might be drugs involved. *Either that, or the woman needs them.*

"Have some of this pineapple juice," Sami told Alex. "You'll feel better."

He sighed, massaging his temple, and reluctantly reached for her glass, which she pulled away from him. "I'll pour you some of your own."

Alex gave her a weak thumbs-up and a half-hearted smile to go with it.

Sami set her glass in a cup holder and started to get a fresh one from the bar in the back of the limo. She was halfway through pouring when Luisa sprang from her seat and landed on Alex's lap, her knee banging Sami's, her skull knocking against Alex's. Sami spilled pineapple juice and nearly dropped the empty glass.

"Luisa, come on!"

She laughed and hugged him, immune to being admonished. "Wake up, handsome. Carpe the fucking diem. You're in Hawaii with your gorgeous wife. You're about to get on a boat worth more than any of us make in a year. I can promise you some topless sunbathing, lots of drinks, and late-night reminiscing. If

I can get her drunk enough, I'll even make out with Sami."

"Oh, you will?" Sami said. "Do I get a say?"

Luisa hugged Alex tightly, grinning at Sami even as she smushed her face up against his. "Of course you do! You get to say 'yes!'"

Sami wanted to drag her off Alex's lap by the hair and remind her whose husband he was, and yet she couldn't help grinning. Luisa might be a handful but promised to be entertaining as hell, as long as nobody decided to throw her overboard.

"Lulu, come and sit down," Nils admonished her. "Behave yourself. We can taunt Alex later when he's puking off the side of the boat."

"That," Alex said, "is likely to be prophetic."

Nils smiled.

Patrick glanced up from his phone, amused. "Glad to see you seem to be coming around."

The limo slowed and began to turn. Luisa finally crawled off Alex's lap and went to kneel on the bench and peer out the window. Ten years out of college and she had the energy and general demeanor of a sixteen-year-old. Sami arched an eyebrow at Alex, who smiled tiredly. They'd been together long enough that words were unnecessary in times like this. She didn't need to say a word to her husband about him having other women sit in his lap, regardless of whether he'd ever slept with them. In Luisa's case, that would be a no, but Luisa wasn't the only female among this group of old friends.

The limo rolled to a stop and the driver hurriedly threw it into park and jumped out to open the door for them. Sami had been disappointed that Kahale had been assigned to take the other group—this driver had been silent and serious—but when she climbed out of the back of the limo she saw him holding the door for his own passengers, the second car parked just a dozen feet away.

"Good morning, Sami!" he called to her. "Bon voyage."

Alex slipped an arm around her. "You have an admirer," he whispered.

Their driver had opened the trunk and begun to pull out their suitcases. Luisa took hers and turned toward them. "Come on, you guys!"

"You too," Sami whispered back.

Alex laughed. His hangover seemed to be fading and Sami was glad. One glance at the various boats lining the marina and she felt herself drifting into fantasies of sailing away from the world forever. Not that she'd ever go without Tasha. Their little girl was home and in good hands. If the temptation to run away and start life over again ever turned into reality, she would happily have Alex and Tasha with her—anywhere she landed would be home, as long as she had them. But for this week, it felt good to be on their own, with no one to answer to but themselves.

Nils and Patrick took their time, mostly because Patrick had stopped to text someone. Luisa squeaked and ran over to the group climbing out of the second limousine. Nalani Tjan unfolded from the backseat, drawing Sami's eyes to her long legs. She'd grown up in Hawaii but now lived in San Francisco with her tech exec husband James, who climbed out of the car behind her. With his beard and shoulder-length hair and weathered sandals, he looked very much at home in the islands.

They'd shared the car with Alliyah and Dev Basu, as well as Cat Skolis, who seemed the quietest of them all. Dev had a scruffy charm and had done his best to chat with the other spouses, bonding with what he called the outsiders. Alliyah worked for Goldman Sachs doing something that Sami had trouble under-standing, which she suspected came partly from not caring and partly from the air of chilly indifference that surrounded the woman. That might have been jealousy talking—Alliyah and Alex had dated briefly in college—so Sami promised herself she would hold off judgment, give the woman a chance.

"You guys ready to go?" Dev called happily.

"Raise the anchor, Mr. Basu!" Sami replied. "Hoist the mainsail! Or whatever."

Dev laughed and bumped Alliyah, who smiled at him and started to drag her suitcase toward the ma-rina dock. The sweet glances they exchanged sug-gested a couple infatuated with each other, and Sami felt herself soften toward the woman. *I guess I'm the bitch,* she thought. But the jury was still out.

"You managing, baby?" she said to Alex.

"I'm such a lightweight. The only one with a

hangover." He gave her a sheepish look as they started down the pier after Dev and Alliyah, Nalani and James, and Cat.

"Oh, I have a feeling there will be a lot of hangovers this week," Sami replied.

Luisa rushed up between them, matching their stride, dragging her bag behind her. "I'll drink to that!" she cried happily.

They all laughed, and suddenly they were *together*. A group. Nils and Patrick caught up to them, Nils enthusiastically extolling the virtues of Harry's sailboat, which apparently belonged to a category people actually referred to as "luxury sailing yachts," as if that weren't obnoxious to say out loud. Sami figured she'd just keep calling it a sailboat, although as they walked out onto the pier and she took in the hundred-foot ship she had to admit it was something far more than that. The name of the boat, emblazoned on the back, was *Kid Galahad*.

Sami slowed down to let Luisa get ahead of them so she could slide up next to her husband. "What does that mean? The name?"

Alex smiled. "A combination of two things, I'd assume. It's the title of an Elvis Presley movie, and Harry always loved Elvis. Plus he always wished he could be one of the Knights of the Round Table."

Sami slipped her arm through Alex's and kissed his cheek. "Boys."

"What? I never said I wanted to be a knight."

"You didn't have to, my love."

Luisa dropped back, having overheard. Cheerful as

ever, she fell into step on Alex's other side and shot a conspiratorial glance at Sami. "Your man didn't want to be a knight. He wanted to be the Dread Pirate Roberts. Forever. We must have watched *The Princess Bride* a dozen times."

"He still loves it," Sami said. "Don't get him going or he'll start quoting."

"To the pain," Alex said, grimacing.

Luisa laughed, but Sami only smiled. There was a presumptuousness about old friends, the idea that they knew her husband better than she did, and it made her uncomfortable. In her head, she understood that these people had been intimate with an earlier Alex, a man who had no wife and no daughter and no career, and so could not really know him as well as his own wife. She knew it was a foolish thing to allow herself to be irritated by and she would have to get used to it.

Samantha Simmons, she thought, *who ever knew you had such a jealous streak?*

They were walking along the pier when they heard Harry's voice booming from the deck of the boat.

"Come on, you lazy fuckers! Paradise is waiting!"

CHAPTER 5

Alex had arrived in Hawaii with some doubts. All his life, he'd grown up with the impression that the islands were the closest the world had to paradise, that a journey there would take his breath away, that he'd fall in love with the place. By the time he'd graduated from high school, he'd been too cynical for that kind of whimsy to take root in his brain. He and Sami had a good life, but he didn't believe in some Shangri-la that would cure what ailed him, ease his spirit, or do any of that happy crap.

Now he'd spent a day on the island of Kauai, and he had to take back all of his hard-earned cynicism. As he climbed the ladder up from the dinghy, he smiled to himself. He knew the effect would fade, that the memory of the island would diminish and the once and future Alex Simmons would begin to doubt the vivid colors of the flowers, the honeyed purity of the air, the way his whole body had lightened. The hours they'd all spent together jumping from waterfalls and swimming in their natural pools . . . the peace he'd felt today would never be recaptured. It had been the single greatest vacation day of his life and the week was just getting started.

"Well, look at you," a voice said above him.

Alex looked up, saw he'd reached the top of the ladder and that Harry waited for him, reaching down to take his hand and help him aboard. With a grin he failed to hide, Alex took his hand and scrambled onto the Kid Galahad.

"What did you think of Kauai?" Harry asked.

"You could just leave me here."

Sami had been right behind him on the ladder. Now she called up to them, "I heard that!"

Alex and Harry both laughed—an easy camaraderie that had eluded them for so long—and turned to help Sami up together. She'd slipped her shorts back on, but they didn't cover much more than her bathing suit, and her shirt remained tied around her waist. In her bikini top, with that flat belly, she looked like she belonged in this paradise.

"Don't worry, my love," Alex said. "I'd never let myself get marooned on a tropical island without you."

Sami punched him lightly on the arm. "You'd better not."

Half of their party were already on board. Nalani and James and Cat were down in the dinghy, taking turns climbing the ladder. The guy piloting the dinghy had been the surprise of the journey thus far. Harry's first mate, Gabe Hogan, had been born in Harrisburg, Pennsylvania, but had moved to Hawaii at the age of seventeen and had never returned to the mainland, not even to visit family. Quiet and competent, with a confident, easy smile, Gabe somehow managed to be Harry's friend and employee at the same time. They'd all been wondering how Harry would handle this boat himself, and Gabe had been their answer.

"We'll set sail as soon as the dinghy's stowed!" Harry called down to the water.

Gabe had Nalani by the hand, helping her to steady herself on the ladder. With his left, he waved the *shaka* hand sign up at Harry, which seemed communication enough.

"He's a good guy," Alex said.

The boat swayed beneath them. The sunlight had turned golden as evening approached, and maybe that accounted for the shadow that crossed Harry's face. Alex couldn't be sure.

"You're wondering what he's doing hanging out with me," Harry said.

Sami slid her arm around Alex. They could hear laughter from below, where the others were showering and changing clothes, maybe mixing some cocktails.

"He didn't say that, Harry," Sami noted.

Harry shrugged. "Gabe's a good influence on me. I pay him well, yeah, but if he quit he'd have another job in a day."

"I'm sure . . . ," Alex began, but he pressed his lips together, refusing to finish the sentence.

"You're sure what?" Harry asked.

He seemed at ease with the past, like he knew he might not be able to erase the hostility and resentment Alex had brought with him on this trip and he could live with it. Alex envied him that.

As always, Sami stepped in. "He's sure there are brightly colored cocktails with little umbrellas in them somewhere on board," she said. "And he's going to drink one with me, just as soon as we put some clothes on."

Harry arched an eyebrow. "Don't get dressed on my account."

Once, it would have irritated Alex, but Harry's flirtation seemed almost by reflex, and besides, Sami didn't need him to be her knight in shining armor. If she felt like Harry ever stepped over the line, she'd make it very clear.

Instead, Sami paused with a hand around Alex's waist. "I'm sure we'll all be skinny-dipping before the week is out, Harry, but meanwhile, I have to thank you. Truly. Alex will pretend otherwise, but today was the most relaxed I've seen my husband in years and we both owe you for that."

Harry's eyes softened and he seemed genuinely touched. "You don't owe me anything. If the two of you really had that kind of day today, that makes me very happy."

The ladder rattled against the railing and they all looked over to see Nalani scrambling to climb on board. With a quiet laugh, Harry went to help her.

"Go and get that drink," he said over his shoulder, and then he was flirting with Nalani, threatening to cut her husband loose so they could sail away together.

The boat swayed and the rigging clanged against the masts as the wind picked up. Alex and Sami moved together toward the cockpit. Harry hadn't been exaggerating when he'd described the *Kid Galahad* as a sailing yacht. The staterooms belowdecks were nicer than most of the luxury hotels Alex had ever slept in, all wood and brass and colorful cushions. The bathtub had Jacuzzi jets. The staterooms were forward, ahead of the living area, which comprised two large areas, one below and one slightly higher—not quite level with the boat's deck. The inside cockpit, as Harry called it, had sofas and a mahogany coffee table and shelves loaded with books for anyone who wanted to get comfortable. Continuing aft, there were port and starboard doors that led out onto the deck and into the "outside cockpit," which was covered only by a tight awning yet seemed even more comfortably and elegantly appointed than its indoor cousin. This was the place to sprawl and share meals and talk late into the night over too many drinks.

Half a dozen steps led up into the wheelhouse, which was situated on top of the inside cockpit. Gabe called it the pilothouse, which Alex thought was more accurate, though he was going to leave the argument to the actual sailors on board. The wheelhouse was claustrophobic, fine for one or two people, but not suited for a group. Harry had given them all the tour when they'd gotten on board. The wheel was attached to a black instrument panel festooned with throttles and dials and readouts for weather and radar and Neptune-knew-what-else. How two guys could sail this thing without help he didn't know, but they had done a beautiful job on day one.

Now, as Alex and Sami passed through the starboard door leading to the inside cockpit, they heard laughter from within. Alex let himself exhale again. He didn't want to lose all of the peace he'd found ashore.

They walked into the cockpit and found Luisa, Alliyah, and Dev putting glasses on trays. Gabe had brought their group back to the boat first, and they'd all changed out of their swimsuits into loose, soft, clothing. Alliyah had on a light cotton sweatshirt. She always said she had thin blood because she got cold so easily.

"Hey!" Luisa cried. "We were headed out onto the deck to watch the sunset. Come with!"

"Coconut mojitos!" Dev promised, gesturing to the drinks on the two trays they'd prepared.

"Sounds good," Sami said. "Let us put on something dry and we'll be right there."

The others were barely listening, laughing and teasing one another over some joke that had been made before Alex and Sami had walked in. They were gone from the cockpit, out on the forward deck, moments later, leaving Alex alone with his wife.

Sami slid into his arms and kissed him softly. "Maybe we'll get lucky and be shipwrecked here."

"We can dream," Alex said as they started toward the stairs that led to the staterooms below.

"I have to admit . . . It was hard to keep hating him today," Sami said quietly.

She didn't have to use Harry's name for Alex to know who she meant.

"I agree, but don't worry, honey. He'll remind me why I hate him soon enough. He always does."

The phrase "coconut mojitos" had inspired a certain amount of dread in Sami's heart. It sounded like the kind of drink someone had invented just to sound trendy and that people had claimed to like for the same reason. She changed her mind as soon as she'd had her first sip. Luisa smiled knowingly at her and nodded, like they'd both just been caught lusting after the same handsome coworker on an elevator.

"I'd better eat something if we're going to just sit on the deck and drink," she said, mostly to Alex but also to Luisa.

"Why?" Luisa said, sliding closer to her. "What are you afraid you'll do if you have too much to drink?"

The woman's grin had annoyed her before, but now it just seemed playful. It occurred to Sami that maybe Alex hadn't been the only one who really needed to unclench and unwind.

"Life makes you uptight," she confessed, taking another sip of coconut mojito. "If I relax too much, I might unravel."

"I'd like to see that," Luisa said.

Alex laughed and sipped at his own drink. "So would I."

Sami glanced at him. "Careful what you wish for, sweetheart."

One by one the others joined them. There were two lounge chairs and a hammock just forward from the cockpit, in view of the wheelhouse windows above, and they all gathered around these. She admired the colorful surfboards strapped to the back of the cockpit, additional testament—if any might be needed—that Harry had dedicated his boat to fun and adventure.

Sami had to admit that she was, indeed, having fun, and she knew Alex was, too. But it felt strange to be so far away from their daughter, Tasha, to look at the water and think of the thousands of miles separating them. It would only be a week, and Tasha was only six—likely too young to remember much about their absence as she got older—but Sami still felt guilty. She had called her mother earlier and asked her to put Tasha on the phone. The little girl had sounded happy enough to play with her grandmother, and excited to know that her mommy and daddy were going to bring surprises back from Hawaii for her, but that didn't completely erase Sami's guilty feeling. And it didn't keep her from missing her little girl.

Coconut mojitos were helping.

Nils and Patrick claimed the hammock together and Alliyah and Dev landed in the loungers while the rest of them sprawled on the deck, seated on cushions Harry kept packed away for just this purpose. While Gabe got the dinghy hoisted up at the back of the boat,

Harry had gone below to prepare dinner. Sami drank and laughed, but her thoughts drifted to their host. The guy had gone to great expense and great trouble for this trip. It was only the first day, but he had to be exhausted already, and now he was down in the galley making dinner. Maybe he didn't know how to talk to people without coming off like an arrogant prick, but if he truly was as selfish as Alex remembered him, it hadn't shown today.

When Gabe had secured the dinghy, he passed them on the way to the wheelhouse. Luisa leaped up from the deck, spilling a few drops of mojito, and practically sashayed over to him. Whatever her relationship might be to her home-alone husband, she seemed intent on forgetting his existence on this trip. Quiet as Gabe was, Luisa's head tilt, hair flip, and girlish laughter drew a smile from him.

"Like a lion on the veldt," Alex said, nuzzling at Sami's ear. "Luisa stalks her prey."

"He's not unattractive," Sami noted with another sip of her drink.

"Hello? Husband sitting right here."

She smiled. "Wife just stating the obvious."

Alex sighed and spread out on the deck, enjoying the breeze as the sun slid toward the horizon. Sami ignored him. They both knew she wasn't about to try to seduce the first mate, or anyone else for that matter. But Gabe did draw the eye, and not just hers. She'd noticed Alliyah watching him as well. Cat, however— the only single woman on the boat—didn't seem interested at all. That was all right, though. Sami would check him out on Cat's behalf. Bronzed and blond, Gabe would have looked like an aging surfer if not for the scars on his hands from ropes and fishing line and the weathered wisdom in his eyes.

Over by the starboard railing, Luisa touched Gabe on the arm and then sauntered back to the cushion she'd been sitting on earlier. She dropped down beside Sami while Gabe walked by, headed up to the wheel-house. They'd be setting sail now, which meant Harry and Gabe would both be occupied for a while.

No more drinks till dinner, Sami promised herself.

"I can't decide if that guy's life is sad or romantic," Luisa said, resting on her elbow.

"You mean because he never sees his family?"

Luisa's gaze wandered to the horizon, where the sun had turned a vivid orange as it touched the edge of the world. "He doesn't seem to mind. They come see him every few years, apparently. He just told me he never wants to go anywhere he can't sail to on a boat half the size of this one."

Sami took another sip of coconut mojito. "Both."

"Say again?"

Alex spoke up without opening his eyes. "She means it's both. Romantic *and* sad."

They were quiet for a few seconds before Luisa spoke up. "I need another fucking drink."

They'd been under way for more than two hours, all gathered under the awning of the outside cockpit. Harry had outdone himself with Kalua pig, slow roasted at home before the trip and prepared with long rice, with a spicy pineapple salsa on the side. Throughout the meal, the drinks flowed and Alex kept stealing glances at Harry, wondering how the guy he'd been so angry at for so long had the patience and generosity of spirit to prepare this food for them. He'd assumed Harry wanted to show off, to swagger around the deck taking credit, but he brushed off every compliment and expression of gratitude, seeming more at ease out here on the water, among the islands, than Alex had ever imagined he could be.

They all laughed about old times and their spouses put up with it. Cat brought out her guitar at Nalani's urging and the two of them sang old songs from Paramore and The National. Stories of their college days came out like knives in the Roman Senate, but none of them minded so much, and the knives weren't as sharp as they could have been. Alex knew stories about his college friends that would have horrified their spouses—if those respective significant others didn't already know. For his part, he'd told Sami his own ugly truths long ago, the things he wasn't proud of, but he wasn't going to assume that about his friends' lives. Luisa, of course, needed no prodding. She talked freely about the two shy Japanese high school boys she'd bedded when they were visiting the campus for an overnight, trying to choose a college. She'd been a junior. The tale of a drunken blow job that ended with vomit gave the gathering a good laugh, but also a chance to recoil in disgust.

"Really?" Alliyah said, tucking her legs beneath her on the cushioned bench. "You'll tell that story but not tell everyone who you puked on?"

Luisa smirked and shrugged.

Harry raised his hand. "I confess, I was the puked-on party."

"I've heard that story a thousand times," Nils said, curling a bit closer to Patrick. "It's nasty every time."

"Really?" Luisa sprawled back on the bench like a queen among her subjects. "All the dicks you've sucked, and you've never gagged a little?"

Alex bristled, thinking they'd all relaxed too much, that spending time with friends from another era didn't mean they had to behave as if they hadn't matured in the years since. But Nils only rolled his eyes and glanced at his husband. Patrick leaned his head forward as if to confide something to Luisa, though they could all hear him.

"Here's the thing, Lulu," Patrick said. "The experts never gag. You just need more practice."

Harry hooted and clapped his hands. A ripple of laughter went around the circle, there under the awning as the *Kid Galahad* glided across the Pacific, its sails full and ghostly against the night sky. For a moment, it really did feel like they were back in college, all of them together. Alex smiled and took another drink, glancing at Sami and then pulling her close. He kissed his wife, drawing whistles from Cat and Nalani, who snuggled up to her own husband as well.

"I was twenty," Luisa said with a comical huff.

"Though if I'm drunk enough to be honest, I haven't had nearly as much practice since then as I'd have liked."

"Is that why you left your husband at home?" Alex asked.

The laughter died. They all stared at him, mouths open in shock like a bunch of Christmas nutcrackers.

Alex threw his hands up. "What? You were all thinking it."

Cat strummed a chord on her guitar, played a few ominous notes. "We were. But nobody thought *Alex Simmons* would be the one to say it."

Luisa touched her nose and pointed at Cat. "There you go."

"To be fair," Dev piped up, "you do have a reputation as the righteous one."

Alex laughed. "I'll take it."

Sami kissed his cheek. "Give him a drink too many and you'd be surprised what he gets up to."

"Oh, really?" Alliyah said. "Do tell."

"That's enough of that," Alex said. "Let's put the spotlight back on Luisa, where she likes it."

More laughter, and then Cat's fingers danced along the neck of her guitar and she played the complicated opening notes of something Alex almost recognized, knew he ought to remember. Something from their glory days.

Harry cleared his throat. He stood, sea legs easily handling the tilt of the boat.

"I've got to thank you all for coming. You honestly don't know what it means to me. I've got to confess,

I really didn't think you'd all come." He didn't identify Alex by name, but a glance said it all. "I'm truly grateful to have you—"

"And we're grateful for this gift you've given us," Nalani said.

Harry nodded. "It's my pleasure." He raised his glass. "But you all know there's one person who should be here but isn't. I never understood why he left us—"

"Don't," Alex warned.

"—I think about him all the time. About what I could've said, or should've said. So after this perfect day, with what I hope are more perfect days to come, I just wanted to take a second to remember Derek Li."

Alex shifted on the bench. "Are you serious with this shit?"

Sami grabbed his arm to keep him from getting up.

"Come on, Alex," Cat said, narrowing her eyes. That gave him pause. Cat was the calmest, most rational, of them. If she thought he was the one out of line, he knew he had to rein it in.

"Cat . . ."

"It's okay," Harry said, with what might have been faux sincerity or genuine regret. With him it had always been hard to tell. "I was a prick when Derek died. I didn't know how to handle it and it scared the shit out of me that someone I knew could take his own life. It shook me."

"You hid it well," Alex said.

Harry sat down, perched again on the edge of his own bench, across from Alex. He kept his glass raised.

"You don't have to forgive me, Alex. I'm sure I

wouldn't, if I were you. But I hope we can all agree that Derek deserves to be remembered. I just wanted to toast to the guy, to share a moment with you all so we could shout out to the universe or whatever and say we wish he was here with us tonight. Can we do that?"

Alex exhaled. He glanced around at the others and then back to Harry, and finally nodded and raised his glass. "Yeah, man. Of course we can."

"To Derek," Harry said.

They all chimed in, those who'd known their lost friend and those who'd only heard stories about him. Alex drank, and thought of Derek, and wished that Harry hadn't been the one to make the toast. Derek deserved to be remembered by the people who'd actually grieved for him.

"Hey," Harry said. "We good?"

Alex nodded, raised his glass, and took another sip, as if toasting to the uneasy truce between them.

"Good, because there's something else I wanted to talk to you all about."

"That sounds ominous," Nils said.

"No. Just personal," Harry replied. "And I hope you'll indulge me, because as great as it is to have you all with me, it's not the only reason for this trip."

Sami shifted on the bench. "Go on."

"I don't know how many of you ever knew this, or if you'd remember," Harry said, "but my dad was in the Coast Guard, once upon a time."

Cat kept her fingers over the strings of her guitar to keep them silent, as if they had a voice of their own. "I remember."

Harry raised his glass to her but didn't drink. "If anyone would, it's you, Cat. Anyway, my dad passed a few years back. He was a good man, better than me by a hundred miles. He always talked about his time in the Coast Guard as the most peaceful time of his life, which is ironic, right? He was stationed at a place called Orchid Atoll, said it was paradise, hundreds of miles from anything. The Coast Guard station there has been shut down for years, but if it's okay with all of you, I'd like us to visit Orchid Atoll tomorrow. Pay my respects and . . . I don't know, connect with that part of my dad's life. We'll come back to Hawaii the next day, do all of the islands, but if nobody minds—"

"Nobody minds, Harry," Nils said, glancing around at the others for confirmation. "Right?"

They went around the circle, reassuring Harry, enthusiastic about the adventure and sympathetic over the loss of his father, about which it seemed only Luisa had been aware. Sami told Harry they were honored to go with him and intrigued by visiting an atoll. Alex agreed, though he couldn't help wondering what their precise heading might be at that moment. They'd left Kauai hours ago and had been sailing ever since. Had they been sailing toward Orchid Atoll all along without Harry bothering to bring it up until now? If so, how much did Harry really give a shit about getting their blessing? Alex didn't mind the side trip. Sami was right; it was an honor and an intriguing prospect and he'd never have denied Harry the moment he was obviously searching for. But this was quintessential Harry, doing exactly what he wanted and manipulating others into going along, even making it seem like they'd volunteered.

Alex raised a glass and offered a toast to Harry's father, for which Harry looked genuinely grateful. Alex meant it, too. However his son might be wired, Alex wasn't going to blame a dead man for it.

"Can I just ask . . . ," Dev began.

Alliyah smiled at her husband. "He's nervous."

"Terrified, actually," Dev confessed with a self-deprecating laugh. "I think I've been hiding it pretty well till now, but . . . okay, the Coast Guard station is closed. Is there anything else out there? I mean, how far will we be from civilization?"

"At least three hundred miles," Harry said. "But I promise you, Dev, you're in good hands. I know what I'm doing, and Gabe is the best first mate I could ask for."

Sami chuckled. "I know someone who'd like to be in Gabe's good hands."

Luisa shot up her hand to volunteer before anyone could ask. "Me, oh, me."

Later that night, when Harry had gone down to relieve Gabe at the helm for a few hours and many of the others had gone to bed, Alex stood at the forward port railing and gazed out at the moonlit water. He didn't share Dev's fear of the sea, but out here, with only the night and the waves and the hundred-foot boat seeming so very small, he could understand that terror. They were so alone, so separate from the rest of the world, that they might as well be the last people on earth. In that moment, head still a bit muzzy from the drinks, heart soaring with the sounds of the wind in the sails and the clank of the rigging and the power of the wind, it was easy to imagine they truly were the last of the human race.

"Hey."

Alex nearly missed the word on the wind, but he turned and saw Alliyah sidling up to him. She'd tied her hair back, but a curling lock had escaped its band and whipped across her eyes. She tried to tuck it away but to no avail, so she ignored it.

"How's Dev?" he asked.

She smiled. "He'll live. Half a Xanax a day will do the job. I don't want him to take a whole one because I'm afraid he'll fall overboard."

"Good thinking."

"Listen, Alex, we're off to bed, but I just wanted to say I'm really happy you and Sami came. I know it's not easy for you with Harry, but I think it's good. For you and for all of us. And on a personal note . . . I thought it might be weird, being here with you and my husband and your wife."

He leaned on the railing, giving her a sideways glance. "Alli, you and I dated for a month."

"I know. Just a month. But it wasn't like Luisa hooking up with Harry—"

"Thank God."

She laughed, lifting a hand to hide her smile when she did. "That's what I'm saying. You and I were a bad idea as a couple, but we did have a romantic something, as opposed to a couple of torrid nights and a vomit-inducing blow job. I just thought it might be awkward, but I'm glad it's not."

"Well, it *wasn't*," Alex teased. "Until now."

He glanced past her and saw Dev and Sami talking to Luisa alongside the cockpit. Sami wasn't the jealous type, but Alex saw her forehead crinkle with curiosity when she spotted him talking to Alliyah.

"Listen, I think we're going to turn in, too," he said.

"Holy shit, look at that."

Alex turned to see Alliyah pointing out at the night-black sea. The moonlight frosted the water, but he spotted the fin immediately.

"Wow."

"Tell me that's a dolphin," she said.

"Nope. They usually surface and go right back down. I'm no expert, but swimming along like that . . . pretty sure it's a shark."

"Wonderful," Alliyah said. "I don't think I'll be sharing that with Dev."

Alex watched the shark knifing through the water. "I don't know, maybe it'll make him feel better. After all, he was worried about us being alone out here."

CHAPTER 6

Isko knew death must be close. He sensed it nearby, looming in the shadowed corners where the nighttime darkness seemed painted even blacker. Sweat beaded on his forehead and along his arms and he felt the fevered flush in his cheeks. Even with the breeze that snuck through the broken window and whispered along the floor, he could not cool down, could not catch his breath. His eyelids drooped and he drifted off into a gray nothing.

Blinking awake, he inhaled sharply, as if for a moment he had stopped breathing. And maybe he had. Death had tried to steal upon him while he'd slept. As he opened his eyes, a swarm of black dots fled toward the edges of his vision. Like death, they'd crept in while he'd slept, dark little spots of brain death, but now they hid themselves away as if to keep the truth from him.

He frowned, eyes slitted, heavy enough that he knew he might fall unconscious again at any moment. A scent had reached him, a smell of flowers that reminded him of his little girl. Dalisay liked to make rings of flowers, to choose the most vividly colored blossoms and knit them together into chains she'd hang all over their small, neat home. Sometimes she'd put one on her head as a crown. Sometimes she'd do the same to her daddy to make him the King.

And she'd smile, his Dalisay.

Isko tried to say her name, but it came out a croak. He wetted his lips with what little saliva remained on his tongue, thirstier than he'd ever been. His stomach had become a tight, aching ball. He shivered, the fever giving him a chill in spite of the heat trapped inside the room. He thought of his wife, cleared his throat, and managed her name.

"Tala."

His eyes damp with tears, he shifted, hugging himself as he tried to fight the sudden chill. The stink of blood filled his nostrils and his torn pants stuck to the drying crimson puddle on the floor. His leg had been mostly numb, but now pain spiked up along the bone and he gasped and went rigid, trying to ride it out. But the darkness swallowed him again, just as if he'd sunk into the sea and never made it to shore.

In the dreamless sea of his fevered unconscious, death swam nearer. In the shadows of his mind, it had rows of sharp, gleaming teeth and merciless black eyes. Somewhere down deep, lost in that fever, he prayed for death to be swift.

CHAPTER 7

Alliyah stood at the bow of the *Kid Galahad* and wondered how the footsteps of her life had led to this place. Eighteen months ago, she'd walked out on her husband. After years of offering him noncommittal assurances that yes, she would like to be a mother someday, the guilt of her lies had become overwhelming. Unconsciously at first, but later very much on purpose, she'd built an icy distance between them, punctuated by a two-week affair with a corporate attorney she'd met at the gym. The sex had been furious and intense. No one else had ever made her come hard enough to pass out. She'd told Dev the truth in order to enrage him so that he would leave her, although she'd secretly feared his forgiveness.

It turned out she'd had nothing to fear. The plan to drive Dev away had worked perfectly, and it had torn her apart. With their house still echoing the shouts and the slam of the door, panic and regret had flooded through her. She'd never screwed the lawyer again— never talked to him again, even switched gyms to avoid it. Instead, she'd tracked down a therapist she hadn't seen in years. When she'd received a text from Dev saying he intended to file for divorce and asking if she'd agree to a mediator, she'd broken down completely.

I owe you the truth, she'd texted him.

Isn't the truth what broke us? he'd replied.

Yes. But not the way you think.

To her surprise, he'd reluctantly agreed to come by the house. She made coffee. Only coffee. A meal would have frightened him away, and she didn't feel like she deserved the sort of forgiveness that him sitting down to a meal with her would indicate. Over coffee, she told him that she didn't want to be a mother. Part of her wanted to burst into tears, as if she ought to be flushed with shame over her disinterest in bearing children, but she found that her only shame came from what she'd done to avoid this confession. Saying it out loud, saying it to Dev, helped her focus in a way she never had before.

"Why did you never—" he began.

"It didn't start as a lie," she'd interrupted. "I always thought the idea would grow on me, that I just wasn't ready, but someday I would be. But years went by and I realized that somewhere along the way, going along with the idea that we'd have kids one day had *become* a lie. I hated how it made me feel, every time we talked about it, every time you'd get that look in your eyes. I knew how much you wanted to be a father—"

"I wanted to be your husband more."

That had silenced her. Alliyah had stared at him, fiddling with her coffee mug, knowing the coffee had started to go cold and she'd only taken one sip.

"You deserved the life you'd imagined for yourself," she'd said quietly.

Dev had gone quiet, too, then. He'd rocked back in his chair—the same chair he always sat in when they had breakfast or dinner together—and stared at the ceiling for what seemed an eternity. Then he'd tilted his chair back down, lifted his mug, and drained the rest of his coffee. Sliding the chair back, he'd set the mug down and stared at her.

"It's too late for me to have the life I imagined. You destroyed that."

"Dev—"

"You abandoned me emotionally long before you cheated."

"I—"

He'd stood up from his chair, coffee mug forgotten on the table. He'd looked tired; she remembered that now. Weary and thinner than usual, his clothing rumpled, but he had also seemed more like the man she'd married than he had in years. Even then, she'd realized that probably had more to do with her perception than it did with reality, but in the moment she saw him with utter clarity.

"I'm going," he'd said. "But I'm not going far. I can't see past betrayal right now, Alli. But I know the person I used to love is under there somewhere, and I'm willing to give you a little time to find her."

Two months later, dancing around each other like boxers before the first punch is thrown, they'd gone out for dinner together. A date, which had seemed absurd, except that it had led them here. Their close friends knew, and their families, of course. Dev's family had never been happy with him marrying a Pakistani woman in the first place, and after what she'd done they were furious. He'd never told them that she didn't want children; that would have driven them over the edge. It turned out that Dev could imagine a life without kids. It saddened him, but he could imagine it.

Still, nothing was certain between them. None of the people on this trip were privy to their secrets, and Alliyah had no intention of sharing them. Coming to Hawaii had felt to her like the final piece of the puzzle of repairing their life together, and she had no intention of dredging up painful memories. Dev seemed on the same page. He'd been enthusiastic about the trip from the beginning, wanted to know her friends from college better. Even the fact that a lifetime ago she had briefly dated Alex seemed to amuse him. In a month or a year or five years, Dev might decide he had made a mistake, that he couldn't really forgive her or that in the end having children was more important to him than having her.

For now, though, they were in paradise.

They were practically on top of Orchid Atoll before Sami spotted it, and even then what her eye picked out was a landmass at least fifteen miles distant. Fortunately for them all, Harry and Gabe knew what they were doing. Had she been piloting the boat, they'd have grounded themselves on the outer rim. The boat banked south and slowed. Gabe lowered the sails and Harry used the purring engine to glide them through the largest of the openings in the atoll's ring.

Someone stepped up beside her at the railing. "Vanishing beauty."

Sami glanced to her left and saw it was Nalani who'd spoken. Without James, which seemed strange. The pair had been almost inseparable since Sami had first laid eyes on them. She reminded herself not to make assumptions. Maybe Nalani and James often ranged apart—what did any of them really know about one another except what they'd learned in the past day or so? Even these old friends were having to learn who they were now.

"Vanishing how?"

Nalani shrugged. "Sea level. The larger part of the ring there, with the building on it? That'll stick around longer. The rest of it will be gone, probably in our lifetimes. Maybe sooner than we think."

The atoll was already not what Sami had imagined. She'd thought the ring would be mostly unbroken, but instead the circle of land had numerous breaches in it. As they sailed inside the ring—six or seven miles from side to side—she couldn't make out much of the distant edges, but Harry navigated toward the western rim, and though there were long stretches here and there, the breaks were frequent, the water flowing in and out as if each piece of the shattered ring was an island unto itself.

They sailed toward the single significant landmass on the rim. Trees and flowers grew there, as if a piece of the paradise of the tropics had broken off and been forgotten out here, hundreds of miles from the nearest fragment of civilization. A small gray two-story building sat in the center of an open space in the midst of this, as unwelcome as Dorothy's house dropping from the sky into Oz. Featureless except for its rooftop radio tower, the building had a familiar utilitarian drabness that screamed of governmental lack of imagination.

"Must be the Coast Guard station," Sami said.

Nalani laughed. "Nothing else out here."

She wasn't wrong, but Sami loved the isolation. Out on the water she'd begun to have a breathless feeling of wild vulnerability that both frightened and excited her. Now that she saw the Coast Guard station, she wished that she could erase it. With the tropical eruption of color represented by the trees and flowers on the largest part of the atoll, the man-made thing marred the land-and-seascape. Still, there was something wonderful—something she'd never experienced in her life—about being so far from everything and everyone except this boat and the people on it. They were sailing at the edge of the world, and all the troubles of life at home had been cut away. They were untethered, and she loved it.

Alex slid up beside her at the railing. Others joined

them, until finally Harry arrived, having left Gabe to pilot them toward the Coast Guard station.

"A hundred feet deep," Harry intoned, as if he'd dug beneath the water himself. "And look how clear the water is. In my father's letters, he wrote about spearfishing in the water here. He said it was so clear they could have caught the fish by hand if they'd been fast enough."

Sami put her arm around Alex. "God, it's so blue."

"Sapphire," Nalani said. "I love the way the sun flares in the water."

Sami stared down into the water. A fish zipped past, and it was true, the water was perfectly clear, but only near the surface. Toward the beach and the rocks, where the water grew shallower, it was clear as glass . . . but out here they could see only so far before the Pacific blue turned deeper and darker. A beautiful mystery.

"Okay, it's my nature to give Harry shit," Alex said, "and I know we have a lot of Hawaii to see. But this little stopover may turn out to be the best part of the trip. It's breathtaking out here."

"Why, you old romantic," Harry said with a grin.

The two shared a truly amicable moment, and for a second Sami had an idea of what it might have been like when they were younger, in their early days at college, when their similarities had been more important than their differences.

"Has this place really been abandoned since they closed the Coast Guard station?" Sami asked.

"Most people don't even know it's here," Nalani

replied. "I'm sure there are day-trippers and sojourners who've come out this way over the years—"

"But not many," Harry said, beaming as he gazed at the shore. "One thing's for sure; nobody's lived here in that long."

The engine hummed a bit louder and Harry glanced back at the wheelhouse. He gave a wave and then shot them an excited look. "Time to weigh anchor."

He rushed off, leaving Sami and Alex, Nalani and Nils, Dev and Alliyah, all gathered at the railing.

"Our own private paradise," Dev said quietly.

Alliyah put her arm around him. "Damn, I needed this."

Sami smiled, leaning her head on Alex's shoulder. "We all did."

Nils shot them a mischievous look. "Patrick and I just want to know if there'll be skinny-dipping."

Alex shook his head. "Some things never change."

Nils laughed and rushed off, presumably to find his husband.

"Is he serious?" Sami asked.

"You've seen his abs," Alliyah said. "Nils is always looking for a reason to strip."

Moments later, the anchor splashed into the water. A little shiver of excitement went through Sami and she turned and kissed her husband. Grinning, she leaned in to whisper into his ear, soft and intimate, the words only for him.

"I love you. And I'm so glad we came."

Alex kissed her forehead. She thought he might have said something in return, but then Harry cried out to them.

"Grab your gear and get ready!" Harry shouted. "All ashore that's going ashore!"

CHAPTER 8

It took three trips for all of them to go ashore, although *all* turned out to be minus two bodies. Despite Nils's talk of skinny-dipping, he and Patrick decided to stay on board, taking advantage of the opportunity for some private time on the luxury sailing ship. As Patrick had put it, "The wine is already on board, and the deck won't get sand all over my ass." Nobody begrudged them the desire for time alone. On the contrary, when they'd announced they were staying on the *Kid Galahad* Alex had felt a twinge of envy, wishing he'd thought of it first even though he knew it would have been the wrong move. Harry had taken no offense to Nils and Patrick's decision, but if Alex and Sami had done it their host would definitely have felt slighted. Alex wished he didn't have to take diplomacy into consideration, but the history was complicated. Some of the tension had finally started to bleed out of the atmosphere between himself and Harry, and for everyone's sake—including his own—Alex wanted that to continue.

Alcohol was helping.

Cat lay sprawled on a thick woven beach blanket, big mirrored sunglasses covering her eyes as she took a puff on a joint that had appeared in her hand as if by magic. She'd shared it around at first but now seemed to be relishing it with the passion of a connoisseur. Luisa sat beside her on the blanket with a cold beer between her legs. The rest of them were arranged along a twenty-foot stretch of beach. Alliyah and Dev, Nalani and James, Alex and Sami. On the raised table of rock Gabe had brushed sand away and spread out a red-and-white-checked picnic blanket.

"Come on, folks," Gabe announced. "All of this food isn't going to eat itself."

"Damn, man," Alex said, "how much can you fit in one basket?"

"He's a magician," Dev declared.

"There's more than one basket," Gabe replied. "You guys helped carry it. Or have you already had too many beers to remember that?"

"Amateurs," Harry sniffed. He lay propped against another stone nearby, this one jutting from the sand, the surf rippling and frothing around its base. On a green towel between his legs was a small cooler from which he'd produced an enormous pineapple, which he now proceeded to carve up with a wickedly sharp blade.

Alex had to hand it to them: Dev wasn't wrong.

These two men, one a sailor at heart and the other an elitist prick trying to figure out where he'd gone wrong, were more than they seemed. They had navigated the boat and sailed it here, and by the time they'd dropped anchor they'd had a picnic prepared for the entire group consisting of vegetable wraps, sushi, an exquisite chicken salad, and a selection of fresh fruits. Three separate coolers of beer and wine had also come ashore.

"I know you're all getting spoiled by all the fresh pineapple," Harry called, "but who wants some?"

"Are you kidding?" Sami said. "I might stay forever just for that."

Alex chuckled. It felt good, like the carefree potential of this journey had finally begun to settle in. He glanced around again at the people arrayed on the shore, old friends and their mates. They'd lost one of their own when Derek had taken his own life, but the rest of them were not just alive; they were thriving. Cat had softened a bit in the decade since college. Nalani's hippy husband, James, had a bit of flab on him. Dev had a few gray hairs already. But as far as Alex could see, they were all healthy. It struck him in that moment how lucky they all truly were. Cat wore cutoffs and a bright peach tank top, but the other women all wore bikinis of vibrant color and varying style, some more daring than others. Dev wore a shorter suit than the other men, stylish and with a younger vibe. Harry had a red floral Hawaiian shirt, threadbare and unbuttoned, like he'd gone to the beach or to sea a hundred times and the fabric had been bleached by the sun and salt.

"I know we keep saying it, but this really *is* paradise," Alex said aloud.

Only when he caught Sami, Harry, and several of the others looking at him did he realize the words had traveled from his thoughts to his lips.

"It is," Sami agreed.

Alex glanced at Harry, who lifted one corner of his mouth in what seemed a rueful smile, an expression that took into account the tension that had lingered between them, and the friendship they'd once had.

Sami tapped Alex's arm. She had her eyes closed now, reclining in the sun, but she'd put out a hand to nudge him. "How about some of that pineapple, baby?"

"I live to serve." He climbed to his feet and strode over to Harry, who had produced a sleeve of blue Solo cups and was putting sliced-up pineapple into several of them.

"Good man," Harry said. "A smart husband knows when it's time to obey."

A day—even hours—before, Alex might have snapped at him. Instead, he only smiled and reached out to take a cup of the sliced fruit.

Harry cocked his head. "No riposte? I'm almost disappointed."

"Nah, man. You're right. I'm a smart husband."

"But you're wondering how I became such a font of wisdom on marriage. Trust me, it happened after I was divorced. You learn a lot when your life falls apart."

Harry reached into the cooler and drew out a bottle of Kona Lemongrass Luau, a Hawaiian beer. "You want one?"

"More than my wife wants fresh pineapple."

Harry opened the bottle of beer and nestled it into the sand, then plucked another from the cooler and did the same. He drew out a lime and expertly sliced it into wedges, twisting two of them and garnishing the mouths of the beer bottles before he handed one to Alex.

"To better days," Harry said.

Alex took the bottle of beer. "These might be the better days."

"I'll drink to that."

They clinked bottles. Alex pushed his lime twist down into the neck of his beer while Harry squeezed his lime, letting its juice drip down into the bottle. A kind of quiet covenant formed between them in that moment, more than just a détente. Alex knew he could never forgive Harry for the past, but he found himself willing to judge an old friend by the man he'd become, not the man he'd been.

Each of them took a swig of beer.

"You're still a jackass," Alex said quietly, wanting this part of the conversation to be private. It felt intimate, this moment of reparation. Gabe was close enough to hear them but courteous enough to pretend to be minding his own business.

Harry smirked. "But absent malice, my friend. Absent malice."

They both drank again. Alex hoisted the cup of pineapple. "I need to deliver this."

"Of course. After you do, though, I'd like to go and take a look at the Coast Guard station. It's a weird little pilgrimage I've undertaken."

"You want to see where your father spent his time here," Alex replied.

"I guess I want to see if he left any echoes behind."

"Echoes?"

"Just to see if I can feel him," Harry said. "Not like a fucking medium or anything. I'm not that spiritual. I don't mean actual ghosts. But if I can imagine him there, inside that building, maybe I can know him a little better."

Alex tilted back his beer and took a long sip. "You've been in a lot of therapy since the last time I saw you."

Harry laughed. "What gave me away?"

Alex turned on his heel in the sand. "I'll go with you. Just give me a second."

As he walked the pineapple back to Sami, Harry stood and faced the whole group. "This is a personal journey for me, guys. You should absolutely stay here and chill. Have another drink; eat your fill; go for a swim. Just enjoy this place. Hardly anyone in the world will ever see it, and none of us is likely to ever see it again. But if you're curious and you want to check out the Coast Guard station, I'm happy to have you along."

Alex crouched by Sami. She took the cup of pineapple from him, reached in for a piece, and popped it into her mouth.

"Okay if I stay here?" she said quietly.

"Absolutely. I'm going with him, though."

"I'm glad. It obviously means a lot to him."

Alex sipped his beer thoughtfully. He knelt and kissed Sami on the cheek, and by the time he rose once more to his feet Cat and Luisa were also standing. The three of them joined Gabe and Harry, and then all five were walking along the shore of the atoll. The flowers were splashes of vivid, joyous color and the ripple of the surf was calming, but the abandoned Coast Guard station loomed quietly ahead, and the five of them were strangely somber as they walked, drinks in hand, into Harry's unknown history.

Sami used her fingers to pluck another chunk of pineapple from her cup as she watched the quintet walk along the shore. A rustling of sand beside her made her turn. Alliyah had knelt there, some kind of tropical mixed drink in one hand. She offered it to Sami.

"Orchid Sunrise," Alliyah said. "I just invented it."

"What's in it?" Sami asked.

"Secret recipe. Just try it."

Curious but a little afraid, Sami took the cup. She narrowed her eyes in suspicion, but Alliyah stayed mum, so Sami took a sip. At first she could only taste fruit—orange, pineapple, plus something else, some kind of berry. Then the alcohol kicked in, a rush of heat that inflamed her throat and brought a flush to her cheeks. The fruit flavors rolled back over the burn, soothing and sweet.

"Wow," Sami said, eyes watering a little.

Alliyah laughed. "Good?"

"Very good. And very dangerous."

"My trademark," Alliyah said. "You have that. I'll mix another."

Her husband had overheard the exchange. From his

spot on the sand he raised his own drink. "This is when the party starts."

Sami lifted her cup to toast the thought, then saw that Alliyah's gaze had drifted up the beach.

"There's a sight I never thought I'd see," she said.

"You mean Alex and Harry?"

"Acting like they don't hate each other," Alliyah replied. "Yeah. It's new. I like it."

The drinks flowed nicely after that. Everyone seemed to have adopted the Orchid Sunrise, its name inspired by the atoll. Sami had finished her first and happily accepted a second from Dev, who had taken over his wife's mix-master duties. By the time the others returned, Sami knew she would be hammered. Not on the second drink—as powerful as these drinks were, she had a fairly high tolerance. But she anticipated being offered a third, and didn't intend to say no.

"Whoo, Sami," Alliyah said as she took a long sip. "Nice to see you loosen up."

Sami could have taken offense at the implication, but after all, Alliyah wasn't wrong. There'd been plenty of tension on this trip, and she and Alex had been tightly coiled from the beginning.

"Alli-honey," Sami said, "look around. You put the devil in this place with a drink in his hand and pretty soon he'll be an angel."

They sat with their feet in the water, the surf rippling up past them. Sami felt the sand shifting under her with each white-frothed wave. Her feet and her butt sank deeper and she lay on her back and let her body sink in. She thought of snow angels. *Sand angels, now.*

A smile touched her lips as the surf tickled her, and even with her arms spread out to either side she managed to keep her drink aloft.

"Psst."

Eyes closed behind her sunglasses, Sami opened them reluctantly. She lolled her head to the right and saw Alliyah looking at her. In the moments her eyes were closed, Dev had joined them, the three of them making sand angels in the froth. Alliyah's eyes sparkled with mischief.

"Notice anyone missing?" Alliyah asked.

Sami frowned. She sat up, wet hair plastered against her neck. She took a sip of her Orchid Sunrise and then glanced around. The three of them were alone on the rocky stretch of sand. Nalani and James had been there, tangled together, kissing and whispering to each other.

"They went for a little stroll," Alliyah said. "Very romantic."

Dev sat up and craned his neck. The broken pieces that made up the atoll were a ring, but these island fragments were the upper edges of a volcanic formation below the water, like the teeth of the volcano's mouth. The inside edges of the broken ring were sandy, while the outer edges had rocky shores with slightly higher surf, waves that crashed and flowed between the fragments of the ring. Some of the fragments, including the one they'd chosen for their picnic, had coral ridges at the waterline. A ridge of coral and stone, as well as earth and flowers, rose a few feet behind them, and Sami assumed Nalani and James were on the other side.

"They went swimming on the outer edge," Dev said. He raised his drink in a mock toast and gave a little shrug. "I think they're fucking in the water. If you think that sort of thing's romantic."

Sami rose on her knees and turned to survey the fragment of atoll they were on. It was about eighty yards in width. There were trees far off to her right, where the Coast Guard station silently sat. Over the top of the ridge and the flowers, she could barely make out Nalani and James in the water, their heads above the waves. Whatever they were doing, it was intense and intimate and not meant for prying eyes.

"Actually, I think it's very romantic," Sami said, averting her gaze and settling back onto the sand. "I just hope they don't end up drowning out there."

"What about you, love?" Dev asked his wife. "Do you think it's romantic? Should we go for a little swim ourselves?"

Alliyah gazed out over the water inside the atoll's ring. She seemed lost in thought, and it seemed to take a few seconds for her to realize Dev had been talking to her.

"What?" she said. Then she must have realized what he'd said, for she shot him a lopsided grin. "Maybe *you* should go for a swim. Cool off a little."

Dev drained his drink, set the cup down, and ran into the surf. He dove into the water, knifing under the surface. The crystal-blue clarity made it easy to follow him until he kicked deeper. Down there, a shadow seemed to envelop him. Sami could still make him out, but now the details were gone. For a few moments, Dev might have been anything down there, a dolphin or a sea monster. He broke the surface and waved to them before swimming farther from the shore.

"I'm a little more conservative than Nalani," Alliyah said quietly.

Sami turned and propped herself on an elbow, studying the other woman. "At the moment, I'm starting to think even Luisa is more conservative than Nalani."

Alliyah rolled her eyes. "Luisa's all talk. Or mostly talk, anyway."

"I understand it, though," Sami said. "Nalani and James. We're only here for a few hours. Some lunch and drinks and a chance for Harry to visit with the ghost of his father."

"Ghost?"

Sami ran her fingers through the surf that rippled along the sand, washing in and washing out. "Not a real ghost. The memory, I mean. It feels like an early midlife crisis or something—whatever he's going through. Whatever it is, we're here. Feels like we're out on the edge of the world, the kind of place sailors used to worry they'd reach the end of the Earth and sail right off a cliff into space."

"Your husband called it paradise," Alliyah reminded her.

"It is. It's the wild, out here. That's all I'm saying. If a place like this makes Nalani and James feel . . .

liberated, like the ordinary rules don't apply, I understand that."

Alliyah smiled without looking at her. "Is that your
way of telling me that you're ready for your third
Orchid Sunrise?"

"I might take a swim first. You going to come into
the water?"

"Not just yet," Alliyah said.

Sami sat up and brushed sand from her elbow. She
rose to her feet. Alliyah had kept staring out at the
water, presumably watching her husband. But as Sami
looked on, she realized Alliyah wasn't tracking Dev's
movements at all. Instead, the woman's eyes scanned
the expanse of water inside the atoll's ring as if searching for something.

"What are you looking at?" Sami asked, swiping
sand off her butt.

"I thought I saw something."

Sami frowned. "In the water?"

Now Alliyah stood, too. She didn't bother to brush
herself off.

"A fin," she said.

Sami smiled. "You're funny."

"I'm not being funny." Alliyah stepped into the surf,
walking until she was thigh deep, still scanning the
quietly undulating surface of the expanse of ocean
within the atoll's ring. She hadn't started to call to Dev,
to ask her husband to get out of the water, but she
looked like she was thinking about it.

"Maybe it's a dolphin," Sami offered.

"Do you ever see just one dolphin, by itself?"

"I think so. I don't know. But even if it's a shark, they don't normally just attack people without being provoked. Do they?"

Alliyah glanced at her. "Maybe not. But that doesn't mean I'm in a hurry to go swimming with one."

CHAPTER 9

Harry kicked the door hard enough to crack the frame.

Alex wasn't so drunk that it didn't concern him. "You sure this is a good idea?" he asked. "Breaking and entering on federal property?"

Harry ignored him. Luisa and Cat hung back, drinking, watching from a respectful distance. If they were troubled, neither one showed it.

"The place is abandoned," Gabe explained, as if he spoke for Harry. And maybe he did.

"Even so. If nobody cared whether we went in there, it wouldn't be locked up."

Harry shot another kick at the door, his foot landing next to the knob. Another crack, and this time a gap opened. Just a quarter of an inch, but it was clear the door was about to surrender.

"Nobody's been here for at least a decade," Harry said, pausing between kicks. "Anywhere else it would already have been wrecked and covered in graffiti by kids using the place to party."

The rationalization didn't work for Alex, but he'd said his piece. He kept his mouth shut as Harry launched one more kick. The frame split around the lock and the door swung inward with such force that it cracked against the inside wall. The doorframe had been weak, but the lock had been solid. Strong.

Alex hung back while the others entered, first Harry and Gabe, then Luisa and Cat. When he stepped over the threshold, he expected the place to smell musty. And it did, but not nearly as bad as he'd anticipated. There were floral smells here, the salt tang of the sea, the damp reek of dusty concrete and wood swollen with humidity. He followed the others past a reception desk, staring at the walls as they moved deeper into the building. He'd expected posters or banners on the walls, portraits of whoever was President when this place shut down. Typewriters, Rolodexes, maybe even some rotting mattresses on top of rusting bunks. Instead, the large room just past the reception area looked like Whoville after the Grinch had been there, not even a crumb left behind.

"Wow. Scrubbed clean," Luisa said.

The room was so barren that it took a few seconds for Alex to realize it must have been office space. He could picture cubicles in here. There were phone jacks spaced about ten feet apart on each wall. The front and back walls had small box windows that were rimed with salt on the outside, making them almost opaque.

Cat went to the back of the room and tried to scrape

at the window to look out, but she had no success. On the far wall was another door, which hung partway open. Harry paused as if to collect his thoughts before he went through the door with Gabe in his wake.

"How many men do you think were stationed here?" Cat asked.

"Not sure," Luisa replied. "Any women, do you think?"

"Depends what year, I guess," Cat replied. "Tight quarters for men and women who are far from home."

"You're suggesting lots of hot sex took place in this building?" Luisa said.

"If these ugly walls could talk."

Alex drained the last of his beer. It had gone warm and the lime had overwhelmed the flavor. The fruit lodged in the neck of the bottle and he gave up on the last few drops, setting the bottle on the floor in the corner of the old office space.

When he looked up, Gabe had returned, filling the doorway.

"You guys should get in here."

Something about his tone made the small hairs prickle at the back of Alex's neck. Cat started asking questions, but Alex figured the answers were beyond that door. Gabe stepped out of the way to let them pass. They moved down a corridor with several doors on either side—the quarters for the Coasties stationed here, Alex figured. Some of the doors were open and others closed. Through one open door, Alex saw a bed-roll on the floor. Blankets and a pillow. Someone's dusty, crinkled shoes. A small tower of empty beer cans. Through another open door he saw an actual bed. Metal frame, thin gray mattress—U.S. Armed Services issue, most likely—so the Coast Guard had left something behind after all. He imagined the other rooms also had beds in them.

But the Coast Guard hadn't left the beer cans stacked like that and those shoes weren't government issue.

"Gabe?" Alex asked, glancing over his shoulder.

Cat and Luisa had stopped to look into the room with the bedroll and the beer cans.

"In the mess," Gabe said, gesturing for Alex to keep going.

The mess. What the military called the kitchen—or, really, the cafeteria where their meals were eaten. During his time in the army, Alex had eaten some of the worst food of his life in the mess, but usually he'd been so tired he had barely tasted it.

He reached the end of the corridor, turned left and then right, and found Harry standing alone, studying an enormous map of the Pacific that had been affixed to the wall of the mess hall. There were other maps, but it wasn't the maps that drew Alex's attention now. Jackets and sweatshirts were draped over abandoned office chairs. A weathered Oakland A's baseball cap hung from a hook on the wall. Most of the tables were dusty but otherwise bare, but several . . . at the front of the room . . . were stacked with cases of bottled water, beer, and coffee pods. A gleaming Keurig sat on one table, plugged into a wall socket, barely any dust on it at all. There were sleeves of cups, plastic tubs of sugars and creamers and utensils.

Blood smeared the floor by that table and there were streaks on the table itself. On the plastic packaging of a case of water. A bottle of water lay on the floor, bearing a bloody handprint. On the sill of the small window above that table, someone had lined up dozens of empty bullet shell casings.

We shouldn't be here, Alex thought. An image of his daughter, Tasha, rose in his mind, and he wished he and Sami were at home with their little girl.

"Harry," he said. "What the hell is this?"

Harry turned to face them. "Looks like the station's not as abandoned as we thought."

"This isn't just casual boaters crashing for the night and partying in here," Alex said. "You see those shell casings. And that map—there are markings on it. Shipping routes or something."

Cat and Luisa had come into the mess hall. Luisa whispered a variation on the same question. Something else had caught Gabe's attention, though, and he walked to the back of the mess hall. Above a huge industrial metal sink, a window had been smashed in. His Birkenstocks crunched broken glass underfoot.

"Someone came in this way," he said. "Glass in the sink, too. All over the place back here."

"That makes no sense," Harry said. "Someone's been using this place, but it's definitely not just one person. Whoever brought all that stuff in here—a fucking coffee maker—they didn't come through that window."

"We shouldn't be here," Luisa said, all of her usual mischief gone. Her voice had dropped an octave and all trace of playfulness had vanished. "Alex is right. Those bullet casings are a dead giveaway. No fucking pun intended. Whoever's been using this place, they're not going to like the idea of unwelcome visitors."

"The lock," Cat said. "It seemed . . . too new."

"But if they put their own lock on, what about the broken window?" Alex asked.

Gabe had joined Harry, staring at the map.

"Drug smugglers, you think?" he said.

"Or guns," Alex said, pointing out those shell casings again. There was something ominous about them, the boldness of the way they'd been lined up on the sill, no different from the beer cans that had been stacked into a pyramid in that bedroom. Someone didn't see any difference between empty beer cans and empty shell casings.

"Could be pirates, for all we know," Luisa said.

"Or care," Cat asked. She walked over to Harry, took his face in hers, and made sure he met her gaze. "You've been here. Whatever this pilgrimage was about, you've done it. Say hello and goodbye to your dad and let's get our asses out of here."

Harry nodded. "Yeah. Okay." He glanced around the room again; then he turned to leave.

Alex exhaled. They were alone, but this had spooked him. Orchid Atoll might have been paradise, but he thought it was a very bad idea for the *Kid Galahad* to stay anchored in the bay, or lagoon, or whatever the water inside the atoll's ring was called. They were all walking back the way they'd come, heading out of the mess, when they heard a very clear thump behind them.

"Kitchen," Harry whispered.

Gabe raised a hand and gestured for the others to stay back. He moved back across the mess hall. Luisa stayed where she'd been, but Cat and Harry started following Gabe, padding quietly, all of them on tenterhooks now. They'd all been drinking, their thoughts softly blurred not only by alcohol but also by the beauty and serenity of the atoll. The blood had been a surprise to them. So had the bullets. They hadn't expected a mystery, or any hint of violence. Now the thump seemed to linger in the room, the silence yawning, waiting to absorb whatever sound might come next.

The mess hall had two doors on the far wall. Alex calculated quickly. If the bullet-laden windowsill faced south and the broken window north, then they'd entered the mess from the west side of the room. There were two doors in the east wall. One had a heavy padlock that still gleamed, just like the knob and lock they'd broken to get in here. *Too new,* he thought now. They should have seen it right away.

The other door in the east wall—the door Gabe now crept toward, his big hands empty, his body tensed and ready for a fight—had no knob. No lock. Harry had mumbled about the kitchen, and Alex knew it had to be. Probably a swinging door for servers to pass back and forth.

Cat and Harry followed four or five steps behind Gabe. Alex blinked, realizing that he ought to be with them—that if someone familiar with blood and bullets waited on the other side of that door they were going to need help.

He took two steps across the room and nearly jumped out of his skin when Luisa clamped a hand on his shoulder. Spinning, right hand clenched into a fist, he felt his heart thunder in his chest as he stared into her eyes.

"What are you idiots doing?" she rasped.

Gabe froze. He, Harry, and Cat all turned to glare at her for breaking the silence. But Alex understood. She was right, of course. Luisa thought they should all be going the other way, getting the hell out of there, which had been their initial instinct.

"Harry," he said.

Cat held a finger to her lips. Gabe gestured for all of them to freeze. He pushed gently on the swinging door. The hinges creaked and he let the door swing closed again. They all waited. Despite Luisa's caution, Alex freed his arm from her grip and took two more steps. He felt flushed, muscles taut, ready for whatever came next.

Gabe put his fingers on the door again and slowly pushed it open. Harry, Cat, and Alex all moved closer, coming within just a few feet. Alex watched over Gabe's shoulder as the kitchen revealed itself—the massive sink, the antique stove, the long metal cooking island in the middle of the room.

"What the hell—" Gabe began.

Cat passed Harry and joined Gabe in the doorway, quietly cautioning him.

Only now, as Cat and Gabe moved into the kitchen and propped the door open, could Alex see what had caught Gabe's attention. The thump hadn't been the wind, and it hadn't been wildlife. A shirtless man lay on the floor, sprawled in a bloody heap in front of the stove. His clothes were caked to his body with what Alex thought must be blood and sweat and maybe salt, for he looked as if he'd been in the water at some point. He had tied his bloody T-shirt around his left thigh and cinched it tightly. Through the tatters of the trouser leg below, Alex could see a ragged wound in the meat of his thigh, crusted with dried blood but also still weeping crimson.

Alex stared at the wound as his thoughts raced. Had this guy broken the window? Had he ripped his leg open on the glass? He hadn't gotten there without a boat, so where the hell was it?

"Gabe?" Harry said. "Is he alive?"

As Gabe glanced back at them all, frowning in frustration—of course he didn't know if the guy was alive—the man on the floor moved. With a whisper and crackle of stiff, dried clothing and a cry of pain and anguish, the man rolled over. In a single motion, as he rolled, he whipped his right arm around, a cast-iron skillet in his hand. The skillet hit Gabe's skull with a wet crunch. As Gabe collapsed to the floor, the man scrambled onto him, still screaming. He swung the skillet again. Alex and Cat were both in motion, but Harry reached them first. He grabbed hold of the man's arm, trying to check his swing. The skillet glanced off Gabe's forehead, the edge slicing skin, spraying blood, but even as Alex hurled himself at the man and ripped him off Gabe he knew that if Harry hadn't interfered that blow would have been the end of Gabe.

"Oh my God, oh my God, oh my God," Luisa kept saying, like it was a prayer that didn't seem to be working. She'd come into the kitchen when the screaming started and now Cat took her hand.

Alex held the bleeding man down, saw his bleary eyes and the scruff of beard, and wondered how long this man had been here. At first he'd thought the guy must be old, but he was just withered.

The guy whimpered. He fought, but so weakly it was clear his attack on Gabe had used up all the strength he could muster. Alex turned to look at Harry.

"Gabe?" Alex said. "Is he . . ."

Harry knelt by Gabe. Blood sluiced down Gabe's handsome face. The first mate tried to talk, but the words were halting gibberish.

"He's in shock," Cat said. "And that hit—it didn't sound good, you guys."

"Jesus," Harry rasped, and he stood and glanced around as if it had just hit him that they were on Orchid Atoll, in the middle of the Pacific, hundreds of miles from anyone who could help them.

With one exception.

Alex ripped the skillet from the guy's hand and stood up. The guy moaned, then rolled onto his side, closing his eyes as if this had all been a bad dream. Alex pulled off his T-shirt and threw it to Luisa.

"Rip this up. Tie his hands. You and Cat are going to have to take charge of him. Bring him with us. Harry and I will carry Gabe."

"Carry him where?" Harry said, freaking out more than a little. "All our first-aid crap is on the *Galahad* and Gabe's got more training than I do anyway. Fuck, man, what are we gonna do?"

Alex tossed the skillet across the room. It hit the floor with a clatter as he hustled over to Gabe, knelt, and reached under his arms. "We're taking him back to the beach and then to the boat. More important, we're taking him to Sami. You know, my wife? The doctor? Now get his legs."

Cat moved toward the door, empty-handed.

"What are you doing?" Alex called.

"Being the smart one," Cat said. "Yes, get him outside. Carefully. Or at least to the door. Don't get that wound full of sand. Otherwise sit tight and I'll be back."

She bolted, her footfalls echoing back to them.

"Where are you going?" Harry called after her.

Alex knew. He'd been in shock, not thinking straight. "She's going to bring the doctor to the patient."

Luisa started to rip Alex's T-shirt, staring down at the scruffy, wounded man on the floor. "I'll tie his hands, but I'm not sure there's much point."

She nudged Gabe's attacker with her foot. "I think this guy is dead."

When the man groaned, she jumped backward.

Unleashing a string of profanity, she turned the whimpering man onto his stomach and began to bind his wrists behind his back.

Alex looked at Harry. They exchanged a silent nod and then hoisted Gabe off the floor. Harry's anguish was plain on his face, but he glanced around, moving swiftly and efficiently, careful with the swinging door.

Kneeling on the floor, cinching the lunatic's wrists, Luisa called after them, "Harry. I'm sorry, but I've got to ask you—"

Harry and Alex paused halfway through the door with Gabe heavy in their grasp, unconscious and bleeding, the wound in his skull glistening.

"What?" Harry snapped.

"If Gabe's out of action," she said, "can you sail the boat without him?"

Alex felt his skin go cold. Ice trickled down his back. The question hadn't even occurred to him and now he stared at Harry.

"Not alone," Harry said. "But I can teach one of you what you need to know. And we can call for help. We'll get home, if that's what you're worried about."

He said this last with disdain, as if he wanted Luisa to know how disgustingly selfish it was to be thinking of herself when Gabe's blood spattered the kitchen floor. But now that she'd asked the question, now that he'd seen the uncertainty in Harry's eyes, Alex found his concern for Gabe fading. He hoped the guy would be all right, but getting away from Orchid Atoll seemed more important now.

Someone had left the crazy son of a bitch here.

Someone had lined those bullets up on the windowsill in the mess hall, and pinned those maps on the walls. This place belonged to them now. Whoever had claimed this place, they weren't the Coast Guard.

"Come on," he said. "Let's move. Gabe's in serious trouble."

Harry knew that. He glared at Alex as they staggered across the mess and then down the corridor, Gabe swaying between them. It had been a stupid thing to say. Harry knew very well what kind of trouble Gabe was in. He'd only said it to speed them along.

Whatever might happen to Gabe, that chapter had already been written.

It was the rest of them that concerned Alex now.

Come on, Cat, he thought. *Move your ass.*

CHAPTER 10

Sami lay stretched out on her towel, sunglasses on, the last few ounces of her third Orchid Sunrise tilting in her cup as she drifted in that lovely gray space that wasn't quite a nap but sure as hell wasn't wakefulness. She listened to the water. Listened to the voices of the new friends around her. Dev and Alliyah had gone for a walk—the opposite direction from the Coast Guard station—to see how deep the channels ran between the fragments of the atoll's ring. Nalani and James had come back from whatever they'd been doing during their swim, laughing together and talking about all the places in the world they hoped one day to see. They were focused completely on each other and that suited Sami just fine. Their voices were a pleasant background buzz to go along with the other buzz she was working on.

At first the shouting along the beach sounded like

the cries of seagulls. Mixed with the shush of the surf, the noise melded with her expectations of the sorts of noises to be expected here. But there were no gulls here.

Her hand twitched, spilling a few ounces of Orchid Sunrise onto the sand. Her eyes opened.

"Sami!"

Now she sat up. Nalani and James had dropped their conversation, finally turning their focus to someone else. Alliyah and Dev were returning from their stroll.

"What's going on?" Alliyah called.

By then Sami had started to rise, blinking sleepily behind her sunglasses. Her cup lay forgotten beside her towel. She stared at the lone figure running along the beach toward them. Cat Skolis shouted her name again—not anyone else's, just hers. Sand flew up behind her as she ran, legs pumping. Sami looked past her in confusion, wondering where the others were, wondering why Cat was alone.

Alex. No no no. Something had happened to Alex.

"What the hell—" James began.

Sami left him there, left them all there. She started running to meet Cat, listing badly to first one side and then the other. She stumbled in the sand and nearly fell. Her thoughts were muddled and she understood now that somewhere between the second and third drinks she'd entered the strange twilight zone of drunkenness. Sami wasn't shit-faced, not so intoxicated that she wouldn't remember this moment or that she'd slur her words or vomit or pass out, but this was more than buzzed.

And something had happened to Alex. They had their little girl at home and she needed her dad.

The two women closed the distance between each other so quickly that Sami nearly collided with her. They caught each other by the arms, leaning together, Cat breathing hard from the run and Sami unsteady with drink.

"What is it?" Sami asked. "Is Alex okay? What happened?"

Catching her breath, Cat waved the words away, a deep frown on her face. "It's not Alex . . . it's Gabe. This guy jumped him . . . bashed him . . . in the head—"

"Guy? What guy? Alex is okay? What guy? How badly is Gabe—"

Cat took her arm, started her moving back the way she'd come. "It's bad, I think, but you're the doctor. All I can tell you is that we need to move fast."

The others called to them, asking questions. Cat did her best to answer on the run, but Sami had tuned them all out. She and Cat reached the dinghy. James and Nalani were there helping, pushing the little motorboat off the beach. Cat climbed in and then reached down for Sami's hand, eyes imploring.

"I'm . . . ," Sami began. "Oh, shit, Cat, I'm drunk."

Cat only frowned deeply and narrowed her eyes. "Sober the fuck up, honey, or I think this guy's as good as dead."

This is a nightmare, Sami thought as she let Cat help her into the dinghy. *I'm having a bad dream.* But she knew it wasn't true. As Cat fired up the engine,

Sami lost her balance and fell on her ass in the boat, sprawled across a bench with her legs in the air, feeling like a fool. By the time she hauled herself into a sitting position, the dinghy was roaring through the water, skipping across waves, with the Coast Guard station growing larger ahead of them. Something moved in her peripheral vision and she glanced to the right and spotted a fin in the water. It blurred and she rubbed at her eyes, realizing there were two of them, one about thirty feet away from the first, sharks cruising in the bay inside the encircling arms of the atoll. When Sami blinked again, one of them had vanished under the water.

Tracking the progress of the other fin, she shuddered, but then she heard more shouting and turned to see the others running along the beach, unable to keep up with the boat. The sharks were forgotten.

Cat cut the engine fifteen feet from the sand but kept it aimed for the station. The dinghy skidded onto the beach, tipped to one side, and Cat was already jumping out. She turned and reached up for Sami.

Reality crystallized for her. She stood, empty-handed. "What the hell am I supposed to do? I've got nothing."

Harry ran down to meet them. He had to have anticipated this moment. "First-aid kit under the pilot's seat!" he barked. "Let's go!"

Blinking hard, breathing deeply, Sami forced herself to focus. The alcohol made her throat dry and her head ache and her ability to think clearly seemed to ebb and flow like the surf, but she grabbed the first-

aid kit, unclipped it, and then scrambled off the dinghy without crashing, limbs splayed, onto the sand.

"Come on," she said, hurrying unsteadily toward
the Coast Guard station.

"She's drunk," Harry said.

"Obviously," Cat replied.

To his credit, whatever Harry thought about Sami's
condition, he said nothing more. Alarm bells were
screaming inside her head and she felt like throwing
up not from booze but from the weight of this crisis
that had just fallen on her. Instead, she ran, weaving a
bit, to the door of the station and stepped inside.

Alex knelt beside Gabe, who lay on the floor with
half of Alex's T-shirt under his head. Farther into the
building, Luisa held what looked like a broken chair
leg and kept guard over a bearded, blood-caked, filthy
man who sat propped against the wall, hands tied
behind his back, eyes slitted, mumbling and barely
conscious.

Sami dragged the back of her hand over her lips,
as if wiping away the taste of the alcohol could erase
its effects. She took a breath and dropped to her knees
beside Gabe, across from her husband. Alex watched
her quietly. He knew her, must have seen that she wasn't
entirely herself, but he also knew that she worked
best when she could tune out the rest of the world.

A shadow fell across Gabe. She snapped a look up
at Harry. "You're blocking the light."

He leaped aside. Sami gave a cursory visual examination to the rest of Gabe's body.

"Any injuries other than the head?" she asked.

"Fuck, isn't that enough?" Luisa asked. "Do you see the blood?"

Sami ignored her. She looked at Alex.

"Nothing else. Two blows to the skull. Cast-iron frying pan. Glancing blow tore the scalp." He wasn't a doctor, but he'd listened to her for long enough that he knew what she needed to know, more or less.

"Okay. Most of the flowing blood is from the scalp wound. I can sew that up."

"But the first one . . ." Harry edged closer, careful not to block the light. "I heard . . . I think it cracked his skull."

Sami carefully parted Gabe's hair, wishing for more light but not wanting sand in these wounds. Blood had already started to congeal around this spot, and the injury was far more concerning than the second. Either blow could have caused a variety of brain injuries, but she could see the white of bone beneath the blood. Cranial trauma was certain, but she wasn't worried about a concussion or even a skull fracture. Out here, in the middle of nowhere, so far from help, what worried her was cranial edema—swelling of the brain. If she had to relieve intracranial pressure here, with no tools . . .

"Harry, are there more towels on the dinghy?" she asked, opening the first-aid kit. Her vision blurred a bit and the heat inside the dusty walls made her stomach churn, but she held it together, fighting off the effects of the alcohol she'd had.

"Maybe. Probably."

"Cat, please get them," she said, digging through the small kit. If she'd had surgical glue she would have used that, but all she had were bandages and gauze. She could suture if she had to, but not here. Not like this.

"How is he?" Luisa asked.

"How does he look?" Sami snapped before reminding herself she wasn't dealing with med students. She took out the small bandages, removed their adhesive, and used them to close the tear in Gabe's scalp.

"I'll need plenty of fresh water to clean this right," she said, ripping open a packet of gauze. She pressed it gently but firmly over the torn scalp, then looked up at Alex. "Hold that."

As he obeyed, she used surgical tape to wind around Gabe's head, just to hold the gauze in place for the moment. Then she rose unsteadily and stepped around Gabe and Alex, heading for Luisa and the shuddering, muttering man against the wall.

"Wait, what the hell are you doing?" Harry barked.

"There are two injured men here," Sami replied.

"Are you shitting me? That's the guy who did this! Gabe's still got a gaping wound in his skull, for Christ's sake. What the fuck are you doing?"

Sami knelt by the stinking, unshaven man. He hadn't eaten in some time. Along the way, he'd obviously pissed himself. She looked him over, her eyes drawn to the torn-up fabric that had once been his trouser leg, and the blood that had soaked through. He had a dirty T-shirt tied around his upper left thigh. She wished she'd washed her hands—cursed herself and the alcohol she'd drunk for not having done so—and she parted strips of fabric to find the source of the blood.

"Damn it, Sami!" Harry roared.

"She's doing her job," Alex said.

Before Harry could snap at her again, Cat ran back in with two clean, folded towels.

"Good," Sami said, her head fighting a booze fog. "Wrap Gabe's head, carefully. I'd like to keep those wounds clean. They're going to bleed more, but hopefully not nearly as much. Then you guys are going to put him in the dinghy and we're going straight back to the boat. If he's suffered real damage, there's nothing I can do for him here."

"So you can help him if we get back to the *Galahad*?" Harry asked.

"Whatever you've got there for first aid has to be better than this. And we should head for the Hawaiian islands as soon as everyone's back on board."

Harry took the first towel and worked with Cat and Alex to prepare Gabe.

Sami took a closer look at the wound on the other man's leg. Luisa helped her turn the guy to take advantage of the light coming through the boxy foyer window.

"We taking him with us, too?" Luisa asked.

"Of course," Sami said.

"Not a chance," Harry snarled.

They all ignored him. Alex moved to Sami's side.

"We have to be careful. If he wakes up again—" Luisa said.

"I know," Sami interrupted.

"There's a broken window in the other room," Alex explained, gesturing toward the man's bloody leg. "We figure he slashed himself up climbing through."

Sami blinked, a fresh wave of Orchid Sunrise–induced queasiness washing over her. "You didn't get a good look," she said. "No broken window cuts like that. And he's given himself a tourniquet, or he wouldn't have survived this long. The guy was bitten."

They all stared at her. Sami rolled her eyes. "Come on. Move it."

"His leg," Harry said. "That's a shark bite?"

Luisa and Sami helped the disoriented man slide himself up the wall, staggering, leaning on them both.

Sami shot Harry an urgent look. "Well, I sure as hell didn't bite him."

Then they were moving. Alex, Harry, and Cat hefted Gabe and carried him gingerly outside and down to the dinghy. By then the others were there, but they could only stand and watch and ask a dozen questions. There was nothing else for them to do.

Nothing else any of them could do.

Whatever was going to happen now was going to happen.

Sami wished she'd stayed on board the *Kid Galahad*. She wished they'd *all* stayed on board.

CHAPTER 11

As it turned out, they had to leave the guy with the shark bite behind. Harry wouldn't allow them to put the poor bastard in the dinghy with Gabe, and Alex didn't blame him. Sami argued, but not for long. The little boat and the sailing yacht both belonged to Harry, and in the end that won out. They left Luisa on the shore in front of the Coast Guard station. Cat promised to come right back for her. Harry sat by the motor and held tightly to the throttle, using it to control their speed and direction.

They hit a wave and the boat bounced. Sami shot Harry a hard look. "Slow down."

"I'm doing my best," Harry said.

Alex, Cat, and Sami sat in the dinghy, arranged so that Gabe was stretched out across them. They tried to keep him from bouncing too much, tried to keep his head supported, keep the towel wrapped around his skull. Moving him like this was a huge risk—Alex knew it, just as he knew that Sami wouldn't have gone along with it if she thought she'd had a choice.

For a time, no further words passed among them. Harry's fingers were white where they gripped the throttle. Alex and Sami kept glancing from Gabe's still form to the *Kid Galahad* as they buzzed nearer and nearer. Cat seemed the only one among them who wasn't tense or terrified. Her legs were across the dinghy so that Gabe's lower body rested on them. Somehow she had blood on her chest and hands—from moving him or wrapping his head in that towel.

Then they'd reached the *Galahad*. Harry slowed them as he drew alongside the starboard side and cut the engine. He leaned over to grab the ladder as the dinghy drifted over to bump against the yacht. Two heads appeared above them—Patrick and Nils must have heard the engine and come to help them aboard. But as Alex glanced up, he saw the horror on the faces of the two men.

"My God," Nils said. "What happened?"

Harry ignored the question. "Help us."

Working quickly, they secured a line from the dinghy to the boat. Alex reached out and held on to the ladder. Sami kept her focus on Gabe's head—she bent and said something into his ear, maybe some quiet exhortation or an apology for whatever pain they might cause him—and then she, Alex, Harry, and Cat all hoisted Gabe upward. The dinghy rocked beneath them. For half a second, Alex tensed and held his breath, thinking they were going to tip, that they were all about to spill into the drink. Then Patrick and Nils lifted Gabe's upper body and hoisted him carefully upward.

"Watch his head," Sami warned. "Just wait for me."

She scrambled up the ladder and for a moment Alex felt relieved that the crisis was out of his hands. He exhaled, even as Harry stepped past him—the dinghy listing with his weight—and followed Sami up the ladder and onto the deck. Voices carried back down, Sami barking orders at Patrick and Nils, putting them to work.

Cat shifted into the back of the dinghy. Expressionless, eyes cold—so unlike her—she gripped the throttle.

"Cast me off before you go aboard, would you?" she asked.

Alex untied the line from the ladder, holding on, studying Cat more closely. "You okay?"

Cat smiled thinly. "Why wouldn't I be okay?"

"Stupid question," Alex acknowledged.

"Let's just get everyone on board and get out of here," Cat said. "Between smugglers or pirates, or whatever, and the sharks—"

Alex cocked his head. "Sharks?"

"You didn't see them? Look around, Alex. They're creeping me out."

He scanned the water but saw nothing. Cat's urgency didn't allow him time to linger, so he climbed the ladder. The motor revved and the dinghy leaped away from the yacht, motor growling as the little boat powered back the way it had come, headed for the

Coast Guard station to pick up Luisa and the delirious lunatic who'd started all of this.

At the railing of the *Kid Galahad,* he watched the dinghy skid across the water. Cat bent low as if to urge the little boat on, trying to give it extra speed just from her will alone. He had always thought of her as a person of great serenity, though her innate strength and ferocity had shone in her love for music and her performances. This determination was a different side of her, a different sort of strength, but Alex was glad to see it. They all needed to focus right now.

From somewhere behind him, Harry called his name. Just as he turned, he caught sight of something in his peripheral vision. Alex looked again and this time he saw the fin surfacing. Then, as if they'd been invisible until he'd spotted the first one, he noticed two others. The sharks were at least seventy-five yards from the yacht, and not all swimming in the same direction, but he had the strangest sensation that they were aware of the boat's presence. As if the sharks were purposely keeping their distance from the *Kid Galahad,* waiting to see what might happen next.

Alex saw movement below and he glanced down to see another fin passing by, this one within a few feet of the hull. He realized he didn't know a damn thing about sharks. The army hadn't taught him that, and his graphic design and marketing career hadn't prepared him for this. Whatever the sharks were doing, they certainly weren't keeping their distance.

Harry shouted again, so Alex turned and hurried across the deck, past the wheelhouse. They'd laid Gabe out. The towel around his head had been unwrapped and lay open beneath his skull. His chest rose and fell, so Alex knew the first mate hadn't died, but his tanned features had gone pale and there were beads of sweat on his face. His eyes scrunched together and he mumbled something, not conscious but not completely out.

Nils stood back, watching. Patrick had vanished. Sami knelt over Gabe while Harry loomed expectantly.

"What do you need, Doc?" Alex asked his wife.

"I sent Patrick to fetch freshwater. I need plenty of it. Harry needs to get me the entire first-aid tool kit, whatever's on board—"

"Alex can get it," Harry said.

So that was why Harry had been shouting for him. He listened as Harry described exactly where to locate the kit and then he hustled into the wheelhouse. Unlike the little box that had been on the dinghy, this was like a mobile emergency room, a trio of colorful cases. Alex grabbed a red duffel labeled OXYGEN and a fat, heavy blue case labeled FIRST AID. A stiff yellow backpack labeled DEFIBRILLATOR he left behind. He couldn't carry all three, so he'd have to make another trip for that one.

When he rushed back onto the deck and set the two cases down, then unzipped the FIRST AID case, Sami's eyes lit up with relief. Alex couldn't tell how drunk she really was—still buzzed, at least, despite the adrenaline rushing through her. But now she was in familiar territory—sober or not, she could work with this. She started barking orders and the men around her followed them. Harry opened the duffel and took out the oxygen tank, hurriedly responding to Sami's instructions. She checked Gabe's airways. A thin, clear mucus ran from his nose and he saw the way her brow furrowed at this discovery. Harry didn't notice as he was turning on the oxygen while Sami settled the mask over Gabe's face.

Patrick returned with the water, but Sami made him wait as Nils became her nurse. She used antimicrobial wipes to clean her hands, then opened a package of surgical gloves and slipped them on. Alex knew this wasn't ideal, but he didn't question it. Circumstances were dire and he didn't need to give Harry any additional reasons to get agitated.

Moving quickly through the supplies, checking what she had, Sami pulled up Gabe's eyelids to check his reaction to light. He groaned. She studied his pupils for dilation.

"Well?" Harry asked.

"I'm just starting, Harry," Sami said, not looking up.

She pinched Gabe on the arm so hard that his eyes went wide and he let out a gasp of pain.

"What are you *doing*?" Harry snapped.

For a moment, Gabe focused on him. "Wow," he rasped. "That . . . Harry . . . it hurts."

His eyes fluttered and he started to pass out. This time Sami took him by the ear and pinched the lobe.

"Stay with me," she said. "Do you know your name? What about your birthday?"

He licked his lips like they were dry, face etched with pain. "Gabriel . . . Anthony . . . Hogan. July . . . something . . ."

With a sigh, he passed out again.

"Get him back," Harry demanded.

"One thing at a time," Sami said, and now she did glance up, a little bleary-eyed but steady. "It's good. He knew your name. Knew his own. He's suffered a traumatic brain injury, but there are no convulsions, no vomiting. I think he may have some swelling in his brain, but if the brain is not bleeding—"

"There's a lot of blood," Patrick said quietly.

Sami nodded. "From the wounds. Maybe not from the brain. We'll see."

She kept working. Alex cleaned his hands and helped her remove the little bandages they'd put on the scalp laceration back at the Coast Guard station. With Patrick pouring clean water, she confirmed that this wound, at least, was superficial. She placed a layer of thick gauze over the gash, then opened another packet of gloves and made Alex put them on.

"Light pressure on the gauze," she instructed.

He knew not to argue. Gently but firmly, he added pressure and when Sami turned Gabe's head a bit Alex tried to keep that pressure steady.

"Patrick," she said. "Wash out this wound. If you think you're going to be sick, tell me. Do not throw up."

"He's got a strong stomach," Nils said.

Alex caught a glimpse as Patrick washed the wound. In the midst of hair and torn scalp, a little bit of Gabe's skull showed through, glistening wetly in the sun. Sami had kept pressure on it during the boat ride and so the bleeding had subsided. Alex tried not to think about how much blood Gabe had lost, telling himself it couldn't be that big a problem or Sami would already have mentioned it.

"There is a skull fracture," Sami confirmed, almost as if talking to herself.

Harry exhaled loudly. "Shit."

"Isn't it bad for him to be passed out?" Patrick asked. "He's in shock, right? I mean—"

"It's sure as hell not good," Alex said. "Let her work."

Sami used her gloved fingers to feel the crease in Gabe's skull and the area around the wound. "Definitely some swelling of the brain. No way of knowing yet how bad it will get. The only thing I can do right now is clean and bandage the wound."

"Are you kidding me?" Harry asked.

Sami sighed. She held up her gloved hands so she wouldn't accidentally touch something unsanitary and she stared at him. "I know you're upset, Harry. I'm doing what I can. If it's not to your liking, try thinking about what you would've done without a medical professional here. These kinds of wounds can heal on their own, believe it or not. The skull can repair itself. That depends on severity, so he might need surgery. But I'm not the one we want performing that surgery and we sure as hell don't want to do it on a boat, rocking on the sea, without the proper equipment."

"Is he going to be all right?" Harry asked.

Sami opened a small packet of iodine. "I don't know. I told you, I'll do what I can."

She looked at Alex. "What about the other guy? Cat went to get him?"

"Fuck the other guy!" Harry growled. "You're going to take care of Gabe. The son of a bitch who did this can rot on the beach. He's not getting onto this boat."

They all stared at him for a moment, but Harry looked away in disgust and then dropped to his knees by Gabe. He took the injured man's hand. "You people don't get it. The last couple of years, Gabe's about the only person in the world whose friendship I never had to doubt."

Alex would have put a hand on Harry's shoulder, but he didn't want to take pressure off Gabe's scalp wound, or waste the sterile gloves he'd donned. Instead, he bent low over Gabe and made sure he caught Harry's eye.

"Sami's going to do all she can. We all are. As far as the other guy's concerned, he was bitten by a shark and left here to die. The guy looked half-starved and completely disoriented. He's clearly out of his head. The state he's in, there's no telling who he thought was coming through that door. Probably thought he was defending himself."

"Fuck him," Harry said quietly.

Nils rose and went over to crouch beside Harry. "My friend, listen to me. The best thing you can do right now is put clean sheets on Gabe's bed and get a clean blanket we can use to carry him below. Then make sure we're ready to sail as soon as the others get back to the boat."

Harry squeezed Gabe's hand, then nodded.

"I'm sorry," he said as he rose. "This was supposed to be a new beginning for me."

For me, Alex thought. *Not for us.* But he would never point out the word choice. Harry had done some soul-searching over the years. He wanted to be a better man. Alex wasn't going to judge him for how far he might still have to go. At least he was trying.

Sami wiped her face with a damp cloth Alex had fetched from the cabin. He'd brought her a bottle of raspberry seltzer, cold from the fridge, and the moment she tipped the bottle to her lips she wanted to marry the man all over again. Relief trickled through her with that icy, fruity water and she sighed. Nothing had changed. Gabe would be in critical condition until they were able to get him to a mainland hospital, and even then she had no idea what the outcome might be. She wouldn't be getting any sleep until then, so she knew she had a lot of coffee to look forward to. Coffee would definitely help. As the alcohol buzz started to wear off, it would keep her from getting a splitting headache. For now, though, she took another sip of her seltzer and kissed her husband.

"You're a good man," she whispered. "When this is all over, I'll show you just how good."

Alex kissed her back. He smiled sweetly, but then his expression soured. Sami turned to see what had wiped away his smile and found that Harry was staring at them. He'd been pacing back and forth beside Gabe while he waited for Patrick and Nils to prepare a clean bed and bring back a blanket with which to carry Gabe into the cabin.

A whining buzz drew Sami's attention, the dinghy returning with Cat at the throttle. Sami glanced again at Harry, but he'd started pacing again, so she left him to watch over Gabe and went to the railing. Alex stood beside her as Cat guided the dinghy up beside the *Kid Galahad*. She had Nalani and James with her, but no sign of Luisa.

"Let's move," Cat said as James tied the dinghy off.

"Do you need me to come down there?" Alex asked.

"You're better off on the deck," Nalani said. "This guy is skinny as hell. James and I can lift him."

She was as good as her word. The slender, stinking, unshaven man whimpered and opened his eyes, but he didn't fight as Nalani and James hoisted him from where he'd been stretched across the dinghy's benches.

"Where's Luisa?" Sami asked as she and Alex hauled the injured man up onto the yacht.

Cat glanced up. "Nalani and James met us at the Coast Guard station. They knew something had gone wrong and were checking it out. Luisa's gone to tell Dev and Alliyah what's going on. I'm headed out to get the three of them now."

Nalani climbed the ladder. James waited for her to reach the deck, holding on, not bothering to tie up the dinghy since Cat was leaving immediately.

"Did you see the sharks?" Alex asked.

"I keep trying to pretend they're dolphins," Cat replied as she turned up the throttle. From her thin smile, Sami couldn't tell if she was joking. Then it didn't matter, for the dinghy roared away without so much as a backward glance from its current pilot.

As Alex gave James a hand up onto the deck, Sami crouched by the injured man. He looked as if he might be naturally slender, but she had no doubt he was also emaciated. The leg had been tied off for far too long to slow the bleeding, and now that Sami could tear aside the tatters of his trouser leg she saw that the skin was badly discolored. Part of the stench coming off him was the stink of that leg. It had been deprived of blood flow for so long that flesh had started to die. Whatever else happened to this guy, he was going to lose the leg.

"Damn it," she whispered.

"His name's Isko," Nalani said, standing over them.

Sami glanced up at her. "Sorry?"

"He was conscious for a while. Or conscious enough to answer when I asked his name. Pretty sure he said 'Isko.'"

"Thanks. What about you?" Sami asked. "You okay?"

Nalani gave a tiny nod, but now her attention was elsewhere. "Is Gabe gonna live?"

Sami stood and turned her back so Harry wouldn't hear. She kept her voice low, so not even an errant breeze could carry her words to him. "I think so. I hope so. If we were in port somewhere and could get to a hospital, I'd say almost certainly. But we're a long way from port."

Nalani swore quietly.

James slid past them. The boat bobbed on the water and the breeze blew, a chill in the air. Sami glanced into the distance and saw clouds far off. So strange to have the blue sky above and still see clouds.

"Harry, brother, listen," James said, "I'm sorry all this is happening, but I have to ask. Can you get us back?"

"You too?" Harry sneered. "Yes, I'll get you back. Gabe's got a fucking hole in his head, but you don't even ask about that. The first question is about yourselves."

Long seconds passed as everyone froze. The boat rocked. Awkwardness had paralyzed them all.

It was Nalani who broke the silence. "That's not fair."

Harry scoffed, rolling his eyes.

Sami knew how upset he was. She saw in the set of his shoulders, in the weight he suddenly carried, that he blamed himself. If what he'd said was true, if Gabe truly was the only friend he had whose friendship he trusted, that had to make it even harder for Harry to bear. But his stomping around and glaring wouldn't help anyone.

"James, could you go below and see what's taking Nils and Patrick so long? I want to get Gabe somewhere comfortable," Sami said. She ought to have told Harry to get started on whatever preparations needed to be made to get them under way, but she knew he wasn't in the frame of mind to listen. Not while Gabe remained out on the deck.

She walked over to the medical kit, crouched and gathered items back into the case, and put the strap over her shoulder.

"What are you doing?" Harry asked.

Something in his voice froze her for a moment.

Then, quite deliberately, she rose to her feet with the bag over her shoulder.

"I'm going to examine the other patient. See what can be done for him. I'm probably going to have to—"

She would have said *amputate* next. That was the word on her lips when Harry reached out and ripped the strap from her shoulder, tugged the whole medical kit away from her.

"Hey!" Alex shouted, hands up, moving beside Sami. "There's no call for—"

"This is my boat," Harry said coldly. "All of this shit . . . it's mine. Every last bandage. You're not giving that piece of garbage so much as an aspirin until you've done everything you can for Gabe. Maybe not even then."

Sami stood up to her full height and squared her shoulders. Her husband had served in the U.S. Army in Iraq, but Dr. Samantha Simmons had dealt with angry, grieving assholes of every stripe in the emergency room over the years. She might still be a bit unsteady on her feet thanks to the drinks Alliyah had mixed for her, but she didn't need her husband to intervene.

"I've done what I can for Gabe," she said. "I'll continue to do that. Whatever Isko—"

"Fuck Isko!"

"Whatever that poor, desperate son of a bitch did, you know circumstances had a lot more to do with it than malice," Sami went on. "Look at him!"

She gestured at Isko. His eyes had opened again, but he looked around slowly, head lolling, as if he saw things in the air that the rest of them couldn't see. He was obviously delirious.

"Gabe first," Harry said.

"She's doing what she can, damn it," Alex rasped.

"I won't leave the man untreated," Sami said. "I won't do that."

She reached for the medical kit. Harry slapped her hands away, stepped forward, and gave her a shove. In the same instant, a wave rolled beneath the boat, causing it to list enough that Sami—off-balance—toppled to the deck. She sprawled there, skidded a few inches, and hissed in pain when her elbow smashed down on the wood.

Alex had Harry around the throat a second later. "Motherfucker. You do not lay hands on my wife."

Sami cradled her elbow as she sat up. "Alex, don't. I can speak for myself."

Harry broke his grip and threw a punch. Alex tried to dodge, but the blow still clipped his chin and he stumbled backward. The two of them started shouting and swearing at each other as Sami stood. Nalani tried to get between the two men and Harry shoved her away. Nalani careened across the deck and would have tripped over Gabe if she hadn't jumped to avoid him.

The masks of politeness and the effort to repair old friendships shattered simultaneously. Ten years of mutual resentment boiled to the surface. Sami didn't need Alex to fight her battles, but what she saw unfolding now—this had been his fight all along.

"Should've known you couldn't change," Alex said. "Never met an asshole as selfish as you. Even this, with Gabe . . . it's not about him; it's about you!"

Harry swung a left, but Alex dodged it, stepped in, and tackled Harry to the deck. Alex hit him once, hard, before Harry got his hands around Alex's throat and bucked upward, throwing him off. Wary, ready, they climbed to their feet, each man like a serpent rising from a snake charmer's basket. Sami and Nalani looked for openings, tried to talk to them, but these two were beyond listening.

"*I'm* selfish?" Harry said. "I brought you all halfway around the world, and I'm selfish?"

"You didn't do it for us," Alex said. "You did it so you could come out here and say goodbye to your dad and pretend there were people still on this side of the grave who loved you."

Scuffling sounds off to her right made Sami turn. Made them all turn.

Patrick, Nils, and James were there carrying a heavy blanket and the door to one of the staterooms. Sami understood immediately—they'd taken off the door to use as a backboard, a method of transporting Gabe the way medics would have. Now the door was forgotten, and so was Gabe. The three men stared at Harry and Alex.

"Guys," Nils said. "What the fuck are you doing?"

Harry feinted with his left, then delivered a punch that staggered Alex. Sami winced. She could feel the impact of knuckle to jaw, the clack of bones. Her own fury and impatience boiled over. She'd thought, mostly unconsciously, that boys would be boys, that the fight had been brewing for years, that it was unfortunate after old wounds seemed to be healing. She'd thought she ought to keep out of it, that it would end in a wrestling match on the deck and the others would pull them apart. But this was her husband, and she wasn't going to just watch this violence, regardless of who might win. There were no winners here.

"Alex, stop!" she called. "Let it go."

As she spoke, her husband blocked another punch, raised his fist to deliver one of his own, and hesitated. Even Harry hesitated. The others had been on the verge of jumping in, dragging them apart. For a moment, even the breeze blowing across the *Kid Galahad*'s deck seemed to pause.

Then Isko began to shout, "Machii, no! *Huwag! Maniwala ka sa akin. Mga Diyablo Pating ay nandyan sa ilalim.*"

Sami didn't understand the words, but the man's fear needed no translation. Disoriented, perhaps feverish, even hallucinating, he cried out in anguish and began to smash a fist down at his rotting leg.

"Damn it!" Sami snapped. "Stop him. He's lost way too much blood already."

She was thinking of surgery, of the possibility she'd have to amputate right here on the boat if she wanted to save his life. The calculus of that was racing through her head as she turned away from Alex and Harry and started toward Isko. If he tore open the shark bite, the decision might be taken away from her.

"It's Filipino," Nalani said. "Tagalog. Something about—"

Harry marched across the deck. Five strides brought him to Sami. He grabbed her by both arms and shook her. "Are you fucking kidding me?" With a grunt he shoved her backward, and she stumbled and fell on her ass; then he pointed a finger at her. "You can worry about this bastard after we're sure Gabe will be okay. Not before. I'm not going to—"

Alex grabbed him from behind, one arm around his throat, choking him. Harry clawed at his arm, shot an elbow back into his gut. Alex took the blow and held on.

"Enough, goddamn it! Sami's right. I'd like to knock your head off, but we've got to—"

Harry slammed his head backward, his skull smashing Alex's nose. Sami shouted and tried to scramble to her feet. Nalani and Patrick and Nils started moving in, everyone talking at once, hands reaching out as Alex stumbled away, blood streaming from his nose. Freed now, Harry turned. Nalani, and Patrick reached out for him, but he brushed their hands away and ran at Alex. Shoulder low, arms raised, he plowed into Alex and tried to tackle him to the deck. Bleeding, furious, Alex grappled with him. The two of them staggered together, careened toward the railing, smashed into it, and then toppled over the side.

In the last sliver of an instant, Sami saw the realization light both men's eyes. The melee ended in that heartbeat. Harry and Alex both tried to reach for the railing as they went over, and then they were gone.

Alex plunged into the water with his arms and legs flailing. He went under, sinking deep, and for a few seconds as his heart galloped in his chest and adrenaline surged through him he couldn't tell which way was up. His eyes were pinched shut—he hated to open them in salt water, but now he forced himself. They stung and he blinked but turned his head around as he started to swim, thinking he must be clawing toward the surface, desperate for breath. The beating of his heart thumped inside his skull and he told himself to *calm down, calm down, calm down. Think. Feel the water. Look for sunlight.*

Which way was up? He'd had a few beers and taken a few punches and his thoughts were fractured by anger and fear and chaos. He spun around again, forcing his eyes open wider.

The sun glinted. The clear water refracted it, but now he could see shapes through the crystal blue—out of the shadow of the boat. Maybe the bottom? Rocks or fish or coral . . . did they have coral out here?

Alex swam. His chest burned. He thought about Sami and Tasha and how badly he wanted them in his arms. The base of his skull ached as he held his breath and his lungs screamed for air. He broke the surface and gasped, drawing ragged breaths, heart still clamoring. Voices shouted from overhead, but he couldn't respond, not even to lift a hand and wave. Not without more oxygen. His anger seeped out of him and now all he felt was despair. They'd had a few hours of paradise and it had turned into a shitshow. He hated Harry, but he felt bad for him, too.

The boat, he thought. He needed to get out of the water. This childish bullshit was a distraction. They had real problems.

Overhead, Sami shouted his name. Alex turned to see Harry, head above water, reaching for him with a face still carved by anguish and fury. Alex slapped his hands away, just done with it all. Still catching his breath, he swam for the ladder that still hung alongside the boat.

"Motherfucker," Harry grunted, swimming after him.

Alex ignored him, stretching out, bending into the swim. Fifteen feet away now. He tasted blood on his lips and for half a second imagined it must be Harry's. Then he remembered his nose, felt the ache, knew the copper tang came from his own blood.

Something brushed against his leg under the water. A bump. At first he thought it must be Harry, but Harry swore at him again and Alex knew it couldn't be him. Eight feet from the ladder he twisted in the water, glancing around, a terrible certainty catching in his throat.

"Swim, Alex!" someone screamed above him. Not Sami. Maybe Patrick or James.

Then Sami's voice, much softer: "Oh, my God."

He kicked toward the ladder, glancing back as he

did so. He'd hated Harry a moment before, but none of that mattered. He saw Harry's face, and he saw the moment when his anger turned to surprise. Harry's eyes went wide and his mouth gaped with the recognition of pain. He screamed and reached toward Alex, not in rage but for help. His whole body jerked once, and then he disappeared, yanked under the water.

A cloud of blood blossomed beneath the surface.

Alex's fingers touched the ladder. He grabbed hold, glanced around, saw several fins, and knew he was fucked. He could practically feel their teeth on him as he climbed, dragging himself out of the sea. His left foot cleared the water, stepped on a rung, slid a little as he reached higher, and then his right foot came out, dripping wet.

A shark thumped against the hull just below him, water splashing, its jaws just missing him. Alex stared into the water as its bulk swept past and he found himself saying a silent prayer of thanks.

Sami shouted at him to climb. He glanced up and saw her waiting just above him, reaching a hand down. The others were along the railing. Some were shouting at him, but Nils and Nalani were staring in horror at the place where Harry had gone down, at the red fog moving beneath the water.

Alex grabbed Sami's hand, stunned to find himself alive, and climbed onto the deck.

In the same moment, Harry bobbed to the surface. Screaming.

They never saw the fin of the shark that dragged him back down.

That was the last of him. The last sight. The last sound. His blood lingered, but it eddied and spread in the water and soon enough it would be diluted so completely that not even a trace of scarlet would remain.

In Alex's mind, however, that last scream would echo on and on. He knew he would remember it as long as he lived.

CHAPTER 12

Alliyah stood knee-deep in the surf, her mouth hanging open. Her breath came in short gasps and she barely noticed the tears that filled her eyes. Luisa had started to scream, her voice blotting out the shouts and cries out on the water, muffled by distance. Numb, hands shaking, Alliyah could only stare.

Cat had beached the dinghy only moments before. She'd climbed out, claimed the beer Luisa had been drinking, and drained the rest of the bottle. They'd begun to gather the towels and coolers on the beach . . . until Dev had started swearing and pointing out to sea. Pointing at Harry's boat.

Now Cat stepped up beside Alliyah in the surf. "Are we . . . I mean, we *can't be* sure. Harry might've gotten out of the water. It's hard to know from here. Maybe he got around the other side. They could've—"

Alliyah turned to stare at her. She tasted salt on her lips and realized this was the flavor of her tears.

"Okay, don't look at me like that!" Cat said, almost angrily. "I heard it, too!"

She turned away, wiping at her own eyes although she had yet to shed a tear. In all the time Alliyah had known her, she'd never seen Cat cry. Even from the first day they'd met, walking across the grass on that September afternoon their freshman year, Cat had exuded a calm wisdom, a kind patience that seemed almost unearthly. Her songs reflected an inner turmoil that she never revealed in her personal relationships. After they'd all watched *The Big Lebowski* together sophomore year, Alex had taken to calling her The Dude, after the film's most enduring character. Alliyah had forgotten about that until this very moment, when Cat's serenity had been shattered.

"Alli!" Luisa snapped. "Alliyah!"

Wiping at her tears, Alliyah let her gaze linger another few seconds on the boat—or more precisely on the dark arc of a fin that cut the water near the *Kid Galahad*. When Luisa shouted her name again, she twisted to stare at her.

"What?"

Luisa pointed at her legs, face ghostly pale. "You're in the water."

Alliyah frowned. "The water didn't kill Harry, you twit."

But the words were in her brain now and Alliyah couldn't help glancing at her feet through the frothing surf, then up and down the shore of this fragment of the atoll's ring. She'd see a shark if it came this close to shore, wouldn't she? The fin? Might she not even see the shark itself in such shallow surf? Almost certainly.

Still, she backed out of the water as if the sea itself might claim her. Off to her left, Cat was bent over as if in physical pain, either losing control or mustering it. Alliyah turned to see Luisa frozen on the sand, hugging herself as she stood amidst the scattered debris of their picnic in paradise. There were blankets and towels, coolers, trash bags full of empty bottles, cans, and cups, as well as the rubbish from their meal. Tubes of sunscreen. Cover-ups, two pairs of sunglasses, the straw hat Nalani had been wearing when they'd arrived.

Beyond it all, Dev sat on the rough, rocky patch beyond the sand. He had his knees drawn up in front of him, his face devoid of all expression. Though he must have seen her looking his way, his gaze didn't shift toward her. Her husband, this man she'd loved and left and loved again, this man whose greatest sin had always been his emotional distance, wouldn't meet her eyes. He stared into some nebulous spot across the water, not at the boat and not toward any of the shark fins they'd seen. He seemed like his mind had left his body.

"Dev," she said, walking up the beach toward him. "Come on. We've got to go."

"Are you nuts?" Luisa said, facing her on the sand. "I'm not going out there."

Alliyah stared at her. She glanced at Cat but found no help. Cat had straightened but now stood with her hands on her hips, back to them all.

Dev still didn't look up.

"Come on, honey," Alliyah said, standing over her husband, her shadow falling across his face. "Let's pack this stuff up and—"

Cat started laughing. "Are you kidding?" she said as she turned toward them at last. Her eyes damp, her expression full of naked pain. "Leave all of that shit there. Come on, Luisa. Get in the goddamned dinghy, right now. Alliyah, your man's gone catatonic or something, but you'd better get him moving. They can't come out and get us from the ship, so we've got to go to them. Harry's dead. Gabe might be dying. We've got to get the hell out of here."

Alliyah turned back to Dev. He still hadn't looked at her.

"I'm not going," he said. "You can go."

The way he said it, with such finality, it felt real. Like he meant it.

For a few seconds, Alliyah was tempted to take him at his word.

"Get in the fucking dinghy," she said darkly.

Dev swallowed visibly, his Adam's apple bobbing. He kept his gaze forward, but he did not reply.

He wasn't going anywhere.

Sami held Alex in her arms. They were curled up together against the railing, and with the chilly breeze blowing across the deck his skin felt cold. The blood from his nose streaked his chin and dappled his chest and it stained her as she pressed herself against him, but she didn't care. A terrible silence had filled her heart, a dreadful void. The shark that had nearly gotten him, that had crashed against the hull, still swam in the water below. They were the only ones on this trip who had a child, and they'd been slightly irritated that the invitation had not included her. Now Sami had never been so grateful for anything in her life.

Alex whispered his love into her ear and she kissed his cheek and neck with a tentative softness, as if her subconscious could not quite accept that he was in her arms. That he was alive. She thought of parallel universes and alternate timelines. Schrödinger's cat. A moment had come, just a minute ago, in which she had imagined Alex both dead and alive.

"Oh, my God," she whispered to him now. A prayer of such gratitude as she had never known.

Her husband began to warm in her arms. Wonderfully alive. But Harry Curtis had just been torn apart. His blood swirled in the water around the boat. His gut-wrenching final scream still hung in the air, somehow filling the silence. And there *was* silence, at least in this moment. Shock enveloped them all.

After another moment or two, Sami heard whispering off to her left and knew those voices. Patrick and Nils, comforting each other. Farther along the deck, curled up where they'd left him, Isko had fallen unconscious but continued to moan in misery and pain.

"I can't believe that just happened," Nalani said, her voice catching. "Poor Harry."

There had been screaming. Sami thought it might have been herself doing the screaming. Then the stillness as the horror set in. Whatever drunkenness had lingered in her seemed to have burned away in a fire of horror and grief.

Alex took a shuddery breath and then exhaled. He kissed her temple and nodded. "Come on, love. You can't help Harry. But Gabe and the other guy . . . they need you."

Sami nodded in return and together they rose to their feet. Nils and Patrick were staring at them both with disdain. Nalani's eyes were full of grief and re-crimination. James stood next to his wife at the railing, but he hung over the side as if fighting off seasickness. He stared into the water below.

"We have to call for help—" Alex began.

"Asshole," Nalani said. "You fucking child."

Sami stiffened. "Are you kidding me? You're not going to blame Alex for what just happened. Harry knocked them both overboard. I'm sorry for him, for this, but he lost his shit. The guy totally unraveled right in front of us."

"And your husband didn't?" Patrick said. He seemed more numb and sad than angry. Lost.

Sami understood. "He did. He acted like a fool—"

"A fucking child," Alex said. "Nalani's right. I was an asshole. But I didn't kill Harry. Jesus, I can't believe I'm even saying that. I can't believe he's dead."

"But he is," Nils said. He leaned into Patrick for a moment, then straightened up. "And Alex is right. Gabe and this other man—"

"Isko," Sami muttered.

"Yes. Isko," Nils said. "They need help. And so do the rest of us. With all of this happening, I understand if you've failed to realize it, but without Harry and Gabe, we're effectively stranded here. We need to call or radio for help and then we need to support Sami as best we can so she can try to keep Gabe and Isko alive."

Sami shuddered. The air had gotten cooler. It wasn't her imagination. But still, it was more than just the chill on the breeze.

"I'm not sure you're thinking about this right," she said, glancing around at the others. "Are you all sure there's no way for us to sail back to port? What about Cat and Luisa and Alliyah and Dev? Are we sure none of them can figure out how to sail this boat?"

Nalani threw up her hands. "We might be able to get the motor running. None of us can sail this thing, that's for sure. But if we could motor back, and figure out the navigation . . . maybe if we radio for help they could talk us through it, but—"

"Why not just sit here and wait for help?" Patrick asked.

Sami glanced at Alex. "Time. If we could get moving now, we can have these guys in an emergency room a lot sooner than if we wait for a boat to come all the way out here and get us."

"So they send a helicopter," Nalani said.

Alex shook his head, thinking about Iraq. "I don't know. We're three hundred miles from the nearest occupied island. I'm pretty sure choppers can't do a six-hundred-mile round-trip without refueling. But we'll radio. We'll find out."

"Meanwhile," Sami said, "let's get the others back to the boat and see if anyone can get us under way."

A thump resonated through the hull, accompanied by a scraping noise. Sami glanced over to see the top of the ladder shake and rattle for a moment before falling still again.

"Was that—" Nalani began.

At the railing, where he'd remained during the fear and recrimination, her husband nodded slowly. "A shark, yeah. They're still out there. At least three, but I have a feeling there are more."

Sami felt Alex squeeze her hand. He gave her a nudge toward Isko. The rest of them hesitated, the thump of the shark against the hull unnerving them. She glanced around and saw the same haunted look in all of their eyes.

"Hello?" a voice rasped. "Is anyone . . . oh, shit, that hurts. . . ."

They turned in unison, all of them staring across the deck. Isko had been moaning, but it wasn't him who'd spoken—it was Gabe. He'd rolled onto his side, almost in a fetal position on the deck. With one hand, he probed gently at the wounds on his head. His eyes roved, unfocused, and his eyelids fluttered as if he could barely keep them open . . . barely focus.

Harry might be dead, but Gabe was alive. Hope ignited in Sami. She couldn't pilot this boat, she couldn't get them to safety, but she might be able to save one life today. She might be able to do that, at least.

CHAPTER 13

Alliyah stood over her husband. "Dev, get in the fucking boat. Now!"

Dev still hadn't moved. He hadn't trembled or wept or gotten angry—whatever terror had seized him, it didn't show on his face. The only expression there was one of fierce determination.

"We've got to go!" Cat called. "Alliyah, seriously."

"I know, damn it! Don't you think I know?"

She knelt on the ground. Not sand here, but rock and coral, a bit of scrub brush growing. Dev would not look at her, but she reached out her hands and turned his face toward her. He didn't resist, and at last their eyes met. She could smell the scent of him, so close now. The familiar scent of the man she had loved once— and had started to believe she would love again—the warm and musky odor that had been on his pillow, in their sheets, in his clothes. She'd missed his scent when they'd been apart, no matter how angry she'd been at him. When she'd first made love with another man—when she'd cheated on her husband—it had been so strange to breathe in that other man's scent after being intimate with only one person for so long.

"You have to get in the dinghy."

His lips quivered as if they were about to form words; then he glanced at the ground between them. When he lifted his eyes again, his determination had returned.

"There is no way I'm going out there," Dev said. "Not into the lagoon."

"It's terrifying. I know. But the sharks are in the water. They're not in the boat—"

"Do you have any idea how big sharks can grow? If they want to get at us, they can tip that stupid dinghy over anytime they want. Then we're in the water. Then we're screaming like Harry. . . . Then we're dying like Harry."

Alliyah stared into his eyes. They had a glaze she'd never seen in anyone who wasn't on drugs. She had known Dev had a fear of sharks, but she had never imagined anything like this. He'd had a few drinks, but that glaze didn't come from alcohol. That was pure, animal fear.

"Listen to me. You're being totally irrational. If we don't get out to that boat . . . Dev, they can't come get us; do you understand that?"

With a wince and a quiet sort of grunt, Dev rose to his feet.

Alliyah stood, dusting off her knees. "Finally."

Cat and Luisa had started to gather up the things on the beach.

"Just leave all that stuff," Alliyah said, turning toward them. "Let's go!"

"I'm not kidding, Alli," Dev said. "I'm not going."

She spun around and grabbed him by the arms. Her face flushed with the heat of her anger and shock, and with the horror of hearing an old friend scream as he died.

"What the hell am I supposed to do?" she said, wanting to shake him. To slap him. To wake him up. "I can't leave you here."

"Wait with me," Dev said. "They'll radio for help. Someone will come."

"You think they're going to just wait? They need to get Gabe to a hospital."

"Then they go. They can send someone back."

"Who won't get here until at least tomorrow! This is ridiculous. I want to be on that boat. I want to be with my . . ."

Her words trailed off.

Dev winced. "Your friends. Right. Not your husband."

"Oh, for God's sake."

Cat marched toward them. Luisa had gone to the dinghy and now waited, muttering urgently and profanely.

"Luisa and I are going," Cat said. "You've got thirty seconds."

With haunted eyes, Dev looked at her. "I'm not getting into the dinghy on the lagoon side. What if you go around—find one of the breaks and go through—"

"How do we get to the *Galahad* if you won't go into the lagoon?" Alliyah asked. "You're not thinking."

Cat exhaled loudly. "No idea who's going to get the *Galahad* moving without Harry and Gabe, but if we can do it, if we get out of here, I'll put the dinghy back in the water once we're outside the ring and come and get you. I don't know why you think there will be fewer sharks out there—"

"Mainly because I haven't seen any sharks out there, but I've seen plenty of them in the lagoon," Dev said.

"Have it your way," Cat said. "Alliyah, you're staying?"

Alliyah felt sick. She glanced back and forth between Cat and Dev. Luisa swore and shouted for Cat, not moving from inside the dinghy.

"I guess I'm staying," Alliyah said.

Dev glanced away, either in shame or with indifference. Alliyah walked to the scattering of towels and coolers and other things left over from their perfect morning. She picked up a towel and shook off the sand, then sat on a blanket and drew the towel over her shoulders. The air had turned chilly as the day wore on. Overhead, the blue sky had gone from vivid to pale.

Cat splashed into the surf and pushed the dinghy off the beach, then climbed in. Luisa sat in the front, scanning the water as Cat fired up the motor. Then they were off, skimming the waves, headed for the *Kid Galahad*.

Alliyah kept her back to her husband. She thought
about Harry Curtis, about the last few days and about
much older days, when they'd all been younger and had
all their years still ahead of them. All their mistakes
yet to be made. Harry had been a complicated person—
much more so than most of their friends had ever recognized. Sometimes he'd been an asshole, but he'd
made her laugh so often in those bygone days that she'd
always thought of him with a smile.

That would never happen again. Now any dream
with him in it would be a nightmare. Any memory of
him would finish with the hideousness of his ending
and the thought of that scream.

Alliyah lay on the blanket and covered herself with
the towel. She turned on her side. Her friends would
come back for her, she knew. One way or another, they
would not leave her out here. Still, she felt stranded.

Her husband sat not fifteen feet away from her, but
she had never felt so alone.

Alex joined James at the railing. Patrick and Nils had
gone off to investigate the wheelhouse, to see if they
could figure out the radio and, more important, how to
start the motor and navigate the boat. Even thinking
such things fed the quiet despair that had been inflating
inside Alex's chest, a red balloon of fear and doubt.
Gabe had started calling out, but that had lasted only
a few seconds before he'd fallen unconscious again.
Sami said it was a good sign. Nalani had named herself the nurse and now the two of them were examin-

ing both Gabe and Isko again. In a few minutes, Sami had said, she wanted everyone to work together and move both men below.

But not yet.

In these minutes when he had nothing to do but dwell on all the things he wished he could erase from the past few days, Alex found that the first among them was coming on this trip to begin with. He'd known better. His heart had kindled a dislike for and resentment toward Harry for a decade. He'd spent his life trusting his instincts, and regretting it when he didn't. The lure of this adventure had been strong. A week in the Hawaiian islands with all expenses paid, a chance to see old friends, and—yes—the possibility that Harry Curtis had changed . . . all of those things had tempted him. A different Harry might mean he could have let go of his resentment. They'd laughed together once. They'd felt like brothers, shoulder to shoulder against the world. It would have been a gift to have been able to erase the past, to resurrect that feeling. That confidence in a friendship.

Alex had barely admitted such hopes to himself, but then today it had felt possible. He'd let his guard down and so had Harry. For a short time, the old camaraderie had returned and it seemed as if past resentments might be erased. Then the world had gone insane. A flicker of nostalgia had been shattered by violence none of them could ever have anticipated.

In fear and fury, the new Harry had fallen apart.

Alex stared out at the water. The fragments of the atoll's ring seemed very far away now. Every little ripple of a wave seemed like a shark's fin to him. How many were out there? Three, at least. But he was sure there were more.

The echoes of his terror kept surging back. The taste of his own blood. With every throb of his possibly broken nose, he remembered Harry smashing his head backward, remembered the pain and then the grappling that ended with them falling overboard. Alex recalled his panic underwater. He remembered swimming for the ladder and the sight of Harry being dragged down and the thump of the shark against the hull. He remembered the screaming.

"I wish we'd never come," he said quietly.

James remained bent over the railing, resting on his elbows, his hair long enough to veil his eyes. "Trust me, man. We all wish we'd never come."

"I can't help thinking if Sami and I had stayed home, this wouldn't have happened," Alex went on. "Maybe the thing with Gabe—finding that guy in the Coast Guard station, him attacking—that would still have gone the same way. But Harry would still be alive."

"Probably," James agreed. "But without Sami here, Gabe would be dead. If not by now, then soon."

The boat swayed. The waves had grown rougher. White ripples topped each rise.

"You know there's no guarantee she can help him," Alex said.

James stroked and tugged thoughtfully at his beard. "She'll do her best. He's a nice guy, but we just met him. I don't know him."

"You barely know me," Alex said.

They both went quiet for a moment, each man alone with his thoughts.

"You going to puke?" Alex asked.

"Not planning to. I'm just watching the sharks. Trying to figure them out."

"What's to figure out?"

James glanced at him, brows knitted. "What do you know about sharks?"

Alex cocked his head. "Mainly that I don't want to be in the water with them."

"I'm no expert, but I'll tell you this much. They don't eat people."

"Excuse the fuck out of me, but—"

James waved his objection away, pushing back from the railing. "No, man. Listen. What just happened to Harry . . . what would have happened to you . . . that's not normal behavior for sharks. Sure, people have been killed. It happens. And yeah, people get bitten all the time. Shark attacks aren't as common as most of us believe, but they're common enough. But what usually happens is that the sharks are disturbed or confused. They see a surfer in a wet suit and they think she's a seal and they take a bite. But once they get a taste, they realize it's not the meal they're looking for. Humans are not the natural prey of sharks. They're not man-eater by nature and they don't get a grudge and hunt us down."

Alex studied him. "You research this stuff?"

"Nah. I'm a tech guy, but I've watched a ton of *Shark Week*. Look, the point is this isn't normal."

"So, why are these sharks different?"

James glanced back out at the water. Alex saw two fins gliding in opposite directions, almost like the sharks had surrounded them and were cruising, waiting for an opening. One of the fins vanished as the shark went under.

"Isko," James said. "Cat said whatever happened in the Coast Guard station, it looked like he'd been abandoned here. Bitten by a shark, but left behind. She also said she thinks the people who've been using this place are some kind of smugglers."

"Drugs or guns, I'd guess," Alex said.

"I saw a documentary earlier this year—"

"During *Shark Week*."

"Probably. These researchers were investigating instances of sharks killing humans. This one spot in Mexico had a ton of deadly shark attacks. Sharks who actually ate people. They couldn't make sense of it— the behavior of the sharks was an anomaly, right? But eventually they found out that some drug cartel had been taking people who'd pissed them off out to this spot, killing them, and dumping their bodies. Fresh blood, drawing hungry sharks. They weren't going to turn away the free food. The cartel killers did it often enough that the sharks got used to it. Got a taste for it."

"Holy shit," Alex whispered, watching that one fin tracing the surface. Another appeared nearby.

"I'm not saying that's what happened here," James said. He looked sick. Hung his head. Breathed deeply. "Just trying to understand. It's not going to matter when we get out of here, but right now, I can't stop thinking about it."

Alex stared at those fins, then turned and looked at Isko. Nalani had knelt beside the unconscious man and now she wrapped his ruined thigh in fresh bandages. Had Isko been one of the smugglers? Had he been just another victim? Had they fed this poor bastard to the sharks at Orchid Atoll, only to have him make it to shore?

Seconds. That was how long Alex had been in the water with sharks trying to rip him apart. How long had Isko been in the water, knowing they were there with him?

"Nalani," he said.

She looked up.

"When he was freaking out before, you said he was speaking Filipino—"

"Tagalog," she corrected.

"The guy was terrified. Like he was having a nightmare. What was he shouting about?"

Nalani paled. She glanced at James and then back at Alex. "With all this . . . after you and Harry fell in . . . I've been so focused on trying to help."

"What did he say?" Alex asked.

"I don't speak Tagalog, but I understand some of it. I have friends who . . . anyway, I missed most of it. He was begging someone not to do something. The phrase that got me though . . . that was *Diyablo Pating*."

Nalani glanced down at Isko. She brushed the matted hair away from his face and then she turned to look out past the railing at the darkening sea.

"It means 'Devil Sharks.'"

"Well, *that's* pleasant," Alex said.

Sami called for him. Alex turned and saw her kneeling by Gabe, packing up the medical kit. When he looked her way, she gestured toward the western sky.

"The day's not getting any more pleasant," she said.

On the horizon, clouds had begun to form. *No,* he thought, *they're not forming. They're on the way.* With all that had been going on today, nobody had been paying attention to the weather. It hadn't occurred to Alex that they might encounter a storm. Out here in the tropics, out to sea, the idea seemed ridiculous, but ocean storms were common enough. If Gabe and Harry had seen a weather report and known it was coming, they hadn't said a word. Maybe they'd figured the beach day would have ended by now, that a little rain wouldn't matter. Still, it only added to how unsettled Alex felt.

"All right," Sami said. "Go get Nils and Patrick. We're going to move these guys below before this day gets any worse."

Luisa had never made excuses about who she was, never apologized for liking attention. All her life she had preferred to keep things light. She liked to laugh and she liked the spotlight, enjoyed how easy it was to get both men and women to look at her, the options it gave her. If she wanted someone to keep her company, to touch her, to be rough or gentle or just be gone when she woke up, it had never been difficult to find. Even married, she'd found power in flirtation, and sometimes more.

She'd liked to keep things light.

Luisa Kershaw had never screamed before today, not even in anger. Not since she'd been an infant, or injured herself as a toddler, and if you'd asked her before today, she'd have doubted that she'd screamed even then. More likely she'd have done a pirouette and wiped away her tears, or made some joke to lighten the moment, or cocked her head in that coquettish way that always distracted from her darker thoughts, even as a child, and let her control the flow of concern or conversation. That was what it had always been about for her—control.

Now she'd lost all control.

The dinghy hit a big wave, smashed upward with such force that she had to grab hold of the edge to keep from being thrown aside. Her heart seized and for a moment she couldn't breathe. The motor came out of the water for a second and she heard it whine like a dentist's drill. Then the dinghy crashed down again, hit the water, and surged forward, resuming its race across the lagoon toward the *Kid Galahad.*

Pulse thundering, Luisa held on, knuckles going white. The ocean had been perfect, its blue a kind of beauty she'd never imagined before coming here, and now that beauty and serenity had turned to terror.

A fin broke the water ten feet ahead. Cat spotted it and turned the throttle and the dinghy shot across the waves right beside the shark, close enough for Luisa to see the texture of its skin and the water rippling on either side of the fin.

"Jesus," she said. "Oh, my God, this is so fucked up."

"Just breathe," Cat told her. "Hang on."

They hit another wave. Again the motor whined as it left the water. The dinghy slapped down and Cat adjusted the angle, keeping them on course. Luisa felt gooseflesh rise on her arms and the back of her neck and she glanced over her shoulder to see gray clouds off in the distance. Even the air above the sea was gray beneath those clouds and she knew that meant rain. A storm coming.

"Luisa—" Cat began, and then she twisted the throttle, angling to the left.

Too late to avoid the shark. The dinghy struck it with a thump that rocked them both. Luisa reached for the edge of the little boat and her fingers missed. She felt herself falling, flailed for a grip on the bench, and in that total lack of control she felt something break inside her. Screaming, she thudded against the other side of the boat. Her left hand splashed into the water, but her hip struck the inside of the dinghy and she dropped onto her butt. Still inside. Still safe.

Swearing, face pale, Cat kept them on course.

Luisa whipped her head around. Three fins. No, four. Racing alongside and behind them. Pacing them as they knifed toward the *Kid Galahad*.

"Shut up, goddamn it!" Cat roared.

Luisa pressed her lips together, forced herself to be

quiet, but the terror continued to rush through her. She stared at the yacht, saw the ladder. It seemed incredibly far away. A shark slid past the dinghy so close that its skin rasped against the little boat. Luisa held in her scream, knowing how small this little dinghy was, how useless it would be to fight if they tipped over.

Then Cat throttled down and they were drifting and Luisa turned to scream at her and saw that somehow they'd gotten within a few feet of the *Kid Galahad*. The ladder was right there. It took every ounce of courage she'd ever had in her life, combined with her desperate desire not to die, to reach out and grab hold of that ladder.

Luisa could hear the shush of the water, the slap of it against the hull. It might've been just the tide, just a wave, but in her mind it had to be the shark that had killed Harry. She hadn't seen him die, not really, not from the shore . . . but the screams had been full of such terror and anguish that she'd thought of her first days in Catholic school, when an ancient priest had described the suffering of the souls in hell to impressionable preschoolers.

She grabbed the ladder and clenched her teeth together as she climbed. Then she was over the railing. Cat must have been tying off the dinghy. Luisa had left her with the sharks, left her down there, but she didn't care. She collapsed on the deck and curled into a fetal ball, all the lightness she'd nurtured for so many years drained out of her. Her body shook as she began to weep, full of grief and fear, feeling as if she ought to be ashamed but incapable of any emotion but relief to find herself on board the *Kid Galahad*. They could get out of here now.

Cat came up the ladder, over the railing, and crouched by her. She took Luisa in her arms and that only made Luisa cry harder, holding on tight, pressing her body against Cat as if her friend might pick her up and cradle her.

"I'm sorry," Luisa said. "I'm sorry I'm such a mess. I'm just so . . . ohmygod, so scared. And Harry . . ."

She couldn't say it. Cat knew, and shushed her. Luisa was so grateful for her, grateful to have someone there who understood. Luisa had slept with Harry in college. It had been a dozen years now, but she still remembered it vividly. She could recall so clearly how torn she'd been, how happy and how confused, how she'd agreed that it would be best for their friendship—for the group, too—if they didn't carry things any further. Luisa had laughed and flirted; she'd tossed her hair back and rubbed catlike against Alex and curled into poor Derek's lap. She'd kept control, let them see that it meant nothing to her. Only Cat had seen past the façade, had realized that Luisa had yearned for more. They'd never discussed it, but the two women—barely more than girls, then—had seen the truth in each other's eyes.

Harry, Luisa thought now. She hadn't carried a torch for him. It wasn't as if she'd been longing to be reunited with him. Her memory of that time carried a certain melancholy weight, but that was the nature of nostalgia. Bittersweet.

Harry's dead.

"We're going to be okay," Cat said, touching Luisa's hair, brushing it away from her eyes.

Luisa nodded and sniffled and thought about sitting up, but instead she curled into Cat's arms even more completely. Just for another minute, she'd take what comfort she could.

"Hey, Lu?" Cat said quietly.

Luisa tilted her head back, there on the deck as the boat listed side to side. She looked up at Cat, but her friend's gaze shifted, glancing around the deck of the *Kid Galahad.*

"What?" Luisa replied.

Cat frowned. "Where the hell *is* everybody?"

CHAPTER 14

Sami sat on the little built-in seat in Gabe's stateroom. She had seen no reason to have them put the man anywhere but his own bed. His spine hadn't sustained any damage she could ascertain, so she'd erred on the side of compassion. She didn't pay any attention to the blood that streaked and stained the sheets and the thin pillow. This might be Gabe's room, but the boat belonged to Harry, and Harry was past the point of caring about bloodstains.

She grimaced. In her head, the thought hadn't arisen as a joke, but now it felt like gallows humor.

On the bed, once more unconscious, Gabe sighed. His chest rose and fell and he blew a little huff from his lips. She bent to take his wrist, check his pulse. Still a bit weak but strong enough. Sami wanted to check his pupils again but didn't want to bother him. If he started to hemorrhage, there'd be little she could do for him with the medical kit she had. She'd been impressed by the supplies it contained, but she couldn't do brain surgery in a stateroom aboard a boat at sea. She could relieve the pressure if the bleeding inside his skull got worse, but real surgery—opening his skull—ended there.

Gabe's skin had been tanned a deep bronze. Now he'd lost enough blood and had suffered enough trauma that he looked sickly even with that dark hue.

A rap came at the door and then it creaked open.

Alex. He'd changed into a clean yellow V-neck T-shirt, linen pants, and sandals. He looked like a man on vacation. Sami had pulled shorts and a floral top over her bathing suit and slipped on a pair of Chuck Taylors to make it easier to walk around the boat.

"Hey, Doc," her husband said. "Nalani and Nils are with Isko. It doesn't look good. Not at all. The guy raves now and again, but that leg—the smell of it makes me hold my breath every time I poke my head in there. They've got the window open."

Sami exhaled. "It's gonna have to come off."

"In his condition—"

"It might kill him, yeah," she said.

"But if you don't take it off—"

"It might kill him, yeah."

Alex shook his head. "Shit, Sami. I'm sorry. This is so . . ."

"Yeah." She smiled wanly at him. No matter what happened, as long as she had this man, she would be all right. Sami knew Alex felt the same way. Together, they would endure. "What about sailing this thing? And the radio?"

"Patrick is working on it," Alex said. "He's turned it on. Just trying to figure out why nobody can hear him when he tries to talk. As for sailing . . . he thinks he can get the motor started. He's working on that now. But using the motor alone will take much longer—this boat's meant to sail. Plus he has no idea what he's doing as a navigator—"

A rasping voice said, "It's not that hard."

Sami turned to stare at Gabe, stunned to find that not only were his eyes open, but they were also clear. The paleness remained, and his eyelids were at half-mast, but he looked more exhausted than disoriented now.

Gabe started to shift on the bed. Sami and Alex moved in unison to prevent it.

"Whoa, whoa," she said, leaning over him to press lightly on both shoulders. "Please don't try to get up."

Gabe's eyes fluttered a bit. For a second it looked as if he might pass out again, but then he inhaled and focused. "Good advice. That hurt so much it made me want to puke. Like someone hammered a spike through my brain."

"Close enough," Alex said.

Gabe looked to Sami for an explanation. She ignored him at first, using the small penlight from the medical kit to examine his eyes. Then she nodded and sat on the edge of the bed, one hand on his forearm to make sure he kept his word about not trying to get up again.

"Please try not to move very much," she said.

Alex leaned against the narrow built-in desk. "Is this normal?"

Gabe winced and gave a small groan. "Define 'normal.' Whatever this is, it sure as hell doesn't feel normal to me."

"You were attacked," Sami said.

"Yeah. Stinky malnourished guy at the Coast Guard station. I've got that part," Gabe replied. He lifted a hand, fingers aimed for the matted blood in his hair.

"No, no," Sami said, grabbing his wrist. "Don't do that."

Gabe looked sick. "See, that's the sort of thing that worries me. How bad is it?"

"It's bad," Sami said.

"You need a hospital," Alex added. "Preferably an ER visit."

"Truth is," Sami went on cautiously, worried about upsetting him, "until you started stringing words together, I'd have given you about a twenty percent chance of regaining consciousness before we got you back to Hawaii, and maybe an equal chance of dying before we got you there."

Gabe lowered his hand slowly. "So, what are my odds now?"

"There are so many factors—" Sami started.

Alex put a hand on her shoulder. "I'm sorry to

interrupt you, baby, but no. We don't have time to play nice here. Be blunt."

Gabe stared at Alex for a second, then turned a reluctant eye toward Sami. "By all means, Dr. Simmons. Blunt away."

Sami took Gabe's hand. "You being conscious and talking is a good sign, but you've got an open cranial wound. Given that this conversation is happening, I'd say the swelling in your brain has lessened considerably, so the intracranial pressure isn't a problem. Right now. You could still suffer a hemorrhage, or any number of other complications. I'll want to clean and sterilize and bandage your wounds again, but right now I just want to get you to a neurosurgeon as soon as possible—"

"And there are problems with that," Alex put in.

"—There's also the matter of my other patient on board," Sami continued. "The guy who attacked you. His name is Isko."

Gabe frowned. "You've got a responsibility. I get that." He glanced at Alex. "But do me a favor? If I die, throw the asshole overboard."

His chin bobbed a little. Exhaustion from his ordeal and his pain, she hoped, rather than any further complications.

"Gabe, listen," Sami began.

"I heard some of what you were saying," he went on. "But maybe you need to lay it all out for me."

Sami glanced over her shoulder at Alex, silently communicating with her husband. How much should they tell Gabe? How much did he need to know?

In the end, they told him everything—about Isko
and the Coast Guard station, about the storm moving
their way, about their debate as to whether to wait for
help or sail for Hawaii . . . and about the sharks. About
Harry.

Wincing, Gabe let his head loll toward the window.
"I thought I'd heard some of that. I hoped I was dream-
ing."

"I'm sorry," Alex said. "Really."

Gabe fixed him with a hard look. "I know you
guys weren't friends anymore. He told me you hated
him."

"I didn't hate—"

"Either way, he knew you hadn't considered him a
friend in a long time. But he also told me he hadn't
always been worthy of friendship," Gabe said. "Thing
is . . . I never knew him as anything but the best friend
a guy could have. Harry had real faith in me. That's
more than I can say for anyone else I've had in my life.
It's not something I could ever take for granted."

"I'm sorry," Alex said. "I know it can't be easy for
you."

Gabe blinked hard, fighting off exhaustion or emotion or both. "Here's what we're gonna do. There are
plenty enough of you all to sail this boat. You won't be
able to get her up to top speed—not even close—
because I'm not going to let you run under full sail.
But I'm gonna give you some instruction right now and
you'd better pay attention before I pass out. I'm not
waiting for help to get here. Not when the beautiful
doctor here is obviously still very worried I'm going

to die. So you guys will radio in—it's pretty damn simple—and then you're going to set sail for home using a combo of the motor and the mainsail. Nalani's got some knowledge and so does Patrick. It'll be enough."

Sami felt a terrible trepidation. "Are you sure? This seems crazy to me. Without you and Harry . . . this isn't some little sailboat."

"If there's a storm on the way it'll slow down a rescue even more," Gabe said. He wetted his lips with his tongue and his eyes fluttered. Sami gave him a sip of water from a bottle on the nightstand. Gabe gestured his thanks and glanced back and forth between her and Alex.

"Get me home," he said. "I don't want to die out here."

The words echoed in Sami's head, and she nodded.

"You won't," she said. "You won't."

It sounded like a promise. She hoped it wasn't a lie.

Luisa wiped her eyes and nose, sniffling a bit. She felt like a total ass. She wore a black string bikini she'd bought from Victoria's Secret three years earlier and never had the guts to put on outside a changing room. If not for the tank top over it, she'd have felt like even more of a fool.

"You okay?" Cat asked.

"Not even a little."

"It's just that you're sitting in my lap."

And she was. Luisa tousled Cat's hair and kissed her

cheek. "You know you've always wanted me to give you a lap dance."

Cat sighed. Smiled. Pressed her forehead against Luisa. "There's the girl I know."

"Not really. Shit, maybe not ever. That was the most . . . I don't think I'll ever get today out of my head, and it's not even over yet."

"We'll be okay now," Cat said. "I don't know what'll happen to Gabe, but the rest of us . . . whether we stay here or try sailing back, we'll be okay. Sharks are not going to get us here."

Luisa touched her face. "Thank you. For being you. For being my friend, despite me being the lunatic I am."

Stronger than she looked, Cat slid Luisa off her lap. "For the record, you were never my type."

"For the record," Luisa said, standing up and brushing off her butt, "you never had a type."

Cat had started to agree with her, but Luisa had stopped listening. She spotted something on the water—out beyond the ring of the atoll—that made her grin. She laughed to herself as relief flooded through her.

"What is it?" Cat asked. "You thought of a great punch line?"

But then Cat must have seen that Luisa's focus had shifted, for she turned to follow her friend's gaze. Only Cat didn't have the same reaction.

"Oh, shit," she said.

Which wiped Luisa's smile from her face. They'd both seen the boat a few miles off, seemingly headed their way. Luisa's first thought had been of rescue, but hearing the tone in Cat's voice, she realized there was another, far more likely truth unfolding.

"My God," she whispered. She reached out and took Cat's hand.

We'll be okay, Cat had said. *Sharks are not going to get us here.* And she was right. It wasn't the sharks they needed to fear.

Alex stepped into the wheelhouse with too much information in his head. Gabe had gotten so tired that he'd started to mumble, triggering a fresh examination from Sami. She'd decided it was exhaustion and not brain damage, but that had been it. Gabe needed to rest. The first mate had argued, but in the end, after extracting a promise to wake him if two hours had passed and they hadn't gotten under way, he'd surrendered to the ship's only doctor.

"So, I don't know if you guys are having any luck," he said as he entered, studying the backs of Patrick, Nalani, and James. "But I've got good news on Gabe, and on getting the hell out of here."

They kept talking as if he hadn't spoken. Something that sounded like a math problem, trying to figure out how long it would be before they met up with the rescue ship.

"Am I a ghost now?" Alex asked. For half a second, he thought maybe they were blaming him for Harry's death, treating him like he wasn't even there. "Hello?

Nobody wants good news? I can tell you how to get the radio working."

Patrick turned to him, charmingly self-satisfied. "We figured it out. Already sent a distress call and had a conversation with the Coast Guard in Honolulu. It won't be fast, but they're coming. We were just debating how much time we could save by trying to meet them halfway."

Alex clapped his hands together. "Yes. Let's do that."

He hurried over to examine the instrument panel. This part of the wheelhouse was cramped even with two people, but now there were four of them. Nalani and James moved aside while Alex put his hands on the wheel. He ticked through Gabe's many instructions in his head, scanning the instrument panel. He spotted several of the buttons and gauges he'd been told would be there, and for the first time he thought they might actually be able to do this.

"Did you suddenly remember you knew how to sail this thing?" Patrick asked.

Alex smirked. It felt so nice to have good news. "Gabe's awake."

"What?" James said. "His skull is cracked open!"

"He's awake," Alex repeated, then waved a hand through the air. "Well, not now. Not this very second. But he was awake and lucid and Sami thinks there's a good chance he'll be okay in the end. But we've got to get him and Isko help as soon as possible, obviously. I mean, time is incredibly important with this stuff."

"Wow," Nalani said. "That's fantastic." She rubbed at her eyes, which were just a little damp. So were her husband's.

Alex sobered. "He's not out of the woods. So every minute is valuable. Not just for him, but for Isko. His leg needs to be amputated, and Sami sure as hell doesn't want to do that out here, on the boat."

"Fuck that guy," Patrick said. He spoke in a sort of bitter growl.

The four of them shifted awkwardly. The argument over Isko had been the thing that brought Harry and Alex to blows. Alex hadn't killed him, hadn't thrown him to the sharks, but that fight had put them both in the water.

"You have something to say?" Alex asked.

Nalani and James just looked at Patrick.

After a moment, he shrugged. "No, man. Sami's doing what she has to. My husband's in there looking after Isko right now, and the guy's obviously been through hell. It's just hard to wrap my head around. If Isko hadn't bashed Gabe's head in, we'd be getting ready to sail to our next destination with Harry at the wheel. I barely knew him, but this is his boat. He brought us all out here just so he didn't have to be alone to make peace with his father's memory. To die like that . . ."

His voice trailed off.

Nalani took his hand. "I know. We all feel like that."

Maybe Patrick didn't mean to, but he glanced at Alex then, as if dubious about the word "all."

"We do," Alex agreed. "It's not right. But it's also over. As soon as everyone's back on board, we'll see if Patrick and Nalani can get the mainsail up, and if Gabe told me enough about piloting this thing that we can get out of here. Honestly, how Harry and Gabe were running this ship with just the two of them I have no idea."

Patrick nodded grimly.

Nalani glanced over at her husband, James. "Where are the others, anyway? Can you go out on deck and see what's taking so long?"

James kissed Nalani on the cheek, then went to the starboard door and slid it open. Immediately, they heard shouting from outside.

Cat's voice. Calling for Alex. Calling for Nils. Calling for Nalani.

"What the hell—" Patrick began.

James stepped back as Cat's voice grew louder. They heard her steps on the stairs, coming up from the cockpit, and then she was there, popping her head into the wheelhouse, staring at all of them.

"You guys," she said gravely, breath coming hard. "Search the boat for weapons. And make it fast."

Alex flinched. He'd been expecting something about the sharks, that maybe something had happened to Luisa or Alliyah or Dev on the way back from shore. But weapons?

"Say that again?" Patrick asked.

"Weapons," Cat repeated, her gaze ice-cold now, her jaw set. "Guns if there are any. Even a flare. Something to fight with."

They all just stared at her, not comprehending until at last Cat scowled.

"There's a boat coming," she said. "You saw the bullets and the maps in the Coast Guard station. There's a boat coming right now, and you can bet your fucking ass it's not a coincidence."

CHAPTER 15

When Alliyah saw the new boat arriving, her first instinct was to cheer. She shot a fist in the air and turned to Dev, but instead of celebrating, he swore and grabbed her arm and tried to make her crouch down.

"What's wrong with you?" she demanded.

Dev shot her a dark look, eyes blazing, and crouched without her. He went to his knees, head ducked, glaring at her.

"Use your head. I'm not putting any faith in whoever that is. Cat said they're talking about smugglers. Guns, drugs, fucking pirates, or whatever. If they called for help, it cannot possibly have come this fast. Even if there are other boats nearby . . . Come on, Alliyah. Just get your head down. If that boat isn't here for a rescue, I don't want them knowing we exist!"

Out of spite alone, years of bitterness she thought she'd put aside, she wanted to jump up and down and wave her arms to get the newcomers' attention. But when she glanced again at the boat making straight for the *Kid Galahad,* she found herself ducking without making any conscious decision to do so.

Within a minute, she and Dev had retreated to the place Nalani and James had been screwing in the water, on the ocean side of the rock and coral ridge that ran along the spine of their little fragment of the atoll. The small rise in the land and scrub was enough to allow them to lie down and to think they might go unnoticed by those on board the newly arrived vessel.

Only after she'd lain down on her belly, like a sniper trying to get a good angle, did she spot the debris of their picnic spread across the sand on the lagoon side. There were red and blue and green towels, colors bright enough to draw the eye, but there was nothing she and Dev could do about that now.

Quietly, her chest aching, gooseflesh rising on the backs of her legs from the cooling breeze, she lay next to Dev and watched the new arrival—a big long-range-style fishing boat—circle around the *Kid Galahad* and then drop anchor fifty yards away. A gray pontoon boat went into the water off the back. Half a dozen crewmen climbed into it and the motor buzzed and whined as they zipped over to the yacht.

Dev swore under his breath.

Alliyah put a hand over her mouth. She needn't have worried about making any noise. No words rose to her lips. She could barely think. The paranoid nightmare Dev had been afraid of had just come true.

The men in that pontoon boat had guns.

The moment Alex saw the guns, everything changed. Nils and Patrick and Cat were just behind him on deck. They'd gathered what weapons they could—the wickedest knives from the galley, a gaffing hook, and the flare gun—but the men in the pontoon boat carried pistols and assault rifles. Alex felt sick, a twist of nausea in his gut, but he knew they had no choice. If they tried to stand against these men with these weapons, right now, they were going to die.

"Patrick," he said. "Take this shit below." He handed over the flare gun. "This was a stupid idea."

"What?" Cat said. "We can't just . . . Alex, at least let's get the ladder up. Don't let them board."

She rushed over to the railing, grabbed hold of the heavy chains at the top of the ladder. Alex followed, put a hand on her arm. Cat turned toward him, and he saw the same sickness in her eyes that he knew must be in his own.

"We'll just end up putting it back down. With those guns—"

"At least we'll buy time!" Cat argued. "We'll hide below. When they come down, we'll fight them. What else can we do? We need *time*."

Alex hesitated a second, seeing it now the way she saw it. Why help them? It would be many hours before help arrived, but the gunmen didn't know that. Pirates, smugglers, whatever they were—they didn't know how long the *Kid Galahad* had been sitting here.

He nodded. Side by side, he and Cat grabbed hold of the ladder. Together, they started to raise it up.

Gunfire ripped the air over their heads, echoing across the lagoon. Cat grabbed Alex and dragged him down. The ladder slapped against the hull as they dropped to their knees. Alex spun around and saw that Patrick and Nils were gone. They'd hide the weapons, and that was good. His thoughts raced. They might need those weapons later—if they had a chance to use them.

"Cat, go below," he said. "Someone's got to stay up here. I want them to know how many are on board and what condition we're in. I'll make them think help's coming soon. But we don't need any extra targets on deck."

"I'll stay," Cat said. "Sometimes your mouth gets you into trouble."

"They're shooting at us," he said incredulously. "You think I'm going to mouth off?"

The engine of the pontoon boat revved loudly, like a lawn mower had just pulled up alongside, and then it cut out completely. Something thumped against the hull. The ladder went taut. Alex could see it from where he knelt on the deck. He thought of Sami, of all the things he wished he'd said to her just now, before he'd left her down below. He told himself that she knew what she meant to him, but still his heart ached. His mouth formed the unspoken words.

Then he stood up. Cat rose beside him.

Both of them put their hands up as the first man reached the top of the ladder. He hung away from the hull as if he might swing on it, one hand grasping and the other aiming an assault rifle through the bars of the railing. Even as the big man grabbed hold of the railing and hoisted himself up and over, Alex could only stare at the gun. The other details he was aware of— the white man's powerful build, his stubbly shaved head, the sleeves of tattoos on his deeply tanned skin— were all periphery. Only the gun mattered.

Till his boots hit the deck and he turned the weapon toward Cat. Then Alex noticed the man's smile and the brilliant blue of his eyes, so vivid they seemed unreal.

"Well," he drawled, his accent unmistakably American. "Ain't you a pretty one?"

Cat exhaled grimly. Her eyes lost any trace of fear. Instead, she looked like she wanted to murder him. Ready to fight. But she kept her hands up.

"If you're here to rob us, take what you want," Alex said as a second man climbed over the railing, and then a third. "But you probably want to do it fast. Our captain's dead and the mate's wounded. We've been here a while and already called for help. Coast Guard should be here any time now."

Blue Eyes and the others ignored him, spreading out across the deck, weapons ready, watching for anyone stupid enough to try to fight them. Several of them had a military bearing. Alex had done thirteen months in Iraq and he recognized the look. Soldiers and other military personnel had a certain aura about them that was difficult to hide. The way they stood, the way their eyes shifted warily, the way they moved. Three of these guys were clearly ex-military, though only Blue Eyes and one other, a tall black guy with a pink scar across his left eye, the eye itself a milky white, were American.

They all stood a bit straighter, weapons trained on Alex and Cat, as the fifth man came over the railing. The sixth had stayed in the pontoon boat, but the way they all reacted to his presence made it clear that this man was the leader. He carried a gun—a pistol, in a holster at his hip—but made no move to draw it. Instead, he glanced around the deck of the *Kid Galahad* as if he'd been invited aboard, and an enormous smile blossomed on his face.

"Now this is a beautiful craft," he said, his accent detectable but not strong. Whatever his native tongue might be—Hawaiian or Tagalog or something else entirely—Alex couldn't guess.

The man clapped his hands together and rubbed them as if he was eager to get to work. "I am not joking. I have been on board some of the prettiest boats on the water, and this one is up there."

He pushed his hands into the pockets of his loose linen pants. His shoulder-length hair was thick and black, like a mane around his pockmarked face. His nose appeared to have been broken at least once, and yet his smile was infectious. If Alex hadn't been terrified for himself and his wife and friends, he'd have smiled in return.

"What'd I hear him saying?" the man asked, turning his focus on Cat. "Your captain's dead?"

Cat only stared. Blue Eyes had moved a bit closer to her and she was all too aware of the way he had been studying her. Alex saw it, too. A terrible calculus had begun in his head. He had always adored Cat, always respected her, but he had begun to wonder, just at the fringes of his thoughts, what he would be willing to do in order to protect her. How far would he go when his own wife was also on board? Would he die for Cat, or would he let hideous things happen to her if it meant he might be able to help Sami later? He needed his wife to live, needed Sami to get home to Tasha, no matter what else had to be sacrificed to make that happen.

Nausea burned in his gut. Shame burned in his heart.

"He said it," Blue Eyes offered, nodding toward Alex, his gun still trained on Cat.

The pockmarked man's smile broadened. He hung his head but didn't look at Blue Eyes. "I didn't ask you."

No apology came, but Blue Eyes knew he'd fucked up. Alex could see it on his face. The man stood a bit straighter. His boss rolled his eyes good-naturedly, but there was something cruel and merciless lurking beneath that good-natured façade.

He turned to Alex. "You were saying? About your captain?"

"Sharks," Alex managed. For the first time it really struck him that none of the men had moved. They had taken up positions on the deck as if they were guarding him and Cat, and watching over their boss just in case anyone came up from below. But they were in no hurry. Not yet.

"How the hell did that happen?" the pockmarked man asked.

"He fell into the water," Cat said impatiently. "Right here. Right off the boat."

"So you haven't been ashore?" the man asked, turning his attention to her. Now his smile vanished. His eyes were small and black, flat and dead as a shark's.

"The Coast Guard is coming," Alex said.

"I have no doubt they are," the man replied without turning. He stayed focused on Cat. "My name is Machii. I tell you that either because I don't care if you tell the Coast Guard or because I don't expect you to be alive to tell them. I'll let you worry about which is true. What is your name?"

She told him.

Machii smiled again. "I like that," he said, and turned to Alex. "And you?"

"Alex."

"Good. Now we're all friends." He glanced at Blue Eyes. "Take Benjie below. Joriz can go up into the wheelhouse. Count heads. Gather up whatever's shiny. I want everyone on the deck in ten minutes. Don't kill anyone unless they don't give you a choice."

Blue Eyes hesitated, then gestured at Cat. "I'm gonna want time with her later."

"That's not going to happen," Alex said quickly.

Machii held up a hand. "We don't have time to waste here. The storm is coming. And if I believe this one"—he pointed at Alex—"then the Coast Guard could arrive anytime. We're in and out."

Blue Eyes sneered. "That was my plan."

"Only if you want to bleed," Cat said, her sneer as hard-edged as his own.

"Oh, honey, you have no idea," Blue Eyes replied.

Machii stepped up to the man. He didn't reach for his pistol or put his fists up, didn't even try to physically menace him. He only moved nearer, making sure he had Blue Eyes' attention.

"Why are you still on deck?"

Blue Eyes sniffed, shot one final glance at Cat, and then nodded to two other men—Benjie and Joriz, apparently—and led them toward the cockpit and the steps that led below. Alex held his breath, praying nobody down there would do anything stupid. Sami was below and he couldn't prevent a zoetrope of horrors from flickering through his mind. After the way Blue Eyes had just laid out his intentions for Cat, it seemed clear rape and murder were very much on the menu of crimes for these men.

Alex glanced at Cat. Despite the ferocity she'd shown a moment before, he could see she was shaken. Of course she was. Alex had been shaken and it wasn't his body being threatened. She'd fight for herself, and he'd certainly fight for her, but against these men he could summon little hope that they could be prevented from doing whatever their cruelty desired.

"Okay," Machii said. "Just me and Damien now." He nodded at the towering man who remained on deck with them. "We're the nice ones."

Machii and Damien both laughed.

"You're taking a risk, staying here," Alex said quietly. "The Coast Guard—"

Damien lifted his assault rifle and marched a few steps across the deck. The ship rocked on the waves, which were higher than before. The sky had begun to turn gray as the huge man pointed his weapon at Alex's forehead.

"We're the nice ones," Damien said. "But I don't think Machii asked you a question."

Alex wanted to fight. He wanted to shout, to threaten, to try to drag the big bastard over the railing and feed him to the sharks. A little sliver of hysteria cut through him as he thought about how much simpler it had all been an hour ago, when all they'd had to worry about was being eaten by sharks.

Cat raised her hands again. "We're good. We're just going to stand here."

Machii faced her. "How long ago did you really radio for help?"

"Late afternoon yesterday. They should've been here by now," she said. No trace of a lie. No wince. She met his gaze evenly. "I was getting really fucking impatient before you showed up. Planning the email I was going to write to them to complain."

Machii looked as if he wasn't sure whether to believe her, but then his gaze cut left and right and he glanced over his shoulder, as if he could feel the approach of a Coast Guard vessel. If one showed up, the situation would get very complicated, very fast.

"Imagine the apology they'll owe you now," Machii said.

Damien laughed softly, the sound of Jabba the Hutt stuck in a well.

Voices shouted below. Alex pressed his eyes closed, listening to the muffled sounds. A gunshot made him flinch. He could feel Cat staring at him but wouldn't look at her. One gunshot, and one only. He wondered if the bullet had been for Sami.

"Who's down there?" Damien rumbled. "Wife? Kids?"

Alex stabbed him with a glare, locked eyes with him and didn't look away. A minute passed. Maybe two. Then people started filing out of the cockpit and he turned to look, silently praying to a god he believed to be fiction. Nalani came up first, then Patrick, followed by Sami and Luisa carrying Isko on a blanket. Blue Eyes followed them out, assault rifle trained on them, his gaze alight with amusement.

In his peripheral vision, Alex saw Damien nod.

"Wife," he said. Maybe he'd seen the relief pass through Alex or maybe he was just assuming they were together because Sami was the only black woman on board. Either way, he knew. If Damien tried anything, if he had the same hungers that Blue Eyes had—if he tried to rape Sami—Alex would kill him. He'd spent his adult life learning that women didn't want some knight on a white horse, but Sami couldn't protect herself from this. Alex couldn't protect her from it, either, but he'd die trying.

James and Nils came up, lugging Gabe on a blanket. Gabe winced with pain and he looked pale, sweat beading on his forehead, but he was alive and alert.

The last two smugglers followed them out of the cockpit. Benjie and Joriz. Alex didn't know which of them was which, nor did he care. He just wanted them gone. The youngest one carried a pillowcase, and Alex didn't have to ask to know what it held—jewelry and cash, maybe passports. They hadn't grabbed any food or booze, not by the look of the bag. Harry'd had drugs on board, and if the smugglers had found them they were probably in the bag as well.

"Have a look at this," Blue Eyes said. He turned to Sami and Luisa. With a deep frown he kicked the blanket carrying Isko. Luisa cried out and jumped back, letting go of her end of the blanket. Isko's legs crashed to the deck. The man screamed in pain and rolled onto his side, clutching his rotting leg. Awake. Conscious.

Machii laughed in what seemed to be amazement. Expression full of wonder, he crouched beside the man.

"Isko," he said before launching into something in his own language.

"You know him?" Cat asked.

"Of course he does," Alex said. "They left him here."

Still nodding in amazement, Machii rose to his feet. "We did." He hooked a thumb toward the railing. "Although really we left him there. In the water. With our hungry friends."

"*Diyablo Pating,*" Nalani said.

Machii noticed her for the first time. "Smart woman." He walked toward her. "Or maybe not so smart. You understand what we call the Devil Sharks, so you know my language. You speak Isko's language. So tell me, smart one . . ."

For the first time since he'd boarded, Machii drew

his pistol. Everyone started to move and to speak, but the smugglers raised their weapons and took aim, and they all froze. Alex held his breath and he was sure that none of the others were breathing, either. The creaking of the boat and the splash of waves against the hull were the only sounds.

Machii reached up to touch Nalani's face. She trembled, breath catching in her throat, as he gently twined his fingers in her hair.

"You don't want to do this," James said. He took half a step, hands coming up in supplication.

Blue Eyes leveled his weapon at James.

"The seconds tick by," Machii told Nalani. "Your friend Alex says I don't have much time, so I'm going to ask you once—"

"I hardly know any Tagalog," Nalani said quickly. "I swear—"

Machii put his pistol against her left eye. "Your man is right. I don't want to do horrible things to any of you. It's an unhappy by-product of what we do. For instance . . . Isko has been with you for some amount of time. I don't know how long. The dirty shit doesn't speak much English. But I have to assume that you, smart one, understood whatever he said. And you've had radio contact with the Coast Guard, which means anything he told you I have to assume you've already told them. About us. About me."

"I swear—" James said.

Machii jammed his gun into Nalani's eye socket. She cried out in pain and tried to tear herself away, but he twisted her hair into his fist.

"What did Isko tell you?" the smuggler asked. His smile had vanished, leaving behind such icy malice that it might never have been there at all. "What did you pass along to the Coast Guard?"

"He raved," Nalani said. "Like in a nightmare. Begging for his life. He talked about the Devil Sharks. I swear that's it!"

Alex pointed at Gabe. "He did that! He was disoriented. He must've thought we were you, coming back for him. He attacked our first mate and bashed his fucking head in."

Machii looked thoughtful. Alex took a step and Damien thumped him in the head with the butt of his assault rifle. He went down on one knee, but he rose immediately. Staying down would mark him as weak, vulnerable, and he could feel the primal tension at work here, the wolf pack mentality. They'd tear him apart. His skull ached, and his maybe-broken nose throbbed, but he stood up straight.

Sami seemed about to say something, but Alex shot her a warning look. He prayed she wouldn't say anything about being a doctor. These people might want a doctor. They might just *take* her. Alex drew only shallow breaths, fighting panic, battling all of the bloody scenarios that played out in his mind. He tried to tell himself that there was a way they might survive this, and maybe there was. But these men radiated violence. They practically stank of it. Alex studied the youngest of them, who might be Joriz or Benjie. The man held the pillowcase with his gun and he kept glancing about nervously. Alex thought if it came to that he'd have no problem wresting the kid's gun away from him. He could kill one or two of them—but which ones? And would anyone else move fast enough to make a difference? Would his friends be quick enough, brave enough, brutal enough, to survive if they had to fight?

He wanted to live, to see his daughter again. But more than that, he needed Sami to live. He'd kill all of these motherfuckers by himself if it meant he could stop them from murdering her.

Breathe, he told himself. *Watch and listen. Wait.*

"So he didn't tell you anything about us? About this operation?" Machii asked.

Nalani shook her head, desperate hope in her eyes.

Machii kept a grip on her hair but swung the barrel of his gun toward James, and pulled the trigger.

Nalani screamed as the bullet punched through her husband's skull, spraying blood and gray matter across the deck, splattering Nils and Patrick. Alex and Sami were both shouting. Luisa fell to her knees, crying, looking like insanity had just claimed her.

"Oh, Jesus. Oh, Jesus," Patrick kept saying, backing up, staring at the blood on him.

"Don't fucking move!" Damien barked, aiming his weapon at Patrick and Nils. Both men froze.

Nalani kept screaming. Machii shook her by the hair and pointed the gun at Nils.

"This guy's next. Maybe you don't love him like you did your man, but I doubt you want him to die. So tell me, smart lady. What did Isko tell you?"

"Nothing!" Nalani cried. "We didn't know anything

about you until you got here. We didn't tell the Coast Guard anything. We didn't . . . Oh, God, James. Oh my God, James."

She kept trying to turn, to twist away from him so she could get a good look at her husband, as if there might be some chance he'd survived that bullet, even with his blood and brains on the deck and on Nils and Patrick.

Machii shoved her backward, releasing his grip on her hair, and she fell sprawling at Cat's feet. Cat, who'd flinched and closed her eyes. Who opened them now, staring at Machii, but kept her mouth shut.

Benjie and Joriz lowered their weapons long enough to pick up James's body. Luisa and Nalani were both crying, screaming at them as they carried James to the railing and threw him overboard. The rest of them stayed silent, not wanting to be next. They heard the splash, and then more noises below, a feeding frenzy.

Blue Eyes stood above Isko, who'd fallen unconscious again. "Want me to finish this idiot?"

"Nah. He's going to die anyway," Machii said. "Traitor piece of shit. No way he lives through that rotting leg and the blood loss. It's a miracle he's lived this long. Let him keep hurting."

Blue Eyes stomped on Isko's ruined leg, but the man was so far gone now that he only groaned, eyelids fluttering. Alex thought this must be a coma now. Machii was right. He wouldn't live long.

The smugglers' leader pointed at Gabe. "That guy, though. Grab him."

Benjie and Joriz moved toward him.

"No," Gabe said, trying to slide away from them. "What the fuck . . . I can't hurt you. I'm no danger to you."

Machii laughed. "None of you are."

The two men picked Gabe up. He started to struggle, trying to fight them, but Damien moved in and smashed him in the skull. Gabe jerked in their arms, not a struggle now but a seizure. That blow had furthered the damage to his head. Bloody spittle flew from his lips.

"Oh, shit," Blue Eyes said, laughing. "What'd you do, Damien?"

Damien glared at him but said nothing. After a few more jerks, Gabe started muttering to himself. Alex heard him call for Harry, but though his hands flailed a bit, he had no fight left in him as they carried him to the railing.

"No!" Alex said, stepping toward them. "He's gonna die like Isko. Just let him die here on the deck. The sharks—"

Machii pointed his pistol at Alex's chest, but it was the look in the man's eyes that stopped him.

"Sharks need to eat, *Alex*."

Gabe whimpered as they hurled him overboard. Alex turned away. He wanted to cover his ears so he didn't have to hear the sounds that would follow, but he worried they would see his hands come up and just shoot him. That they'd throw him into the water with the sharks. The *Diyablo Pating*.

Luisa kept screaming. Nils had taken Nalani in his arms to quiet her. Neither of them seemed to care that her husband's blood stained her clothes now. Patrick had a hand on his husband's back. Cat and Sami stood six or seven feet apart, both with stone faces, careful not to make a motion that would set off the smugglers.

"Okay," Machii said, walking over to put his arm around Alex. "Damien's going to stay here on the boat with your friends. We're making a trade. We leave him, but we take you. See, you seem like you're stupid enough to try something here. We're going ashore. We're gonna make sure there's no trace of us in there, nothing we need, nothing they can use to track us down. And then we're leaving as fast as we can."

He raised the pistol, glancing around at the others. "We're in a hurry, my friends. Our pets are fed. We've had our fun. I haven't decided yet how many of you are going to be alive when we leave, but if you behave yourselves, maybe it'll be all of you."

Machii smiled. "Though I highly doubt it."

He shoved Alex toward the ladder. "Let's go."

Sami said his name. Just once. Not a scream or a cry. She spoke his name.

Alex looked back at his wife and she nodded to him. *Stay alive,* that nod said.

He nodded back.

Then he climbed over the side, leaving his wife behind.

Below, the water churned with Devil Sharks and the blood of two good men.

CHAPTER 16

Alliyah jerked against the ground. The crack of the gunshot echoed across the water. Dev whispered something too quietly for her to hear. She dug her fingers into the hard ground of the little rise that sheltered them from view. When the men threw the body overboard—tossed it to the waiting sharks—she felt the tears come fast. From the way she heard Dev's breathing hitch, she knew he must be crying, too.

Sick with horror, she listened to the distant shouts and screams. They were carried on the wind, drifting in and out like radio stations fuzzed with static. Another body went over the side. She wished she had binoculars, and then was glad she didn't. *Gabe,* she thought. From the hair and the coloring, it had to be Gabe.

Something shifted inside her then. *Hardened.* She felt her tears dry as the wind blew across her back and the light turned gray with the oncoming storm, still a ways off but ominous, full of the promise of hard rain. The wind picked up as Alliyah and Dev lay there watching, waiting to see who would be the next person thrown to the sharks.

The water touched Alliyah's toes. Reflexively, she drew her legs up a bit and glanced over her shoulder. The waterline had been much farther when they had arrived. The tide was coming in.

A motor roared and she settled herself beside Dev again, ignoring the surf as it touched her feet again. In the bay, gunmen were climbing down from the *Kid Galahad,* but they weren't leaving alone. She held her breath as she watched Alex climb down the ladder.

Gunshots filled the air. She flinched with every crack of the air. Then she saw one of the smugglers lean over and fire a longer gun into the *Galahad*'s dinghy, which had been tied up alongside this whole time. This was no crack, no simple gunshot. The boom echoed across the water and she knew it had to be a shotgun, though she'd only ever heard one fired on television or in movies.

"Dev—" she began.

"They're scuttling the dinghy," he said, his voice hollow.

More of the smugglers, or whatever they were, joined Alex and the others in the pontoon boat, and then they cast off. The dinghy would be sinking, even now. No matter what else happened, their friends were trapped on that boat. Nobody would be coming for Alliyah and Dev, at least not today.

Her eyes tracked Alex's head, where he sat in that

small boat, but the gunmen didn't return to their own ship. The pontoon boat cut a diagonal line across the inside arc of the atoll, headed directly for the Coast Guard station.

"There's something there they want," she whispered.

Dev said nothing.

She turned her head, keeping low. "We have to do something."

"Don't be stupid."

Heat flushed her cheeks. "They don't know we're here. Whoever they are, they just murdered two people. They killed our friends."

Dev looked at her as if she were the murderer. His tears had dried, but they were shot through with red. "They killed two people, Alli, and they are . . . I mean, it's pretty clear they're going to kill more. If help is coming, it's not going to come in time."

"*We* can help."

"Alliyah, I want you to listen to me." The wind skittered small stones and bits of sand across the ground around them. The surf shushed up around their feet. The pontoon boat's motor still roared.

"Dev—"

"Alliyah, despite everything, I have been a good husband. We both had fathers who were very different sorts of husbands than I have been to you. I know why you left me, why you hurt me, and you know it was not easy for me to begin again with you. Maybe I was distant and made you feel alone, but I never tried to bully you. I never told you what to do. But you need to listen to me now. We're going to lie here and do nothing. We're going to stay hidden as best we can and hope that nobody discovers us."

Her feelings for Dev had been complicated for a long time. But her feelings about this were crystal clear.

"Fuck you." She slid backward, in the water up to her calves, and rose onto her knees and elbows.

Dev grabbed her wrist. "Stay here! You're going to stay right here with me—"

"Or what?" she hissed.

"Or you're going to get us both killed."

Alliyah exhaled. Deflating. When she looked at him again, she made sure to let her face reveal all the disgust and sorrow she felt.

"One of my oldest friends died a little while ago. Maybe he wasn't a very good friend, but he was one of the best friends I had, once upon a time. Now two more friends are dead, and I don't even know who one of them was. Shot dead. Dumped into the water for . . . for fucking *chum*!"

"Sssshhhh."

She yanked her arm back, breaking his grip. "Don't shush me, you cowardly piece of shit." She felt the rage fueling her, felt the spittle flying from her lips. It woke her up to who and what she was, what she and Dev were to each other, and her sadness deepened. "I'm a broken person, Dev. I think everyone's broken in some way. But I never understood what a tiny, cowardly little man you really are."

"You're going to get me killed," he said quietly. She noticed that he'd said *us both* before, but now it was just about him. At least now his fear wore an honest face.

"There are people I love on that boat," she said. "And Alex Simmons . . . shit, Alex is just about the best guy I ever knew. I got to college, and Alex was the first guy who made me realize that not all men had to be selfish pricks."

"So you slept with him. You're going to get me killed because you once slept with Alex?"

Alliyah had listened to enough. "Dating Alex was a mistake. We weren't right for each other and I was never in love with him. But did I love him? Do I love him? Absolutely, I do. Enough that I can't lie here and let him, or any of the others, die. Not if there's anything I can do about it."

She scuttled sideways, crab-style, and worked her way down into the water.

"They have guns," she heard Dev say, but a wave crashed around her and the words were wiped away.

She knew they had guns. She knew her only advantage was that the smugglers had no idea anyone else was on the atoll. She knew a storm was coming and the tide was rising. But she could see a path along this side of the atoll that would take her into the trees and flowers and eventually, if she kept low and stayed lucky, would let her emerge perhaps forty feet from the Coast Guard station.

More than anything, though, Alliyah knew that if

she'd stayed lying on her belly on the ground like Dev, and she survived, she'd have to live the rest of her life knowing she'd done nothing when her friends were being murdered.

Better to be dead than to live with that.

She stayed low, and she hurried as best she could.

And the sky grew darker, and the tide rose.

Sami sat on the deck with her back against the cockpit wall, the windows of the wheelhouse above her. Cat had asked if she could take Luisa below, but the big man with the gun—Damien—had refused. They were all staying on deck until Machii and the others came back. If the guests of the *Kid Galahad* behaved themselves, they might survive to be rescued. Damien said it as if he believed there to be a genuine possibility of them all living to see nightfall, and Sami didn't judge him as someone who cared very much about lying to make other people feel better.

So she sat—hands in her lap and mouth shut—and she waited. Machii thought the Coast Guard was coming. They'd all be hurrying now, which was good but could also be dangerous.

Luisa had stopped screaming at some point, but Sami had barely noticed. The woman's grief and hysteria had become as much a part of this terror as the rocking of the ship and the sinister presence of the sharks, not to mention the gun in Damien's hands. Sami had never been this close to an assault rifle. The quickness of it, the ability it had to erupt, felt to her like what she imagined it would be to fall into a tiger pit.

Cat sat against the railing with Luisa, arm around her. She wouldn't look at Damien, but she radiated hatred. Sami had no doubt that Cat would kill the son of a bitch if the opportunity arose, which was a thing she'd never thought about another person. Ever. Never had to think about it. If anyone had asked her that morning which of them was least likely to be willing to take another human life, Sami would have chosen Cat. Full of love and music, a kind and patient soul, willing to endure her friends' flaws because she valued their better qualities. But yeah, no question in Sami's mind now. Cat would kill this guy.

Sami couldn't be so confident about herself. Harry and Gabe and James were all dead. Alex . . . just thinking of him made every muscle in her body tense. Alex had been taken at gunpoint off this boat. If she had to do it to protect him, Sami figured she could kill, even though every moment of her professional training had been about saving lives. But in that situation, yes. She thought she could kill a man.

But to get the drop on him, to push him overboard so the sharks would eat him—the easiest method, the method she knew they all had to be thinking about, even Damien—she didn't know if she could do that.

"Oh, shit," Patrick said. "I'm . . . I think I'm gonna be sick."

Damien's upper lip curled in disgust. He swung the barrel of his assault rifle toward Nils and Patrick, who were standing not far from the door into the wheelhouse. Patrick did look pale. He hung his head and gagged, then took shallow breaths, fighting back the urge. He took two steps toward the railing, and nearer to Damien.

"Hey! If you're gonna puke, do it right there."

Nils started to defend him, but Patrick held up his hands, taking more shallow breaths.

"Sorry," he said. "I just . . . oh, shit, no . . ."

He stumbled forward, giving Damien a wide berth but racing past him. Damien shouted at him as Patrick reached the railing, bent over, and started dry heaving. He gagged, making choking noises.

Damien barked again. Then pulled the trigger.

Sami cried out and Luisa buried her head in Cat's shoulder. The bullets punched into the deck, sending shrapnel flying. Patrick dropped to his knees, hands raised again, taking long breaths now as Damien shouted warnings—to get back with the others or the next bullet wouldn't be aimed at the boat.

Patrick started back over to where he and Nils had been standing.

Only then did Sami notice that Nils had vanished. Damien saw it at the same moment.

"Oh, you little bastard," Damien said, and he kicked Patrick in the back.

Patrick sprawled on the deck as Damien marched over to Luisa, who screamed as the big man dragged her away from Cat. He swung his assault rifle left and right to keep Sami and Cat and Patrick from trying to rush him, and then he put the gun barrel to

Luisa's head. Hysteria fled and Luisa fell unnervingly silent.

"Go and get your boyfriend," Damien said. "I'm counting to twenty and this bitch is dead."

Patrick leaped to his feet and lunged through the cockpit door, heading for the wheelhouse steps as he shouted for Nils to stop. He didn't waste seconds trying to plead with Damien or correct the man's observation of his marital status.

"One! Two. Three. Four. Five . . ."

Sami glanced at Cat and saw she had shifted onto one knee, her left hand on the deck as if she might spring at the gunman. Sami would have hissed at her, told her to stay where she was, except that she realized she herself had adopted the same pose. Luisa seemed to shrink, still in silence, awaiting the bullet that Sami hoped would kill her if it came. Better a bullet than the sharks. Better a quick death than screaming the way Harry had as they tore into you, feeling it and knowing what was happening to you.

Damien kept counting.

Sami wanted to weep, but terror had leeched away any chance of tears.

"Thirteen! Fourteen. Fifteen! Six—"

Nils stumbled onto the deck. He glanced around at the others, paused to gaze apologetically at Luisa; then Patrick followed him onto the deck. Damien hurled Luisa back toward Cat and swung the gun at Nils and Patrick.

"You," he said to Patrick. "Go sit with the others."

"Whatever you're going to do—"

"If I felt like killing him, I'd just shoot you both," Damien said, laughing quietly as if he'd just heard the world's dumbest joke. "Go and sit your ass down."

Nils gave his husband a gentle shove. Patrick watched Damien with rapt attention. Sami could see a vein pulsing on his neck as he sat down beside her. She took his arm, looped hers through his, both in comfort and to keep him from lunging.

"You, over here," Damien said, gesturing for Nils to come and kneel on the deck by him. Fifteen feet from the nearest other person—fifteen feet from help.

He kicked Nils in the face.

"Fucker!" Patrick growled, trying to jump to his feet.

Sami held him back and he tried to pull free as Damien kicked Nils again. Blood flew from Nils's mouth.

"That's enough!" Cat shouted.

Patrick broke free. Sami grabbed hold again and was dragged to her feet as she tried to stop him.

Damien pressed the barrel of the gun against the back of Nils's head, staring at Patrick.

"Stop!" Nils snapped, and it was clear he wasn't talking to the man hurting him, but to his husband. "Just let him do what he has to do."

Damien grinned, then swung the gun toward Patrick and kicked Nils in the ribs with enough force to loft the smaller man off the deck. Nils flopped on his side, gasping for air. Patrick's fists opened and closed, but there was nothing he could do that wouldn't end with one or both of them dead.

"Now listen," Damien said. "Machii would've killed you both. I figure you went for the radio, which makes me wonder why. Maybe help isn't coming after all. Maybe all that shit about the Coast Guard was a lie, although you guys were pretty much stranded when we got here, so I don't know. All I do know is that if anyone tries anything else . . . anything at all . . . I'm going to make you guys choose which one gets shot and dumped over the side to our hungry friends. We clear?"

No one spoke. The rigging clanged against the masts. A few droplets of rain began to patter on the deck.

"Are we clear?" Damien asked. "Come on, don't throw mercy back in my face. We could just get all nasty right now if you'd rather."

"We're clear," Nils said, spitting blood as he rose slowly to his feet and stumbled, clutching his ribs, back to his husband.

But Sami saw that Cat remained ready to lunge, and she felt it herself, in every muscle. She glanced at Patrick and Nils, and saw that they too were ready. Waiting for the right moment. Luisa, though . . . Luisa remained utterly silent, barely breathing, almost folded in upon herself on the deck.

Sami had never had a premonition before, but she felt seized by a terrible certainty in that moment. She felt sure that Luisa would die out here.

Then it occurred to her how stupid the thought was.

After all, she felt pretty sure they were all going to die out here.

She just hoped Alex came back before it happened. She liked these people, but she didn't really know them. Alex, at least, loved her. If she had to die, she wanted it to be by his side.

The pontoon boat skidded up onto the sand. Benjie and Joriz were out first, both of them rushing at the Coast Guard station with weapons leveled, as if they expected armed resistance from the abandoned building. Alex watched the crisp motion and professional execution of this simple act, the way they moved without having to be told, and he knew his suspicions were correct. Most, if not all, of these guys were ex-military. They were efficient as hell, and had proven themselves to be ruthless.

When Alex climbed out of the pontoon boat onto the beach, he figured he was never leaving Orchid Atoll.

"You look like I just broke your favorite toy," Machii said as he fell in beside Alex. The surf crashed behind them.

"Or like you just fucked his wife," Blue Eyes added. He didn't laugh. It wasn't a joke.

Alex said nothing. He trudged up toward the Coast Guard station with the two men flanking him. They left the pontoon boat with its pilot, a short, barrel-chested guy named Hannigan, who hadn't spoken a single word while he'd ferried them across the lagoon.

"Not your day, is it?" Blue Eyes asked, marching beside Alex.

"It's not ending the way it started, no," Alex replied. He glanced up at the gray sky, where the clouds were thickening. Raindrops had begun to fall.

Machii clapped a hand on his shoulder. "It's not over yet, my friend."

"Yeah," Blue Eyes agreed. "It could still get worse."

Up ahead, Benjie and Joriz took the door of the Coast Guard station like the ATF busting in the doors of a meth lab. It would have looked foolish if not for the guns, and the two men these ruthless pricks had already killed.

Alex had been inside the station only scant hours before, but it felt different now. Part of it must surely have been the slant of light, the gray sky, the higher tide and crash of waves. But when he'd first entered this building it had been a moment of peaceful camaraderie. The sunshine and the sea and the drinks had created the illusion of rapprochement between himself and Harry, as if all the old resentments could be washed away so easily.

Had it been an illusion, though? It had felt so simple. Maybe the past nastiness couldn't be erased, but as Alex breathed the close, dusty air inside the Coast Guard station and remembered the hope and nostalgia Harry'd pursued to arrive at this place he knew stepping over this threshold had been a fresh start for the two of them. Without hiding from the past, they'd both been willing to build a new friendship on the wreckage of the old.

Then Isko had attacked Gabe, and the eruption of violence had shattered the détente. In his grief and worry, Harry had reverted to behaviors he'd tried to bury, and Alex hadn't acquitted himself any better. Now all three of them were dead—Harry, Gabe, Isko.

"Smells like piss in here," Blue Eyes said.

Machii ignored him. Blue Eyes flinched, staring at his boss's back as Machii hurried down the corridor ahead of them. Blue Eyes hadn't liked being ignored. He ran his mouth a lot. Alex could feel the hunger in the man, his yearning to be the one calling the shots. Didn't Machii feel it, too? Didn't he know that Blue Eyes bristled every time he took an order or was ignored?

Not my problem, Alex thought. But he knew it could become his problem.

Joriz—Alex had managed to tell the difference between him and Benjie now—called to them from up ahead. The words weren't in English, but it had to be an all clear, for Machii quickened his pace. Blue Eyes gave Alex a shove with the stock of his assault rifle.

Benjie popped out of a side room with a small ruck-sack. Alex realized they'd missed it earlier. Maybe it had been rolled into one of the stained mattresses or stuffed into a narrow closet they'd failed to search. Not that it mattered. These men had left very little behind. They just wanted to make sure.

As he stood in the mess hall with Blue Eyes cra-dling that assault rifle beside him, Alex watched Machii step into the kitchen and then emerge again. Benjie and Joriz came into the mess hall as well.

"Nothing but dust," Joriz said. "Can't wipe the whole place down if we're in a hurry."

"And we don't know how much of a hurry we're in," Machii said, eyes narrowing as he looked at Alex. "Depends how much we believe our new friend."

His head bobbed in a slow, thoughtful nod; then he pointed to the bullet casings lined up on the windowsill. "I'm not sure which of you dumb asses put those up there, but grab them. Stuff them in your pockets for now."

Machii turned to Alex. "Your job is to take the maps off the wall and fold them up neatly."

Alex thought about telling him to fuck off, even had the appropriate sneer on his lips, but he thought of what Sami would say. He swallowed his words and his pride, thinking only of her and Tasha—of surviving this with her, and getting home to his daughter. Nothing else mattered. Not the tragic life and death of Harry Curtis or the senseless death of their first mate. Sure as hell not Isko. If he'd been a smuggler, working for Machii, then he'd been far from innocent.

Alex crossed to the wall where the maps had been hung and started to pull thumbtacks out, wanting to keep the maps neat and intact so Machii wouldn't get angry.

"The rest of you," Machii said, "find the gas can for the generator. We're going to burn this fucking place to the ground."

Alex tried not to think about the fire and what it represented. In military history, they called it the scorched-earth policy. It meant leaving nothing behind that might benefit your enemy. With the rain spattering the windows and creating a static rasp against the roof, he told himself Machii would have killed them all out on the *Kid Galahad* if that was what he'd intended to do. But maybe he'd been telling the truth when he'd said he was keeping his options open, that he hadn't decided yet.

A thumbtack gave him trouble. Alex forced his thumbnail under its edge but couldn't pry it out. He tugged the map, tearing off half an inch of paper at the corner. He wanted to move fast now, get out of there before Machii grew impatient—before the fire started.

When he heard the splash of liquid behind him and smelled gasoline, he started just ripping the maps off the wall.

CHAPTER 17

Alliyah moved quietly. With the tide coming in, there was a point on the curve of the atoll, a hundred yards from the Coast Guard station, where the tree line came within twenty feet of the water. Her heart thumped hard against her chest and a little voice in her head screamed at her to stop, to turn around, to go and hide with Dev. In any ordinary life, the fortunate people never found themselves in situations of real peril. They had to wonder what sort of person they would be if the worst happened, if they found themselves in a crisis where pain and horror were looming. Where murder seemed tangible and real and it became difficult to breathe.

The moment had come. Alliyah had never imagined it would, but she'd wondered just the same. What kind of person would she be?

She moved from the tree line and into the water as

quietly as she could. As she slipped into the waves, submerging herself and gliding along, head above water and belly scuffing the bottom, she forced herself not to think about the sharks. They were out there in their feeding ground, not here by the shore, where the tide rolled in. Yet with the sky gone dark and the rain plinking on the surface, every jagged wave appeared to be a fin.

The pontoon boat sat on the sand. The guy who'd piloted it stood beside it, assault rifle held across his chest. He looked bored, not quite at attention. Twice he glanced back across the lagoon, focused on the two boats out there—the yacht and the fishing boat. In those moments, Alliyah slid beneath the water, counting on the gray sea and the rain.

As she glided toward him, the smuggler faced the Coast Guard station and lifted his weapon over his head. "Come on, you fuckers!" he shouted. "It's not bloody moving day!"

Irish, she thought. But she left it at that. Now wasn't the time to try to sort out the whys and wherefores of who these men were and how they'd come to be smugglers.

Twenty feet away, she slid beneath the waves and swam parallel to the shore, rising again when she was behind the pontoon boat. Hidden from view by the bobbing rear of the boat, she swam silently up behind the motor. As her hands reached down and began searching the sand, her imagination plagued her. The sharks must be there, surely. Just out of the corner of her eye, there would be a fin. Only the gun in the hands of the man on the beach forced her to go quietly and slowly. The sharks *might* be there. The bullets *were*.

Her left hand found a rock the size of a grapefruit. Her fingers closed around it and she shifted it to her right hand.

Crouched behind the pontoon boat, she watched the impatient man shifting and sighing on the beach. He swore to himself and turned to look out to sea again. Bobbing in the water, she kept her head down, waiting for him to bark at her, for the gun to fire, or for him to order her out of the lagoon.

Nothing happened. Alliyah crouched in the water. A wave crashed over her and lifted the rear of the pontoon boat. The motor rose and fell beside her. She used her free hand to wipe salt water from her eyes, then peeked around the boat.

"I thought you bastards were in a hurry!" the smuggler shouted.

His back was to her.

Alliyah came out of the water before she even realized she was in motion. She'd wanted to be quiet but could not disguise her rush from the surf. The man muttered some bit of profane surprise as he turned to glance over his shoulder. It was that motion that saved her. Had he simply turned around instead of taking that moment to glance back, the gun would have been aimed at her. But when he saw her—when his eyes narrowed in disbelief and he began to sputter and to turn—it was too late.

Alliyah struck him in the temple. The smuggler staggered. The gun swung loose on the strap he wore around his neck. He tried to catch himself but stumbled and went onto one knee.

Blood trickled down his face. His eyelids fluttered, but his hands pawed at the dangling gun, then took hold. Alliyah felt her heart turn to ice. Jaw clenched, brows knitted, she swung the rock again, aiming for that trickle of blood.

That wooden clack of stone on skull felt satisfying as hell. As the smuggler went face-first into the sand, she knew she ought to be horrified. Instead, she dropped the rock and wrestled the strap of the assault rifle off him before he had a chance to recover. If he recovered at all.

Alliyah picked up the gun. For a moment she just held it, standing on the beach in the rain. The wind gusted, the storm just beginning to strengthen. She'd never held a gun in her life, but she had seen the way the smuggler held it and with a weapon like this she figured it was as simple as not pulling the trigger until she meant to, and making sure the barrel was pointed in the right direction.

Taking a breath, she slid the strap over her head, letting it cross her chest, and she started up toward the Coast Guard station. If anyone inside had seen her attack the man by the boat, she figured she would die. But so far there'd been no raised voices, no gunshots.

At the corner of the building, in view of the door with its shattered frame, she stood in the rain and she waited. Alliyah didn't know how this would all end, but she knew she would finish it on her feet, not lying on her belly and hiding, praying the bad men wouldn't find her.

Better to be dead than to hide while people she loved were being murdered.

If she survived this, she knew she would never be able to look at Dev the way she once had. She hoped she lived long enough to leave him.

The first thing Alex noticed as he stepped out of the Coast Guard station was the way that Machii and Joriz had frozen in place, maybe a dozen paces from the door. He paused, trying to figure it out, and Blue Eyes gave him a shove in the back. Alex stumbled, nearly dropped the maps he'd carefully folded, and went careening out the door. He skidded in the sand but managed not to fall, and as he clutched the maps to his chest he realized Blue Eyes had also gone still as a statue.

"Don't even blink," a voice said.

Alex glanced up. He'd known Alliyah all his adult life. They'd laughed together. He'd gone to her mother's funeral and held her in a claustrophobic little corridor while she cried the tears she hadn't wanted her father to see. In college they'd slept together, and it had been more like making love than just screwing. Not that they were in love, but they'd cared for each other. It had been sweet and healing and awkward and stupid, but beautiful for all of that.

Now she aimed an assault rifle at a bunch of

smugglers—Alex still didn't know what the hell they smuggled, but it didn't matter anymore. Alliyah's hands were steady. She swung the barrel slowly, varying her aim to make sure Machii and the others knew she meant business.

"I don't want to kill Alex," she said. "Honestly, I don't want to kill any of you fuckers, either. I'd *like* you to die. I guess I should be clear about that. I'd just rather not be the one to kill you. But I will. After the things I've seen you do, I'll have no problem forgiving myself."

"Hard bitch," Blue Eyes sneered. His body began to shift, almost imperceptibly. "You don't have the—"

"Cabot," Machii said quietly, and it was the first time Alex realized Blue Eyes had a name. "Put your weapon on the ground."

Alliyah gave a single nod. "That's a good idea, Cabot. All of you, put your weapons down."

They did it. Slowly and carefully, like they'd done it before or made others do it, and learned by watching. Or maybe they were just scared to die, like anyone. Cabot spat on the ground, raised his hands, and backed away from his weapon.

"You know they have others," Alex said, his own hands raised. Not that he expected her to shoot him, but just so he didn't do anything that made her twitch. "Guns or knives or whatever."

"I do," Alliyah said. Then she raised her voice, shouting but with every word clear, "I also know there's still one asshole inside. If I see your face—if I see your shadow—I'll kill all these guys!"

Alex had practically forgotten Benjie remained inside. He'd been splashing gasoline around inside the building, getting ready to burn it all, and hadn't yet emerged. Now Alex quietly hoped he didn't try anything stupid.

"Just go," Machii said. Not in fear. The man seemed not at all afraid. Just practical. A businessman. "Take Alex; go back to your boat. If my people don't kill you on your way out there, you're home free. They'll be busy rescuing us from shore. Of course, that's if you can get your sailboat under way fast enough."

Alliyah frowned. "What are you—"

"I mean, if you get out of here before my people can get me back on my boat, we'll probably never catch you. You should hurry, though."

Alex glanced at him. "She could just shoot you all, right now."

Machii glanced at Cabot and shrugged. "Then she should do that. The gunfire will draw attention and you'll never get back to your boat alive. Seems like your best bet is to go quietly and as fast as you can. It'll be fun. Like a little race. If we catch you before you can get away, you're all dead."

Alex saw the grim light in Alliyah's eyes as she did the mental calculations.

"Let's go, Alex," she said.

He shot one more glance at Machii, Joriz, and Cabot, then crossed the dirt toward Alliyah, keeping well to one side so he didn't block her line of fire. The wind gusted and the rain came down harder, each drop plinking the dusty ground.

Alliyah lifted the assault rifle to her shoulder, taking aim. "Don't try it. Killing me's not worth your own life, is it?"

Alex glanced over his shoulder. Cabot had started to move toward his weapon, where it lay on the ground. Of course it was Cabot. If they all died here, it would be him who triggered the bloodbath. Machii rolled his eyes but said nothing. Cabot only grinned and gave a little shrug, as if it were all some kind of game.

Only when Alex turned toward Alliyah again—just a few feet from her, ready to race for the pontoon boat—did he see motion over her shoulder, and the furious, blood-streaked face looming up behind her.

Hannigan.

Alex started to shout, to reach out. Alliyah gave him a curious look. In a flicker, he saw the recognition in her eyes as she understood what was about to happen. Then she cried out in harmony with Hannigan's own grunt. Her mouth opened slowly, her eyes narrowing in sadness and disappointment, and then widening with the pain as Hannigan yanked the knife out of her back, grabbed her by the hair, and plunged it into her again. This time Alex heard the sound of it going in, the wet splitting of flesh and the crack of bone.

Alliyah sank to her knees. Hannigan touched the blood on his own forehead, a wound Alliyah had to have given him, and then he crouched to retrieve his knife. He yanked it out, wiped it on her hair, and returned it to a sheath at his belt.

"This isn't like me," he said, scowling as he retrieved the assault rifle she'd stolen from him. Hannigan glanced up at Alex, as if he owed some kind of explanation. As if he had a conscience, or a soul. "If I'm gonna kill someone, I do it face-to-face. But she snuck up on me. Could've killed me. I figured it was only fair to return the favor."

Machii had already retrieved his own gun. Joriz and Cabot were doing the same.

"Don't worry about it, Hannigan," Machii said. "Courtesy has to go both ways."

Alex stared at him, the madness of their conversation hurting his brain. Alliyah lay on the ground with a fan of blood spreading out beneath her and these men were talking about good manners and murder.

"Benjie!" Machii shouted into the Coast Guard station. "Light it up. We need to go!"

Numb and hollow, Alex could barely think. Cabot shoved him from behind, moving him toward the pontoon boat as if nothing at all had happened.

"Alli," he whispered.

As he passed her, he fell to his knees and reached out to touch her arm. Her lips moved and her eyes shifted. Alliyah exhaled. Her hands dug into the ground.

"Come on, dickless," Cabot said.

He kicked Alex in the side, knocked him over. Alex scrabbled from harder earth to sand and leaped to his feet, turning with his fists clenched. Cabot smirked and lifted his weapon, fired a burst into the beach. Bullets kicked up sand and Alex backed away, moving toward the pontoon boat.

"Stop messing around," Machii said.

At the door of the Coast Guard station, Benjie appeared. He splashed the last few drops of gasoline onto the threshold and then tossed the bucket inside. Then he dug into his pockets and came out with a packet of cigarettes and a small folding pack of matches. He lit a cigarette, took a long drag that made the tip burn orange, and flicked the match in through the doorway.

The fire ignited with a rush of air and a gust of black smoke.

Benjie took another drag of the cigarette and shot a questioning look at his boss. His captain.

Machii glanced at the sky. "It'll burn. Might not burn *down,* depending how heavy the rain gets. But it'll burn all the fingerprints out of the place, that's for sure."

Then they were moving down toward the pontoon boat, onto the sand, to the crashing waves. As Hannigan passed Alliyah, he hocked a wad of bloody spittle onto her bare back.

The smugglers shoved the pontoon boat off the sand and climbed in. Alex did the same, prodded by Cabot's gun. Rage and shame burned in his chest as he glanced back toward the shore, where smoke had begun pouring out the windows of the Coast Guard station. Alliyah lay there dying, gasping, but his fear for his own life had kept him moving.

She'd want you to live, he told himself. *She risked her life for you, but it's too late to save her. All that*

*blood—those are killing wounds. There's nothing you
can do.*

The words were true.

But the truth didn't help.

Dev couldn't be sure what he'd seen. Not at first.

He'd seen Alliyah make her way out of the trees and
into the water. At this distance her head had been a
bobbing bit of black hair in the waves as she'd moved
up behind the pontoon boat. When she had come out
of the water and rushed at the smuggler standing guard
over the boat, Dev had felt sick. How had their lives
brought them to this moment? But of course people
asked themselves that question every minute of every
day, all around the world. In the grip of desperate pov-
erty and hunger, in the ruin left behind by earthquakes
and floods, destroyed by mental illness or addiction,
ravaged by disease, bereft with loss, or simply undone
by the end of love . . . people asked themselves how it
had come to this.

Dev had never given Alliyah everything of himself.
He'd been faithful before and after their separation, but
fidelity and commitment weren't the same thing. The
woman he'd fallen in love with had deserved a full
partner, a best friend, someone to experience life at her
side. But Dev had not given her that. As the wedding
had drawn closer, he had already started to disengage.
The marriage seemed to have been the goal, and once
the goal had been attained he had shifted his ambitions

elsewhere. Work. The admiration of others. Some indefinable level of achievement he could never have reached. Yes, she'd turned ugly—beautiful as ever, but ugly inside. She'd turned into a stranger, callous and distant. But he had made her into that creature. He'd become a stranger to her even before their vows.

It was why he'd agreed when she had wanted to reunite.

He never should have said yes. It would have been better for her—so much kinder—to let her go on with her life.

And he never would have been on this fucking atoll.

When he saw her come up out of the water behind the pontoon boat, rushing at the smuggler, Dev figured Alliyah was dead. He'd opened his mouth to cry out, but fear had shut his mouth. The smugglers' boat wasn't far offshore and he didn't want to risk being seen. Though the rain and the waves were loud enough that they would surely have drowned him out, and though only the top of his head might be visible from where he lay—half in the water now as the waves rolled up around his waist—he didn't dare draw attention to himself.

Alliyah took the guy down. She hit him with something—Dev couldn't see what—and then she hit him again. He wiped rain from his eyes and watched in astonishment as she took the guy's assault rifle and moved up toward the Coast Guard station.

How was this their life?

Half of him hated her in that moment, sure she would give his presence away. They would kill her, and they would figure out there were other witnesses still on the atoll. But the other half of him—the part of him that remembered what he'd been like when they were younger—felt so much pride that it made him want to cheer. He wished he could stand up and shout, that he could rush along the atoll, wade through the gaps, and go to her side. Help her. That he could tell the world this fierce creature was his wife.

Then they'd come out the door of the Coast Guard station and it had all changed. Dev had seen the smuggler from the beach, the one she'd attacked, getting up and approaching her. *Alliyah!* his mind had roared. He'd even risen to his knees and said her name. Called it out, not too loudly, not a scream. Surely from this distance, with the wind and all, she could never have heard him and he would only have risked giving himself away.

Now the pontoon boat smashed its way across the waves and Dev slithered back onto his belly and kept his head low.

Go to her, he thought. *Help her.*

But if he got up now and ran along the atoll, and waded those gaps, they would see him. No question about it. If they had left Alliyah for dead, then she must be dead or close to it.

Dead, he thought. *She has to be.*

Yes, she had to be dead now. The alternative was that his wife—the woman he'd fallen in love with back when he'd believed himself capable of being in love—lay on the beach dying right now, with her husband so close. Near enough to go to her. Near enough to at least hold her and comfort her while she died, to say the things he ought to say, to let her know that she was not alone. She'd be afraid, and he could make her less afraid.

If she wasn't already dead.

So he told himself she was dead.

He pressed his eyes closed and mourned not only for Alliyah but also for his image of himself. Lying there on his belly, half in the water, would be how he saw himself from that day forward. He turned on his side and drew his legs up into a fetal position, and that was best, because there were the sharks to think of.

Alli, Dev thought, and he wanted to die.

But not enough to put himself at risk.

He stayed there, as hidden as he could manage. Lying there, with no idea how he might be saved, he did not raise his head to check on his wife.

If he had, he would've seen her move.

CHAPTER 18

Alliyah could feel her own blood cooling against her skin. The wounds were different. Where they were open, she could feel the breeze against the split skin and it felt like scouring flame. The blood seeping out had its own liquid heat, running in traces down her rib cage to puddle on the ground. Another rivulet trickled down her back and pooled in the small hollow there, just above the line of her bikini bottoms. The blood in the dirt, pooling against her—that was where it had started to cool, and she found herself keenly aware of that cooling. The warmth leaving that blood felt very much like the dimming of life within her.

"Get up, Alli," she whispered to herself.

It felt impossible. With those two pulsing wounds on her back and the blood around her, it seemed absurd to even consider the idea that she might be able to stand, never mind walk. But though the darkness pulled at her and the temptation to slide into unconsciousness felt almost beautiful, she remained awake. Aware of the hot and cold blood touching her skin. Some of it remained within her, and while it did she was not going to just lie there. Alliyah had no intention of dying out here, thousands of miles from home.

Smoke billowed around her. The smell of rain mixed with it and abruptly she became aware of things other than her wounds. Rain pelted her, falling harder and faster than before. The crackle and pop of a fire built toward a roar. She managed to turn her head, still lying on her belly, and saw that flames had begun to engulf the Coast Guard station. Fire unfurled from each window, charring the outer walls black. Gusts of wind swirled the smoke into strange ribbons.

Alliyah drew her hands beneath her. Even that little motion sent pain spiking into her wounds like fresh knives, so she tried to keep her arms close to her body, tried to mostly use her knees. The pain made her weep. When she'd risen to her knees and managed to get one leg beneath her, the agony of that motion made her scream. She didn't try to hold it in. The blood came out, and she let the pain roar out with it.

She stood. It wasn't graceful. She felt her wounds tug and felt torn muscle rip even further. Pain staggered her, so as she turned toward the water it was more a stumble than a walk. Lurching, cursing, she started toward the water as if each step was the only thing keeping her from falling. Her ability to put one foot in front of the other got her to the water's edge and she glanced to the right, back the way she'd come. Back toward where she'd left Dev.

Dev. She pitied him. She loved him. She hated him. But if she had any chance of surviving until the Coast Guard arrived—many long hours from now— she had to reach him. There were towels on the beach where they'd all picnicked. He could stop the bleeding for her. There'd be no other help, not unless the smugglers decided to leave the people on the *Kid Galahad* alive. If stopping the bleeding couldn't save her, then she would die. And her only chance to do that was the husband she felt like she'd never really known. She'd loved the idea of the man instead of the man himself.

Now he'd have one last chance to be the man she'd imagined him to be.

If she could get to him.

Her eyelids grew heavy. For a few seconds, all was darkness, but another step in the sand jarred her and her eyes snapped open. Somehow she'd kept walking. Her feet splashed in the surf. Waves crashed and rolled around her calves and ankles. Pain speared her back with every stutter step along the shore and awareness kept coming in and out, ebbing and flowing like the surf. She knew she ought to have fallen, but somehow it was like fighting sleep behind the wheel of a car, chin drooping and then head snapping up again, trying to keep the car on the road.

Alliyah glanced across the water toward the place where she'd left Dev, trying to gauge how far she had to go. How many steps. The tide had risen dramatically, so that the gaps between the fragments of the atoll had widened and deepened. The waves crashed harder and it occurred to her that she had no idea what high tide might bring. Would the water rise so high that some of those fragments would be entirely submerged? She thought it would.

Dev was her only hope, but if she couldn't reach him, she'd have no hope at all.

Unless he came to her. Why hadn't he seen her? Why hadn't he tried to get to her?

Alliyah tried to call her husband's name. A memory swam up into her mind—Dev awaiting her on the dance floor with his arms held out, on their wedding day. Their first dance. The smile on his face had been pure peace and contentedness, as if he'd never been so happy or so confident that he was where he belonged. She'd felt the same way that day. It had been the best feeling in the world.

She managed to call his name, but too weakly. She could barely hear herself over the waves and her own legs' splashing in the water.

Her thoughts blacked out again.

This time when consciousness returned, she was falling. Her legs were too heavy for her to put another step in front of her and she spilled headfirst into the shallows. A wave crashed over her. She breathed in a lungful of ocean and began to choke, every twitch of her muscles stabbing freshly at her wounds. The salt stung as it washed the blood away.

Choking, crawling, pushing with her feet, Alliyah

managed to hurl herself up onto the sand. Seawater rippled around her. She coughed it out of her lungs and whimpered as more blood sluiced from her back and into the lagoon.

As the upper trickle of another wave reached her, and the darkness embraced her again, Alliyah thought of the tide rolling in. As she struggled against unconsciousness, she remembered the sharks.

Her eyes fluttered open once, just for a moment.

Alliyah fought the darkness, and lost.

The pontoon boat rocked on the waves, bumping against the *Kid Galahad*. Alex held on to the ladder, steeling himself before he climbed to the deck of the yacht. In his mind, he tallied up the dead. Harry and Gabe. James—he'd almost forgotten that Nalani had watched her husband be murdered, and how hideous a human being did that make him? That he could forget, no matter how chaotic and terrifying his own experience had been?

Now Alliyah had tried to help him, and paid with her life. And Dev . . . Alex had no idea what had happened to Dev.

"Climb, asshole," Blue Eyes Cabot snarled from behind him.

Alex climbed. With every rung on that ladder, he said a silent prayer that he would see Sami when he stepped onto the deck. Damien had been left on the boat. He'd seemed less hungry for violence, less eager to inflict cruelty than Cabot, but that didn't mean

Sami had been safe. Sami, Nalani, Nils, Patrick, Cat, and Luisa. They'd set out with so many, and already they were so few. Alex wanted them all to make it home, but he would sacrifice them all, himself included, to save his wife.

The first face he saw when he climbed over the railing belonged to Benjie. The Filipino smuggler gave him a sardonic smirk and turned his back, not worried about Alex at all. Not seeing him as a threat. Joriz and Machii were there as well. They'd spread out, along with Damien, who had followed orders. All six of the *Kid Galahad*'s remaining passengers were on deck. Nils sat with Nalani against the cockpit wall, holding her hand in both of his. Her eyes were still dull from shock and red from tears. Patrick stood over them protectively. Sami, Cat, and Luisa sat together farther toward the bow, lined up side by side. Luisa had her head hung between her legs, fingers interlaced behind her head, as if she'd submitted to arrest while she was trying not to throw up.

When Sami saw Alex, she didn't smile. Her eyes narrowed and she nodded to let him know she was okay. It was all he needed. A reservoir of strength and determination opened within him and he turned toward Machii.

Something caught his eye, and he realized he'd forgotten one of the *Galahad*'s remaining passengers. Beyond the smugglers, Isko lay on a blanket too near the railing. Wounded and rotting and not quite conscious, he had the air of a task uncompleted, as if death had wrapped him up in that blanket and forgotten to carry him off. It was grim and ugly, but Alex couldn't think about Isko. Like the smugglers themselves, he'd already written the man off.

A hard thought. Coldhearted. But it was how things had to be now.

"So what now, Machii?" he asked.

The smuggler captain had been talking quietly with Damien. Now he turned to face his men, ignoring Alex and the other passengers.

"Benjie, get half a brick of Semtex from Hannigan."

As Benjie rushed to obey, hurrying over the railing and down the ladder, Alex felt the sea rolling beneath the boat and nearly fell over, not from the wave but from the impact of those words.

"You can't do this," Nils said. "Please, you can't—"

Damien aimed his weapon at Nils. "We could just shoot you all. Machii's being kind."

"Kind?" Alex said. "This is kind?"

"What is it?" Luisa asked. "Semtex. What is that?"

Alex replied without looking at her, "Plastic explosive. Easy as hell to get your hands on. Used in construction. Who the fuck would have Semtex on a boat, though . . . that's the question."

"People who don't like to leave evidence floating around," Sami replied.

Machii pointed at her. "Smart lady." He shrugged. "Look, you're all going to have a chance here. Think of it that way. Damien's right. I could just have my men shoot you all—"

"We'd be better off with a bullet than with the sharks," Cat said.

Machii fired two shots into the deck, not far from her feet. Cat drew her legs up beneath her, staring at the bullet holes. Then staring at Machii.

"You I could give to Cabot. He'd like to bring you along with us," Machii said. "But I've let him have pets before, and they always end up causing trouble."

Alex shot a hard look at Cat. He knew she must want to lunge at them, or keep talking tough. Silently, he urged her not to, hoping she knew how close she was to something worse than sinking on this boat.

Benjie climbed back on board, a small plastic bag in one hand. The half brick of Semtex must have been small. Half a pound or less. Alex suspected it would be enough to sink them. Machii would not have suggested it without being certain.

"Give it to Cabot," Machii said.

Cabot slung his assault rifle around behind him and took the plastic bag eagerly. "I always love this part."

"Go up into the wheelhouse and destroy the radio before you go below," Machii added. "It might take a while for the boat to go down. I don't want our friends sharing any secrets while they're deciding whether to sink or swim."

A terrible electricity sizzled through Alex's bones. Every nerve ending felt frayed, every muscle tensed, as he stared around at the smugglers—these killers— and tried to see some way for the *Kid Galahad*'s remaining passengers to survive. He had to get his hands on a gun. Benjie stood nearest to him. If he could get the bastard's gun and kill Machii and Cabot, make the others put their weapons down—

"Hey, Alex," Machii said, eyes narrowed. He cocked his head, smiled thinly, then marched across the deck and slapped Alex in the face hard enough to stagger him.

Fuming, heart thundering with hatred, Alex whipped around with his fists clenched.

Machii jabbed him in the chest with a finger. "No. Don't think the things you're thinking. I'm giving you a chance here, mainly because I like you." He turned and pointed at Cat. "You too, smart one. The odds you guys are going to live are pretty fucking slim, but at least you've got a shot. You all go in the water and the sharks are going to eat some of you, but maybe some make it."

He turned and pointed at Isko, who seemed to have regained some bleary form of consciousness. "Look at this motherfucker. We threw him and some other guys into the water even further from shore than you are right now. Sharks got the other guys, but Isko . . . he made it. Look at it this way, even if only one of you survives . . ."

Machii crouched by Luisa. "It might be you, honey." He glanced at Nils. "Or you."

Alex took a shuddering breath. He wanted this man dead—wanted them all dead—but he couldn't deny the truth. If they fought, they would die here and now. If they let the smugglers scuttle the boat and depart, they had a chance. A tiny one, but that was better than certain death. And any chance at Tasha not losing her parents—or, at least, not both of them—was worth taking.

"Get on with it, then," Alex said.

Sami stood up, back still against the wheelhouse. "You're a sick son of a bitch, Machii. This is a game for you."

Machii nodded happily. "True. But let's not pretend the whole world isn't like this. If I filmed what we're about to do to you and streamed it live on the Internet, millions of people would watch. There'd be bets placed on which of you, if any, would make it to shore. It's not me, beautiful lady. It's people. People are fucking awful."

"That's bullshit," Sami said.

"Is it?" Machii replied. Then he turned toward Cabot. "Do it."

As Cabot started toward the cockpit again, Patrick lunged at him, grabbed hold of his gun, and started to wrestle him against the doorframe. Cabot dropped the bag with the Semtex. Nils and Cat jumped to their feet, shouting. Anguish contorted Nils's features. Everyone kept shouting, smugglers and passengers alike. Alex had been intending to attack these men less than a minute earlier and now he wanted to grab Patrick and tear him away from Cabot, just to protect them all.

Cabot and Patrick grunted and swore and struggled for the gun. Damien raised his own weapon and took aim at both of them, waiting for the outcome. Joriz and Benjie backed away, nervously sweeping the barrels of their guns from side to side, ready to murder all of their captives if Machii gave the order.

"No, damn it!" Alex shouted, moving toward Sami

and Cat, holding up his hands, making sure they saw him. "Don't do anything!"

Cabot got his forearm against Patrick's throat and slammed his skull against the doorframe. Patrick's grip slipped off the gun for just a moment. He scrabbled for it again, but Cabot jerked it around, took aim, and fired. In the last heartbeat, Patrick shoved the barrel downward.

Three bullets hit the deck—one of them passed through Patrick's thigh on the way. Blood sprayed and Nils shouted and rushed toward his husband. Patrick fell into his arms and Cabot lifted his weapon to kill them both.

Machii barked a command and Cabot smiled. He watched Nils and Patrick embracing, watched Nils slide his bleeding husband to the deck, and then picked up the bag with the Semtex inside it and ducked into the cockpit.

Sami took a step toward Machii. She pressed her hands together as if in prayer. "Please don't do this."

Alex heard her fear and sorrow, and it broke him. He took her hands in his and lowered them. Nils held Patrick, whispering to him. Luisa remained seated, as she had throughout the violence, and hung her head between her legs as if she'd gone totally catatonic. Cat began to swear at Machii and to plead with him, alternating back and forth.

The smugglers ignored them all now.

Alex took Sami in his arms. The two of them fell into a stony silence, just waiting together, knowing they could do nothing more as long as these men and their guns were on board.

Machii gestured to Benjie and Joriz. "Abandon ship, assholes."

Joriz laughed and went to the railing, swung himself over, and started down the ladder. Benjie hesitated a second, pointing toward Isko.

"You want to leave him? Something goes wrong and he lives, it could be trouble."

Machii glanced over at Isko. Snot and blood ran from the man's nostrils. With the gusting wind and the rain pelting the deck, they could all smell the sweet stink of his rotting leg.

"He probably won't even live long enough for the sharks to get him," Machii said. "Let him suffer. There's no way he makes it to shore. None of these people are going to risk themselves to drag along a stranger who's that close to dead."

Benjie gave a nod and then followed Joriz over the side and down the ladder. Machii and Damien backed up toward the railing and kept their weapons leveled, ready to fire if anyone did something stupid.

Seconds ticked by.

With a thump and scuffle, Cabot emerged from the cockpit. Gun slung across his back, he ran toward the railing with his head ducked low. Alex held Sami tighter and both of them bent their heads. Cat dragged Luisa away from the cockpit and both of them went flat on their bellies on the deck. Nils didn't move, just kept cradling Patrick.

When the explosion came, it blew the windows out

of the cockpit and the wheelhouse. Safety glass scattered across the deck. Heat blossomed from the broken windows. The deck seemed to heave beneath them with the force of the explosion, but the effect passed instantly.

Machii cocked his head and waited. Smoke billowed from the shattered windows and the boat began to list to starboard.

"There we go," Machii said. He grinned at Cabot. "Nicely done."

The two of them went over the side while Damien covered the passengers.

"We can't let them—" Cat started.

"Hush," Sami said. "It's done."

Damien followed the others over the starboard railing. Alex figured the men in the pontoon boat would be covering the deck of the boat in case any of the passengers tried to attack, but none of them were that stupid.

The smugglers were gone.

The pontoon boat's motor roared. Seconds later, it sped across the rising waves toward the fishing boat. Alex held Sami's hand and the two of them walked to the railing, staring at the men who had just murdered them as much for entertainment as efficiency. From the pontoon boat, Machii raised his hand in a jaunty farewell. One of the sharks paced alongside the pontoon boat, looking for an opportunity. It vanished below the surface and Alex silently hoped it would smash them from beneath, knock them into the water.

Then he saw the water churning at the bottom of the

ladder and a fin broke the surface there. Waves crashed and the boat tilted and rocked and a second shark appeared a short distance away. A rope remained tied to the bottom of the ladder—the line that tethered the sunken dinghy to the *Kid Galahad*. A shark brushed so close to the boat that it jostled that line and its skin scuffed the hull.

The boat listed harder, not just to starboard now but also toward the stern. They weren't just sinking; they were sinking fast. Any thought of waiting for rescue vanished from Alex's mind.

He pushed the sharks out of his mind and locked eyes with Sami. "We swim."

"Maybe," she said, turning away from him and rushing toward the others. "But first we stop Patrick's bleeding. Nils, get out of the way."

Nils wouldn't have listened to anyone else. Alex knew that, just as he knew how much the man loved his husband. But Sami spoke with authority and compassion and it made Nils back away.

"All right," Alex said. "Meanwhile, Cat and Nils and I are going to drag the dinghy out of the water. Whatever it takes."

"There's no time," Nils said. "Never mind the fact it's got holes in it."

Sami had pulled Patrick's shirt over his head and was tearing it into strips. Afraid and in pain, nevertheless Patrick was helping her as best he could.

"Holes can be patched," Sami said. "Alex is right. We've got to try."

"If we have to swim, then we swim," Alex added.

"But this boat isn't going to sink completely in the next ten minutes. We've got a little time—not much, but a little—so let's do everything we can to avoid going in that water."

As if on cue, Luisa shoved Cat aside and lurched to her feet.

"Fuck it," she said, almost drunkenly. Tears streamed down her face and she walked toward the railing. "Fuck it!"

She grabbed the railing, put one foot up.

Even as Cat shouted for them all to stop her, Alex grabbed Luisa around the waist and ripped her away from the railing. She screamed at him, a torrent of the most depraved profanity he'd ever heard, and she tried to claw at him. Alex pulled her close, wrapped her in his arms as she beat at him. He didn't try to shush her and he didn't tell her it would be all right. He just held her and let her know that she wasn't alone out here, even if all that meant was that she wasn't going to die alone.

"Oh, my God," she whispered in a hitching voice. "Alex."

"I know," he said. Nothing more.

With Sami helping Patrick, Nils and Cat went to the railing. Nils started down the ladder. Cat urged him on, promised him that he could reach the line for the dinghy before any shark might attack. She got a gaffing hook from somewhere and stood ready to bring the line up to the deck to make it easier to haul the dinghy up.

They needed Alex's help, but he just held on to Luisa while the boat sank lower in the water and the rain came on harder. He looked out across the lagoon and realized the tide had risen dramatically, that some of the fragments of the atoll were half the size they'd been.

"Hold on," he said.

Cat reached down with the gaffing hook.

Alex walked Luisa a few feet farther from the edge and sat her down on the deck. She wouldn't look at him. Instead, she went along with him as if in surrender, and once she'd sat she returned to her previous position, legs drawn up to her chest, head hung between her knees. Alex stared at her, then glanced over at Isko. At this rate, he wasn't sure which of them stood a worse chance of making it to shore.

"Cat," he said, "wait."

Sami shot him a glance, but Alex ignored her and went to Cat. He leaned on the railing and glanced down at Nils. He could only see one shark now, a fin slicing the water about forty feet away.

"Both of you just wait."

Cat flinched. "Are you fucking crazy? We're sinking. And the sharks . . . do you see them? They're waiting, Alex. It's like they know."

Alex gestured across the lagoon toward the smugglers' boat. "If they think we have a chance in hell of fixing the dinghy, don't you think Machii will come back?"

"They think the Coast Guard's due any minute now!" Nils called up to him.

"Maybe they believe that. Maybe they don't. Just wait. Make it look like you can't get the dinghy out of the water—"

"I don't know if we can!" Cat snapped.

"Please. Just wait. Three minutes. Maybe five."

"We could be in the water in five minutes," Nils said.

"You've seen the way this guy's mind works," Alex said. "You know he'll come back. He wants us to suffer. He wants us to scream."

Cat swore quietly. She put a hand over her mouth as if to stifle a cry, and then she leaned against the railing. Below, on the ladder, Nils tugged on the rope of the sunken dinghy, making a show of how impossible it would be for them to drag it out of the water. Nearby, a second fin surfaced. The rain splashed the waves, leaving little wounds on the water everywhere it touched.

They waited.

The boat shifted, tilting farther astern, and Alex had to lean to keep himself from falling.

But they waited.

CHAPTER 19

Alliyah dreamed of music. Some kind of folkie country thing—the sort of song some scruffy, earnest busker would play on a street corner. Maybe it was half a memory, a scrap of a tune she'd once heard while walking down the street hand in hand with her husband or her lover or one of her friends back in her school days. Or maybe her subconscious had invented it. Were there lyrics? In the dream, it was hard to tell. The scruffy busker sang, but the words seemed to slip through the net of her mind.

She came awake sputtering, choking. A surge of energy pushed her onto all fours as a wave swamped her. On hands and knees, she puked up a quart of seawater that had snuck down her throat while she lay unconscious and the tide came in.

Pain stabbed into her as if the blade the fucker had used remained lodged in her back and was growing and spreading. She'd have screamed, but exhaustion had dulled her ability to respond. The pain had grown, but she knew she had to carry that pain or die.

Alliyah wanted to slump into the surf. She wanted to roll over, but the idea of pressing her wounds against the sand chilled her. With the rain coming down hard, insult to injury, she started to crawl out of the water. A wave swept in, lifted her, carried her several feet. Her hands and feet moved in the water, bicycling, trying to make sure she was in control when she touched bottom again. When her left hand hit the ground it was at the wrong angle and she pitched slightly forward as the wave withdrew. Pausing, breathing, knowing that another wave would be along any second, she grimaced and started to creep forward.

She glanced backward.

For a moment that extended into infinity, she stared at the wave rolling toward shore. The enormous shape inside the wave, slicing parallel to the beach, seemed so impossible that she felt sure this was still part of the dream that included the scruffy sidewalk troubadour. It didn't feel like a dream or even a nightmare, it felt real and tangible and so ungodly painful, but this couldn't be real. Inside the wave, the edge of its fin protruding from the white froth as the wave began to break, was a shark.

Alliyah gave a short gasp. A spike of pain made her blink and she lunged out of the water, stomping through the shallows. Stumbling, she hurled herself onto the soft, sodden sand, making a deep imprint there.

Turning onto her side, she watched the shark skid

past her in the shallows, two-thirds of its bulk out of the water. It caught for a moment on the sand as the wave receded, but then the next wave crashed over it and the killer managed to glide back into the lagoon. Under the gray-black sky with the rain pouring down, the shark vanished in the deep, but she knew it hadn't gone far.

Alliyah stared. She tried to speak, just to curse. A flash of profanity would have made it all feel more real, but the effort of uttering actual words shot a pulse of pain across her back and she hissed air through her teeth. The darkness crept in at the edges of her vision again, but she wouldn't surrender to it. Adrenaline had surged within her and now her heart pumped harder, thudding in her chest. She tried not to think about how much blood she'd lost and how much blood was *too much*. She tried not to wonder if she was just marking time, if there might no longer be any point in trying to save herself.

Instead, she turned and began a slow stutter march down the beach, away from the burning Coast Guard station. Black smoke rose from the building, but she barely noticed it. The rain punished her and the wind gusted into her face, trying to push her back. Alliyah kept going, ignoring the trees on her right, keeping along the arc of the atoll.

Slowly. Too slow, she thought, but still she kept staggering and bleeding.

How much time had passed and how far she'd walked she couldn't be sure, but she came to the first of the gaps in the land. When she'd rushed over here to try to help Alex, the water in this opening had been narrow and less than two feet deep. Now she had to wade across and the water came up to just below her breasts.

The impossible image of that shark riding inside a wave lodged in her brain and she glanced around, watching for a fin. She stared at the dark water and imagined it was waiting for her down there, one of the Devil Sharks, the taste of her blood already in its mouth like the scent of a fox in the nose of a hound. But she had no choice, so she closed her eyes and forged ahead and a few moments later she scrambled out of the water onto the next fragment of the atoll.

Alliyah dragged in several deep breaths and forced her eyes to stay open. The pain lancing into her back made her whimper, but she started walking again. Farther along the atoll there were other breaks. How many were there between herself and that picnic spot? How many between herself and the husband she could no longer bring herself to love or trust but in whose hands she now had no choice but to put her life?

How many steps?

How much more did she have to bleed to get there?

"Dev," she whispered, needing him more than she ever had. Hating him for it. Hating him for how little she believed in him.

But she kept going.

Sami knelt by Patrick. He wore a grim expression. In the rain, he looked more irritated than terrified or agonized. She finished tying a tourniquet around his thigh. The only bandage was a bright purple fleece hoodie she'd managed to fetch from below. Sami tried not to think about the way the ship was listing, or how much water had already poured in belowdecks. She'd waded through it, climbing up into the corridor where things were still dry. While she was there, she had grabbed a raincoat and her wedding ring, which had been in a zippered pocket inside her purse. She'd left the purse behind. All that mattered to her was the ring.

Now, though, she wondered what else they would need if they managed to make it to shore.

"That too tight?" Sami asked.

Patrick grimaced. "Yes."

"Good." She gave the tourniquet another tug and made sure it was tied securely. "You're awfully stoic for a guy with a bullet in his leg."

Patrick huffed and pushed himself up with both hands, bracing his back against the wheelhouse. "You mean I'm awfully stoic for a guy who just got shot and who's on a boat sinking into a lagoon full of fucking man-eating sharks?"

"Yeah. That."

"What are my other options?"

Sami nodded. He had a point. She glanced over at Luisa, who shifted every minute or two. As the boat continued to sink she would clamber farther up the deck to keep her distance from the water roughly the same, as if she didn't understand that eventually she was going to run out of room to climb. Eventually, the *Kid Galahad* was going to vanish into the lagoon. Like a cornered animal, Luisa only looked up to glance fearfully at the water.

"I should talk to her," Sami said.

"No, you shouldn't," Patrick said. "I'm fine for now. Check on Isko and then help them get the dinghy floating. If they can't do that, I'd have been better off with this bullet in my skull."

Sami tapped his shoulder. "Okay. If you find you can get up at all—not that I'm asking you to, not with a gunshot wound—but if we get off the boat, we could really use the flare gun. The Coast Guard's coming, so we can live without food and water for that long. But the flare gun could come in very handy."

"I don't know if I can get into the wheelhouse, but I'll try."

"If you can't, don't worry. I'll go in and look for it—"

"I can tell you where it is."

"Fine. Give me a few minutes with Isko and I'll do it."

Patrick nodded, still stoic, although she could see the regret in his eyes that he couldn't do this one simple thing. They hadn't known each other long, but Patrick impressed her as the kind of person who wanted to be useful.

"Sit tight," she told him.

Sami rose into a slanted crouch and turned toward the others. Alex and Nils and Cat had dragged the dinghy up onto the deck. There had been swearing and the smashing of knuckles and Nils had done something to his back. The dinghy was heavy and not meant to be lifted by three people, but with the current angle of the boat to the water they had been able to drag it across the railing. Now it rested upside down. Nils had also been below, where he'd retrieved a tool kit. He muttered to himself constantly as he tried to get the swamped motor cleaned up enough that it would start if they could get the dinghy to float.

The floating part was another story.

"Where do we stand?" Sami asked.

Alex glanced up. She didn't like the gray cast of his eyes. He wiped rain from his face and gave her a doubtful look.

"Five bullet holes. Shouldn't be a huge problem."

Sami stared at him.

"Okay, yeah," he said with a shrug, "it's a huge problem. But we don't have too far to go. I dried the surface as well as I could and Cat patched one side with duct tape—"

"Duct tape," Sami echoed dully.

"—Then we filled the holes from the other side with Krazy Glue and put another strip of duct tape on *that* side."

"Krazy Glue."

Alex fixed her with a hard look. "We're sinking, Sami. We don't have time for—"

"I know," she said, shivering inside her raincoat. All along she had felt hard and strong. Maybe not brave, but at least determined. Now her left hand rose, shaking, to cover her mouth. It only lasted a moment and then she shook it off. "Duct tape and Krazy Glue. Okay, baby. Okay."

Her husband smiled at her. A wild, nothing-left-to-lose smile. "The bullet holes aren't nearly as much a concern as the damage from the shotgun. Up close, it would've blown a big damn hole in the floor of the dinghy. Instead, there are a lot of little holes from the pellets."

"But you're patching them."

Cat had been ignoring the conversation. Now her head snapped up and she looked at Sami with a dreadful urgency. "We're doing what we can. As fast as we can."

Sami nodded. She understood what Cat was saying—that they needed to get back to it—so she left them to their labor. She turned and crab-walked across the canted deck to where Isko lay. He'd slid up against the railing. In a short time—ten minutes, maybe twenty—he'd be underwater if they didn't move him.

"Hey," Sami said, shaking his shoulder.

Isko took a sharp breath and his eyes opened. They were unfocused and roving for a few seconds before his gaze found her. That quick breath, almost a gasp, unsettled her. It was as if he'd already died and she'd called him back to life.

He said something in Tagalog, but Sami shook her head.

"English," she reminded him.

Isko closed his eyes and exhaled again. "Yes. English. I think I'm dying."

Sami didn't see any reason to sugarcoat it. "You might be. I'm not going to lie to you. But we might all be dying today."

A flicker of understanding touched his eyes. "The boat is sinking?"

"Yes."

Isko muttered in his own language again. Sami felt sure it was profanity. Then he switched back to English. "The sharks—"

"We know. Devil Sharks."

Isko nodded. "They're waiting for a second chance at me."

Sami took his hand. The man's leg had turned septic. The flesh had gone black and rotting and the rot had started to spread upward. He had other wounds, too. Even if they got him to the atoll, there was no telling how long he would survive unless she amputated that leg. Long enough for the Coast Guard to arrive, to give her a place on board a Coast Guard vessel where she could take off the leg in a sterile environment? Did they have an onboard surgeon? Did they have an operating room, or something like it?

It helped her to wonder those things, to imagine that these were the concerns she needed to worry about instead of worrying about surviving the next half hour.

"We're going to get you off this boat," Sami assured him.

Isko lifted a hand and gave a weak wave. His eyes closed. "That's what I'm afraid of."

One corner of his mouth lifted and she realized he was trying to smile. Even with all he'd been through, and although he knew he would almost certainly die today, he had made a joke. Sami squeezed his hand.

Maybe Isko's courage came from his nearness to death, but still she took it as inspiration.

She started to scuttle over to the upside-down dinghy, but as she did she glanced up and saw that Patrick had vanished. For a moment his absence alarmed her—it made no sense—and then she remembered their conversation about the flare gun. They'd talked about it just a few minutes ago, but it had already slipped her mind.

"Shit."

She duckwalked up the slanted deck and grabbed hold of the frame of the cockpit door. From here, going up the few steps to the wheelhouse was like climbing a ladder. She called out for Patrick, but he wasn't in the wheelhouse, so she ducked into the cockpit. The space hadn't filled with water—that time would not come for a while yet. She moved toward the steps that would bring her below. The smell of the explosion that had put a hole in the boat still lingered. The sounds of the rain on the windows and the thump of waves against the boat seemed almost comforting, the sort of thing it would be easy to fall asleep to. A hypnotic rhythm, if not for the fact that those sounds were hastening them all along to their deaths.

"Patrick!" she called.

He ought to have been up in the wheelhouse. Surely the flare gun had been there, so if he'd come in to get it, where the fuck was he?

"Patrick!"

A muffled voice called from below. Sami went to

start down into the cabin, where she could hear the water sloshing.

"Are you okay?"

His head appeared in the opening below. "Of course I'm not okay. I'm shot, remember?"

"Jesus," Sami whispered. She shifted out of the way as he started dragging himself, half-limping, stumping, crawling up the steps. "What are you doing down there?"

"I got you the flare gun. It's on the desk behind you in that yellow case."

Sami turned and saw it there, on the desk in the upper salon area of the cockpit. How she'd missed the case . . . but of course, she hadn't been picturing a case. Just the flare gun itself. Now Patrick reached her and she took his hand and helped him limp down the slanted floor and grab hold of the doorframe. The rain grew louder on the windows. The whole boat shifted a few more inches and Sami tightened her grip on the frame.

"What were you doing down there?" she asked again.

Holding on with one hand, Patrick reached into his pocket and pulled out a sealed plastic bag. Inside it was a cell phone.

"If we die . . . if those pricks murdered us all today . . . I'm not letting them get away with it. I'm going to take a little video. We'll give their names and whatever information we can. I'll tie this to a life preserver. If we die, at least they'll have something to remember us by."

His gaze had turned grim and ferocious.

Sami kissed his cheek. "Thank you."

Patrick gave a quick nod. They would live or die together, and they understood each other.

A scuffing noise made Sami glance back to see Nalani coming down from the wheelhouse. She wore a sweatshirt much too big for her, a faded aqua-blue thing from the Sorbonne in Paris. Sami assumed it had belonged to James, not just from the size but also from the way Nalani tugged it around her as she came out on deck.

"What are we doing?" Nalani asked. She looked tired and pale. Grief crouched on her shoulder, but she was strong enough to carry it.

"Hoping," Patrick replied.

Nalani nodded, as if this was all the explanation she required. And maybe it was. Shifting sideways, she descended the canted deck like a mountain climber, leaning toward the peak.

"Alex," Nalani said. "We need to get off this boat. The cabin's filling pretty fast. You ever try to float a bucketful of water or sand? You keep adding to it and it's displacing more and more water, but eventually it just goes down. Sinks in a millisecond. Pretty soon we're going to take the plunge."

Cat and Alex scrambled back to take a better look at the repairs they'd made to the dinghy. Alex still had a roll of duct tape in his hand.

Nils crouched against the railing. "This is never going to hold. You guys know that, right?"

Luisa had remained against the cockpit wall with

her head in her hands. Now she cried out in frustration and jumped to her feet. Instantly she was off-balance. She pinwheeled a bit, caught herself, bent toward the deck, and started sliding. Alex reached for her, grabbed her arm as she slid past him, but still she struck the railing a few feet from Nils.

"Fuck!" she shouted, smashing her palm against the railing. Her eyes were wide and brimming with tears as she slammed her hand onto the metal over and over. "Fuck, fuck, fuck, fuck, fuuuuck!"

"Lulu," Cat said quietly.

Luisa crumpled into an uncomfortable bundle in the V of the railing and deck. She pointed a finger at Cat. "No. No 'Lulu.' Not a single word to try to placate me. There's no placating this, *Catherine.*"

Sami, Patrick, and the rest all stared as Luisa unfolded herself from that awkward V, shifted around, and forced herself to stand, one foot on the deck and one on the railing. The sharks would be ten feet below her now, maybe less, but she seemed to have forgotten about them for the moment.

"Alex Simmons, you are the reason we don't have Harry to get us out of this—" Luisa began.

Sami gaped at her. "Luisa—"

"That's insane," Cat said.

Luisa underwent a change. Her desperation turned to rage. "It's not insane, *Catherine.* If Alex and his precious Samantha were going to be such uptight douchebags on this trip, they should never have come. Harry did everything he could to make them comfortable, to make amends. Then Alex threw him overboard, where our hungry friends are waiting for us!"

"Jesus, Luisa," Alex said. "You skipped a few steps in there, don't you think? Yeah, Harry and I were getting along pretty well. Then—" He turned and pointed at Isko. "*That* asshole bashed Gabe's skull in. We all tried to help. Sami tried to help. Harry decided to go after my wife. If you recall, we both went over the side."

"Alex didn't bring the smugglers and he didn't invite the sharks," Cat said.

"You want to blame me, enjoy yourself," Alex said, "but it's not going to save any lives."

"Oh, you're trying to save our lives?" Luisa sneered. "My fucking hero."

"What's *wrong* with you?" Nalani asked.

Luisa rolled her eyes. "Are you serious? Look around, woman. You see anything that might be troubling me?"

Nalani skated sideways along the deck until she reached the railing, right beside Luisa. "Look at me."

Luisa did. With attitude.

"You remember me, Luisa? Nalani. I held your hair when you puked . . . nearly every time we went to a party in college. I'm the one you called when you lost your baby. I came to you when your mother was dying. Maybe you never considered me your best friend, but I've *been* the best friend in your life."

That seemed to rattle Luisa. She gave Nalani a petulant look. "And?"

Nalani's face contorted with anguish. "And today my husband was murdered in front of me."

Luisa wiped tears from her eyes with the back of her hand. "You think I don't know that?"

"I think you're thinking of yourself. Like you always do. But right now, we . . . you and I and the rest of the people still on this boat . . . we're all we have."

Luisa wiped her eyes again. She glanced over at Sami, then at Alex. Finally she flapped a hand dismissively and turned to look at Cat and Nils.

"Get the dinghy in the water."

Nils shook his head. "I don't think the patches will hold."

"Not even long enough to get us to shore?" Patrick asked him.

Nils glanced at his feet. "Maybe."

"Maybe is the best we've got," Cat said.

She slid her fingers beneath the dinghy and soon the others were helping her to turn it over. Sami figured there had to be an easier way to hoist it into the water, but they didn't have time to figure that out. And the water was close now. The edge of the deck was only a couple of feet above the water. The rain and wind gusted and a wave crashed across the deck and nearly tore the dinghy out of their hands. Sami slid down and grabbed hold, helping them.

"So who goes first?"

They all looked at her.

Cat started to speak but hesitated.

Luisa didn't. "I go first. Anyone want to fight me for it?"

Nils held on tightly to the dinghy. They all did. The boat rocked and another wave crashed across the deck.

"Patrick goes first," he said. "I didn't fix this thing to have my husband go down with the ship."

"He's been shot," Sami added. "Patrick should absolutely be in the first group. Worst-case scenario, if some of us have to swim for it, Patrick won't have a chance in hell."

Alex studied her. "What about Isko? He's in rough shape."

"Not a fucking chance," Luisa said, turning to Cat for support.

Sami nodded. "I agree with Lulu. Isko can wait. Getting him to the beach first isn't going to help him."

"And if he has to swim for it?" Cat asked, as if Sami needed to be reminded of what she'd just said about Patrick.

From a dozen feet away, Isko coughed and called to them. When they glanced over, the dying man gave them a thumbs-up.

"I'm a very good swimmer," Isko rasped. "You go."

Sami smiled thinly and faced the others around her. "He knows his chances are slim. He needs surgery. There's no operating room on the beach. Without the Coast Guard . . ."

She waved a hand through the air. She didn't need to finish her thought.

"All right," Cat said, glancing at Nalani, Sami, and Alex. "I'll take the dinghy, run Luisa, Nils, and Patrick to shore, and come back for you three. And Isko. Okay?"

Sami and Alex exchanged a glance. He reached out a hand and she took it, holding tight.

"We'll be waiting," Alex said.

But the edge of the deck had slipped under the water and out beyond the railing Sami could see at least two fins in the windblown whitecaps, and she wondered if they really would be waiting when Cat made it back.

They tied the rope to the dinghy and, working together, slid it over the railing. They tried to lower it carefully, but the weight dragged it from their fingers and they dropped the dinghy into the waves.

It bobbed on the water, banged against the hull, but it stayed afloat—for the moment, at least.

Nalani looked at Cat.

"Hurry."

CHAPTER 20

Cat held the throttle on the dinghy. She wanted to twist around and look back at the *Kid Galahad*, but she didn't dare. Alex, Sami, and Nalani had all volunteered to wait for her, but she'd wrestled with the decision. They could have tried to pile everyone on board the little motorboat, but they'd have literally been on top of one another, and even if they hadn't just patched their "lifeboat" up, the risk of tipping or scuttling her would have been strong. Tipping over, dumping them all into the lagoon, was an ending to this story that nobody wanted.

However, risky as it would've been, at least that would have meant only one trip. Leaving her three friends behind meant that she would have to go back for them. She could have chosen to send someone else, but Cat wasn't wired like that. She had promised she would return and ferry them to shore, and she intended to do just that. If it had just been Isko, she might not have dared. To risk her life for someone who was almost certain to die . . . she might have a certain amount of courage, but she wasn't eager to prove it.

No. She would go back for her friends.

"Do you see it?" Nils called.

Cat frowned. Nils pointed over her right shoulder and she turned to see the fin gliding through the water behind them. It vanished beneath a tall wave and then reappeared. Thirty yards farther out, cutting in the other direction so that their trails made a sort of helix pattern, a second shark also seemed to be following.

"Can't you go any faster?" Luisa shouted, the wind and rain carrying the words back to Cat.

Luisa sat at the bow of the dinghy, perched next to Patrick, who sat with his leg outstretched. He ought to have been alone, there at the front, but Luisa had bulled her way up beside him—presumably so she could jump out the second they touched the sand. Nils occupied the middle of the boat, sitting on a bench. While Cat ignored Luisa, Nils wasn't ready to let her off so easily.

"We're staying afloat with tape and glue," he reminded her. "The shotgun blast—"

"Just say 'no'!" Luisa snapped. "If the answer is no, just say it."

Cat glared at her. "No. We can't go any faster."

As it was, Cat and Nils both kept glancing at the floor of the dinghy. Water had already seeped in. Yes, the rain was coming down hard, but with their speed against the wind the rain seemed to cut almost horizontally. The water in the dinghy wasn't rain . . . it had started to seep up through the glue and the duct tape. Not much water—not yet. Cat glanced ahead at the fragment of atoll where they'd picnicked earlier in the day and tried to calculate how long it would take to get there, off-load her passengers, go back for the others, and then reach shore again. How much water in the dinghy would be too much? How much before the saltwater ate away the glue or loosened the tape and the holes just opened up?

She twisted the throttle. The motor growled. A little faster might be a bad idea, but she couldn't decide if it was worse than going slowly under the circumstances.

Luisa glanced back at her. "Thank you! Someone who's not a fucking idiot."

The crispness of the general rebuke cut into all of them, Cat felt sure, but as angry as she wanted to be at Luisa, she was more horrified by the way the woman had snapped. She wanted to tell her old friend to get her shit together, but she had moved past caring very much about Luisa's demeanor. If anyone had ever needed a slap in the face, it was her.

Cat glanced over her shoulder again. No sign of the sharks that had seemed to pursue them. Better for her group, yes, but what of those they'd left behind? She didn't want to think about it.

Instead, she bent against the rain. Nils saw what she was doing and ducked so she could have an uninter-rupted view of the shore. They'd covered about half the distance—still hundreds of yards from shore, but mak-ing progress. Cat tried to get a glimpse of some of the debris they'd left on the beach earlier, the coolers and towels and other detritus of the moments before paradise had filled with horror. The rain lay a thick veil across her vision, but finally she spotted something bright green—someone's towel or T-shirt—and aimed directly for it. The tide had come in and swept much of that debris away. The coolers would be bobbing somewhere in the lagoon now. And the tide kept rising.

She spotted someone moving on the beach. Dev. A wave of relief went through her. Alex had told them that Alliyah had been murdered by the smugglers—stabbed to death—but they hadn't been sure what had happened to Dev.

They were going to make it. She felt it, now. Whether she could get back to the boat and rescue the others remained to be seen, but this group—they were going to reach shore.

Patrick saw it first—saw it just a moment before it hit them. He pointed, started to shout, and then there came the bump that rattled the dinghy so hard Cat slipped off her perch and the throttle slid from her grasp. The motor coughed and purred and they came nearly to a stop on the water. A wave climbed high and lifted them and the dinghy started to turn sideways, almost parallel to the beach. For a breathless moment, she thought it might overturn them. If they'd been nearer to the shore, it might have.

Then the wave passed and Cat gripped the throttle, gave it a twist, yanked it sideways. The dinghy roared and jumped toward the beach again. Cat wiped rain from her eyes and thought they must be playing tricks on her. The beach seemed even farther away.

No. She'd gone slightly off course. Whipping her head around, she caught sight of that green fabric again, and then Dev. He stood on the diminishing fragment of the atoll's arc and waved his hands in the air. In the gray and the rain he seemed barely a silhouette of himself, but she saw him pointing somewhere off to her left.

Cat didn't need to turn to know the shark had returned. Maybe more than one.

"Go!" Patrick said. "Come on, Cat. Please!"

Nils reached out and took his husband's hand, trying to calm him.

Another bump, softer this time but more insidious. A fin glided right beside them, headed in the same direction, the shark's body rasping against the side of the dinghy.

Luisa had gone near catatonic again. Cat stared past her, focused on the shore, not wanting to see the way her friend had closed down. Maniac-bitch Luisa had been terrible, but not as worrisome as this version.

But then Luisa's eyes widened. She wasn't staring out at the lagoon, though. Her shoulders rose and fell with rapid breaths and her brow furrowed as she stared at the floor of the dinghy.

"No, no, no. Look at this! We're dead." She glanced up at Cat, eyes frantic. "We're dead!"

Cat knew what she would see when she looked down. She'd already felt the water at her heels and she knew the leaks in their patches had grown worse. They weren't going to hold. Already she had tried to think ahead and figure out how she might strengthen the patches. She wouldn't leave Alex and Sami and Nalani—and Isko, even him. She wouldn't leave them to die, but if the dinghy had started leaking that badly—

Luisa turned to Patrick. "It's you! You're bleeding. Oh, you fucking bastard, you're bleeding!"

She started to punch him. Patrick had been shot, but he was still strong and he grabbed her wrists.

"Luisa, stop!" Nils demanded. He shifted forward in the dinghy and tried to grab at her again.

Cat started shouting and cursing at them. Patrick gave her a look of protest—he was clearly not to blame—but Luisa kept struggling. She tore herself free of his grip and stumbled backward. Nils lunged for her and caught her arm, yanking her forward so that she splashed to her knees in the thin layer of water that had seeped in. Her eyes were wide, and for a few seconds she couldn't do anything but repeat, "Jesus, God," over and over.

"Lu, what the hell?" Cat shouted at her.

Luisa snapped her head up. With a savage scowl, she scooped water from inside the boat and splashed it in Cat's face. Cat sputtered and reached up to wipe the saltwater from her eyes.

"You nutcase!" Cat barked. "Just sit your ass down, please. We're practically there."

Which was a lie. They were still a ways from the beach, but closing in by the second.

Luisa splashed her palm in the inch or so of water

in the dinghy. "Are you blind? It's his blood, goddamn it! Patrick's bleeding."

Nils threw up his hands. "We know he's bleeding. It's a bullet wound, for Christ's sake! What do you expect him to do, hold it in?"

Luisa knelt in the prow beside Patrick, who still sat on the front bench. She pointed at the water again. "He's bleeding into the boat. The water's coming in through your seal job and that means it's also going out. His blood is in the water. Sharks can smell a single drop of blood in the water from miles away. Don't you get it, he's drawing them after us!"

Nils shook his head. "They did this before. It's the motor. They're used to preying on people. You know—"

Another thump, then. The shark hit the side of the dinghy so hard they could hear something crack. They all cried out, then. The dinghy rocked to one side, but she kept the motor revved, kept them leaping the waves toward the beach. The shark seemed to lift the boat on its back, racing alongside them, and then it vanished below, still so deep here. Still too deep.

"There are more," Nils said, and Cat whipped around to see two more fins on their left.

Patrick had gone even paler, and she knew he must be thinking the same thing she was thinking. Luisa might be right.

"Luisa, sit down," Cat said.

One of the other sharks approached. Luisa started screaming. She splashed her hands in the water again.

"We're gonna die!" she shouted. "We're gonna die because of this!"

The shark rose up out of the water, one dead black eye staring at them, and it hit the side of the dinghy hard. Halfway through Luisa's resulting scream, another struck from the other side, and the cracking sounded more like splintering.

All of the holes were small, but the largest—left behind by the shotgun—burst open. Water fountained up from beside a flapping piece of duct tape.

Luisa screamed in terror, but Cat saw her face twist with rage. Even as Luisa turned toward Patrick she cried out, but she didn't slow them down. They were still more than a hundred yards out.

Then Luisa punched Patrick in the face. As he lifted his hands to shield himself from another blow, she slapped them away, then threw herself against him. Sitting too high, one leg useless, Patrick went off kilter, and Luisa saw it. She felt it. Cat could see from the look on her face that what came next was absolutely intentional. With a mighty shove, she pushed Patrick overboard.

Nils screamed and started to rise. Cat told him to stay down, even as she eased off the throttle. Frozen, she had no idea what to do. Dive in after him? That would be suicide.

"Get him!" Cat said, but Nils didn't need to be told.

This was his husband. Nils screamed and reached out his hand, calling for Patrick to swim. Patrick, with a bullet in his leg, started to do just that. Luisa shouted at Cat, wild-eyed and frantic, not to turn the boat around, but Cat knew she couldn't live with that. She used the throttle as a tiller, got them turning, circling back the way they'd come. Luisa screamed again and lunged at her, passing through the fountain of water jetting up from the floor of the dinghy. They were taking on water fast, but Cat thought they could still make it—they had to make it.

Then Luisa clawed at her face. This woman who'd once been among her dearest friends *clawed at her face*. Luisa's nails raked her skin and Cat twisted away from her. Luisa shoved her, not off the boat but just to get her away from the throttle, wanting to control the motor herself. Cat smashed her in the chin with the flat of her palm, punched her in the left breast, and then shifted and kicked her onto her back. Luisa crashed onto the bench where Nils had been sitting. The jet of water flooding in splashed all over her.

Nils screamed, still reaching for the water.

Cat turned to see a huge wave rolling toward them, understood immediately that they'd gone sideways again. Parallel to the beach. Parallel to the massive wave coming at them. Then she saw the blood spreading out across the wave and Patrick in the water, flailing, trying to swim while a shark tore at his leg. A second shark came in so fast it was like a blur. Its jaws closed on his torso, just below his flailing arms, and then that huge wave passed over Patrick and the sharks and washed his blood toward them all.

The dinghy overturned. Cat heard Luisa's screams even as she plunged into the water. Then the lagoon enveloped her. The power of another wave shunted her forward and she banged her head against the hull of the dinghy. For long seconds she flailed weakly, disoriented, holding her breath by instinct. Then her lips parted and water slid down her throat. Her eyes went wide. The knock on her head had shaken her, but now Cat dragged herself to the surface. She burst up through the waves, coughing hard, and whipped around.

The dinghy lay half-submerged about a dozen feet away. Luisa clung to it—or tried to, her fingers scrabbling against the hull. She kept turning, looking into the water around her. Luisa had stopped screaming now—too terrified to scream.

Of Nils and Patrick, the only sign was blood.

The wind and rain battered her. A massive wave lifted Cat up and lowered her again. In the trough between waves, she spotted a shark. The fin cruised past the sinking dinghy only six feet from Luisa, but her back was turned. Cat could have screamed for her, warned her. She probably should have. She understood that. But she knew it would be pointless.

Someone burst from the lagoon only seven or eight feet away from her. Cat jerked backward in the water, heart pounding, not as numb as she'd let herself believe.

Nils saw her. His eyes were full of an anguish Cat thought no one should ever feel.

"Patrick . . . ," Nils said, and his expression made clear what had become of his husband.

"I'm sorry," Cat said.

Over at the vanishing dinghy, Luisa screamed—and this was a different sort of scream. This was neither hysteria nor terror. This was pain and shock. The scream lasted only seconds. Cat glanced over just in time to see Luisa dragged beneath the sinking dinghy.

Nils tried to say something. Blood spilled from his lips. Bubbling.

A wave crashed over him and rolled him sideways and Cat saw that his left arm had become a ragged stump, a piece of bone jutting out, and an enormous chunk had been taken out of his side.

Beyond him there were two fins, slicing dispassionately through the water at strange angles, as if the sharks wanted to appear nonchalant. As if they wanted her to think they had no further interest in her bleeding, dying friends. In her.

You're in shock, she thought.

Then it all made sense.

She ought to have been screaming. Swimming for shore. Terror and a knock on the head had done something to her and her thoughts had a kind of blur to them. Cat turned to look at the shore. A figure stood ankle deep in the water, waving his hands above his head, too scared to come any farther. Her eyes focused and she knew that face.

Dev. Screaming for her to swim.

As if from outside herself, Cat noticed that the shore was really not so far away now. No more than a hundred feet. If she swam toward Dev, it might not be long before her feet could touch the bottom. The waves would carry her, crash against her, lift her toward safety.

She ought to be swimming.

The water around her warmed with Nils's blood. Cat glanced at the dinghy as the last of it slipped beneath the water and she saw Luisa's red hair fanned out on the surface, some portion of her floating there.

"Oh, Lulu," Cat whispered to herself.

A shark surfaced from beneath the shadow of the sunken dinghy. This one did not seem as shy as the others. It glided toward her.

Almost idly, mostly to stop Dev from shouting at her, Cat began to swim toward shore.

She didn't make it.

Alliyah could see Dev. He stood on the sand only sixty or seventy yards away. A gust of wind staggered her, but she planted her feet and refused to fall. Even to go down on one knee right now might be the end for her. In the rain, she turned and looked out at the lagoon. She could see the *Kid Galahad* in the distance and it was clearly sinking. The boat lay at an angle in the water, its mast out over the waves. Anyone still on board would be sinking along with it.

With the wind and the rain—and with Dev shouting out across the water—she hadn't been able to get his attention. Alliyah raised her own voice as loudly as she could, but his attention was elsewhere. As she was wracked with pain and frustration, it took her a few moments to realize that Dev wasn't shouting across the water at the yacht. He waved his hands back and forth, then beckoned furiously, but his focus wasn't on the boat.

Dev was shouting at people who were *in the water*. Now that she'd seen them, Alliyah couldn't tear her gaze away. She watched as the sharks toyed with someone. Cat—Alliyah though it must be Cat. At this distance it was hard to be sure, but she saw the fins and she saw the head bobbing on the water as someone—Cat—swam for shore. Alliyah saw a shark bump against her. She caught the ghost of a scream in the midst of the storm and then she saw Cat stop swimming. One of the sharks had gone under, gone deep, and a few seconds later, with Dev still shouting at the water, a shark erupted from the lagoon. It breached like a whale, Cat flailing in its jaws, and then flopped back into the water with her in its teeth. They disappeared together.

Alliyah couldn't even cry. All she could do was try not to collapse.

On the shore, Dev's arms dropped. He hung his head, for there was nobody else out on the water for him to wave to.

"Dev!" she called. Barely a rasp. Not a shout or a scream. She lowered her voice, tried to aim his name at him, to push it out of her lungs and make it real and tangible in the midst of the storm. "Dev!"

He lifted his head, looking hopefully at the water for a moment. Then he seemed to realize where the voice had come from and he glanced to his left. Dev saw her and shouted something. The relief that washed over Alliyah clouded out her more complicated feelings. Dev might be a coward and an asshole, but he was her husband and she needed him now. More than she ever had before.

Alliyah glanced at her feet.

Waves crashed in from both directions, the water rising above her knee.

She stood at the edge of one fragment of Orchid Atoll's ring. They should have recognized that the rising tide would change the appearance of the atoll dramatically. The larger fragments, like the shrinking island where the Coast Guard station continued to burn and belch smoke into the sky, would stay above water, but some of the fragments were smaller and lower and now the waves crashed over them and they continued to diminish with every wave.

Alliyah stood at the edge of one fragment. Dev ran toward her along another. He'd remained on the piece of the atoll where they'd picnicked. The water had covered all but the ridge that ran along the spine of that bit of the ring. The gap between the edge of the fragment where Alliyah stood and the one Dev now ran along had been six feet wide and only knee-deep when she'd gone to try to help Alex. Now that gulf was twenty feet wide and the waves from inside and outside of the atoll crashed against each other. The currents were at war in the channel between herself and Dev, but it wasn't the current she worried about.

Dev ran toward her. When he was perhaps a dozen yards away, he got his first good glimpse of how wide the gap was, and how turgid the water. He slowed, his footfalls unsure now. Then he glanced out at where the sharks had been moments before. Where her friends had died.

"Now," Alliyah rasped, trying to be heard over the storm. "While they're busy."

Dev took three more steps toward the edge and stared at the water churning in the gap.

Alliyah smiled at him. *My hero,* she thought, knowing he would never come to her. Not with the water this wide and this deep. Not with the chance of sharks. She bled from the wounds in her back. Where the knife had gone in, parting flesh and muscle, the pain continued to seethe. She thought of fallen angels having their wings torn off after rebelling against God.

You flatter yourself, she thought.

And she jumped.

It wasn't much of a jump, really. She threw herself into the water, her body incapable of much more than that. The maelstrom formed by the conflicting currents tugged at her, but the churning ebb and flow somehow balanced. Her legs began to kick. The water had been knee-deep and now it seemed to be over her head. Her toes brushed against coral.

One arm against her rib cage, she managed to use the other to pull her through the water. Reaching down with her toes, letting herself sink, she pushed off the coral and propelled herself toward the other side. Alliyah tasted blood again, but that might have been her imagination. Or it might have been her wounds, still weeping.

A wave washed across her face. She sputtered and blinked, keeping that one arm pinned and the other in motion, halfway dog-paddling now.

Dev knelt on the coral ridge on the other side of the churning gap. His eyes were wide and fearful as he reached a hand out to her. He called out to her encouragingly and she realized she had made progress. Ten feet, which meant she only had ten remaining. She tried to reach down with her feet, but now her toes wouldn't touch bottom, so she kicked her legs. Every kick dug into her wounds, sending spikes of fresh pain through her.

Eight feet.

"Come on, Alli! Swim! You're so close!" Dev called, and he reached out even farther.

Six feet. She kept kicking, teeth gritted against the pain the motion caused her, but she lifted her right hand out of the water—the other still pressed to her ribs— and reached for Dev. Their fingers were just a couple of feet apart. With a kind of wonder, she watched their fingers move toward each other.

Then she heard Dev swear, and saw his fingers dance away as he withdrew his hand.

Alliyah felt the pressure of the shark's motion, felt the displacement of water—a third current to join the clash of the other two. And she saw the despair and surrender in her husband's eyes.

She lunged for Dev. Pain stabbed at her, but she twisted in the water and yanked her legs forward in an attempt to dodge. The shark's teeth raked her left leg and for a moment it tugged her along with it. Alliyah screamed and reached out again, lunging for the coral ridge. Her hand passed through nothing and she glanced over her shoulder, saw the fin moving toward her again, the water rippling around it.

Again she lunged. Her hand caught rough coral. Her knee struck it beneath the water. Her toes caught on the shifting sand of the bottom.

She felt the shark approaching again. She only had a moment, but it was all she'd need. With a desperate cry, she grabbed hold with both hands and hauled herself from the churning water . . . or tried to. Pain shrieked from the wounds on her back and when she put weight on her right leg, where the shark's teeth had been at her, a fresh, bright wave of agony slammed through her. Her grip slipped. The pain consumed her. Darkness flowed in at the edges of her vision and she hung there, unable to drag herself from the water.

Alliyah didn't want to die, but she knew the shark didn't care.

CHAPTER 21

Alex crouched with Sami and Nalani, all three of them holding on to the railing. They'd been watching in silence while Cat ferried the others to dry land. Soaked by the rain, Sami had started shivering and Alex put an arm around her. On his left side, Nalani began to sob quietly, her body wracked with grief, so he put his other arm around her and held both women close to him. It wasn't his nature to show that kind of physical affection to anyone other than his wife, but there was nothing natural about this moment. Sami reached in front of him and took Nalani's hand. That wasn't her nature, either, but Nalani had watched her husband murdered today, and here they were. Just the three of them left. Sinking. Drowning in a fucking nightmare.

They heard the screaming. Alex squinted and lifted a hand to shield his eyes from the rain. He stared into the gray veil of the storm and tried to make out the individual shapes on the dinghy. They could still hear the motor, but above its dentist's drill whine came shouts of fear and anger.

"Luisa," Sami said. "What the hell is she doing?"

But it wasn't just Luisa. The screams shifted into something else, a plaintive, terrified surrender to fate.

Alex leaned out, peering, trying to get a better view.

"Jesus," Nalani whispered, because her eyesight was better than his. "They're capsized."

Neither Alex nor Sami said a word. What could they do from here? Alex knew all three of them were thinking the same thing, sharing the same clashing worries. Fear for their friends, and fear for themselves. As the screaming rose to a shriek and then faltered to nothing but echoes, Alex kissed Sami on the temple, then rested his head against hers.

"What are we going to do?" Nalani asked.

Alex didn't reply. He glanced over at Isko, who still lay against the railing. The water had come up over the edge of the deck. A wave washed along the boat, splashed the three of them, and engulfed Isko completely for a moment. He gasped loudly as it passed, sputtering, his hands flailing in front of his face as if fighting off a monster in his sleep, or the specter of death come to claim him.

"First thing we're going to do is move Isko," Alex said.

Nalani flinched. "What?"

Sami nodded. "No, he's right." She extricated herself from his embrace and pushed up from the railing.

Nalani lowered her head for a second, but then she

exhaled loudly and levered herself up. Alex rose as well. It was difficult and awkward. The way the boat lay in the water, canted so far over that the edge of the deck rested just below the surface, they were stepping in the water in the V between the deck and the railing. The time had come for them to move, no matter what else happened.

The sharks were there, of course. Alex could see several fins rising and falling in the waves and the rain. How many were there? He had no idea, but certainly far more than the three he'd initially seen. Sharks had killed Cat and the others—friends he'd never see again—but there were still fins near the boat.

"Watch it," Sami said.

Alex glanced back to see one of the sharks coming at them now, gliding silently up beside the submerged edge of the deck. Nalani cried out as all three of them lifted their feet, holding themselves up using both railing and deck. The shark raised its head and opened its jaws and slid the corner of its maw along that corner of the deck, dreadful but impassive, as if it knew their time was running out and merely wanted to remind them that it knew.

When they reached Isko, Alex was startled by the brightness of the dying man's eyes. Copper brown, they glistened as he looked at them. Isko thanked them again and again, in both their language and his own, as they tied him up in the soaked-through blanket beneath him and began the arduous task of shifting him up the slanted deck toward the cockpit. Alex couldn't help thinking how much simpler this would have been if Isko had had the courtesy to just die. An ugly thought. He knew that. But it didn't go away.

They formed a sort of chain. Alex lay on the deck and Sami crawled up it, using her husband for leverage. Nalani dragged and slid Isko in his blanket until he was beside Alex, then helped Alex shift the dying man further. Soon Nalani crawled up until she was above Sami. She managed to grab hold of the ruined cockpit doorframe, and soon, awkwardly and accompanied by grunts and cursing, they had gotten Isko just inside the cockpit. The shattered glass of its windows remained scattered on the deck, and inside the water had flooded the cabin so completely that it had begun to rise into the cockpit, too. Soon it would even flood the wheelhouse. But they were away from the waves for the moment. Away from the sharks.

"How much time will this buy us?" Sami asked.

Nalani laughed. It was a hollow sound. A pragmatic, giving-up sort of sound. "Not long enough for the Coast Guard to get here. Not even until tonight."

Alex looked out at the storm. The sky had gone so dark that it seemed as if night had already fallen, but Nalani was right. Somewhere beyond the rain and the black clouds, the sun was still out.

Sami and Nalani moved Isko around inside the cockpit so that he was resting against the wall. The boat had tilted so much that the wall lay at a forty-degree angle. Nalani started to untie the blanket around Isko and the man glanced over at Alex, his head lolling. His breathing had turned quite shallow.

"What the hell you doing, friend?" Isko asked.

Alex frowned. "Staying alive."

Isko rolled his head, gazing up at Sami and Nalani. They were all propped at odd angles inside the sinking funhouse that the *Kid Galahad* had become.

The dying man smiled. "Pretty ladies. Is the man stupid or just stubborn?"

"The man's trying to save you," Nalani said. "So are we."

Soft, dry laughter floated inside the cockpit, a strange counterpoint to the rain and the slosh of the water that still bubbled up from the cabin.

Isko narrowed his eyes. He took Sami's hand. "What about you, Doctor? You still trying to save my life?"

Alex saw the way Sami shifted her gaze, the way she looked at him without really looking, and they all knew the answer.

"She knows," Isko said. "I'm already dead."

The truth made Alex wince. But he couldn't argue. Now that they were inside the cockpit, even with the wind gusting through the broken windows, the smell of Isko's rotting leg made him want to retch.

"What do you expect us to do?" Alex asked. "Swim? What about the sharks?"

Isko rolled his eyes. He sighed.

"I made it," he said. "Could be you will, too. Probably not all of you, but—"

The boat gave a sudden lurch, as if some invisible hand had been holding it up and had now grown tired of the effort. The water bubbling up from the cabin began to flow. An air pocket hissed and spat like the spout of a whale and then they were going down.

"Shit. Oh, shit!" Nalani yelled. Her eyes were wild as she glanced around, unsure which way to flee.

Alex made a choice. "Up!"

They were moving even before he shouted. The boat had tipped nearly sideways, but now it began to slip backward, the stern sinking fast. They dragged Isko up the steps into the wheelhouse, but the water came up fast after them. Something had given way. This was the end.

Inside the wheelhouse, Alex grabbed hold of the wheel, got a foot on it, and boosted himself up so that he could grab hold of the frame of the broken windshield. His heart hammered in his chest. All he could think about was being trapped in the wheelhouse or the boat flipping and trapping him beneath it, dragging him down. The screams of his friends were still ringing in his ears and the horror of the sharks felt visceral and real, as if their teeth had torn at his skin as well . . . and yet in this moment the idea of drowning, of being unable to breathe until desperation forced him to open his mouth underwater, to suck the ocean into his lungs . . . the pressure in his chest . . . that seemed so much worse.

He climbed out through the broken window, perched on the edges of the frame, and reached his hand back through, expecting to see Sami right behind him. Instead, it was Nalani who took his hand. Alex knitted his brow. Grunting with effort, he lifted her toward him. Nalani got her upper body over the upper edge of the window frame and dragged herself out of the wheelhouse.

Alex ducked his head back in, holding on with one hand. His heart thrummed so fast that it felt like it might vibrate out of his chest. The water rushed into the wheelhouse, filling it quickly, no longer just from below but also from the sides. The aft end of the boat plunged deeper into the water and the ocean swept in.

In the churning water, Sami had her arm around Isko. She tried to keep him afloat as she swam toward the broken windshield, one arm across his chest.

"Sami, goddamn it, leave him!" Alex shouted. "Tasha needs you!"

She ignored him. Dragged herself through the water with Isko weighing her down. The man himself had told them to leave him there, and they all knew death would come to collect him today, that the reaper waited impatiently to claim him. Yet still she tried.

Nalani grabbed at his leg.

Alex whipped around, wide-eyed. "Jump. Swim as fast as you can."

Beyond her, he saw one of the surfboards that had been secured on deck. It had come free and now floated forty feet from the sinking boat. Nalani saw where he was looking and she didn't hesitate. The time had passed for courtesy or recrimination. There were fins nearby. Alex couldn't see them in this moment—this eternal slow-motion torture—but they were there. Each of them had to do what they could to survive.

Nalani swam for the surfboard.

Alex braced himself across the frame of the broken windshield and reached down inside the wheelhouse. Sami caught his hand, lifted by the rising water. Alex pulled, but Isko had caught himself on something. The wheel? Some other navigation instrument? It might have been his leg or the blanket.

"No!" Sami said as the boat plunged.

Alex reached past her, trying to get to Isko, to free whatever had snagged. Then he saw the man's face, awake and aware, and followed the path of his arm in the water to see that Isko had grabbed hold of the wheel and wouldn't let go. He knew Sami would die if she tried to get him all the way to shore, that neither of them had a chance with the added burden.

Sami must have seen, too. Or at least seen the look on his face.

She released him. The boat began to list to one side again, almost rolling as it went under, and Alex held on to Sami's hand as the *Kid Galahad* vanished beneath them. They felt the drag of it sinking, as if the lagoon yearned to claim them along with the boat. Alex let go of Sami's hand and they both swam, pulling away from that suction, and in moments the drag subsided.

Debris popped to the surface, even as the storm-whipped waves rolled through the lagoon. A cooler bobbed up. Hats and beer bottles and a single, cork-heeled, woman's shoe. Something white fluttered and spread under the water. One of the sails had become partially unleashed and billowed like one of the ghosts of the deep.

Rain lashed at Alex's face. He wiped his eyes and glanced around for Nalani. He saw no sign of her.

"There," Sami said. "Alex, look!"

A surfboard. His heart clenched, but he saw quickly that this yellow-and-blue-patterned board was not the one Nalani had swum for.

Sami had already started toward it. Alex swam behind her, glancing around with every extension of his arms, every kick of his feet. Down in the waves, it was difficult to get a broad view, but as one of those swells lifted him high he saw two fins, one of which was not far off at all, and then he stopped looking. It didn't matter where the sharks were. It only mattered that they were in the lagoon—and he and Sami were in the water with them. Isko was forgotten. For a few seconds, while they were swimming toward the surfboard, even Nalani was forgotten.

Alex reached the surfboard first. He threw one arm over it, then held it in place for his wife.

"Get on."

Sami shot him a reproachful glare. "Alex—"

"We don't have time to fight over it. I'm a stronger swimmer. There's only room for one of us. Get on."

Sami couldn't argue with the truth. The waves lifted them and crashed them down again. Just floating out here was exhausting. She dragged herself onto the board and put her arms into the water, starting to paddle. Alex grabbed the rear of the surfboard and started kicking for his life. Together they'd make good speed.

"Do you see Nalani? Or anyone onshore?" he asked.

Sami muttered something he couldn't hear. A wave rose beneath him and he had to lift his head to keep it out of his eyes. She started paddling more to the left and he had to trust in her, knowing she must have spotted the nearest land.

A strange calm descended on him. He lowered his head and put all of his strength into swimming, just kicking his legs under the water, powering the surfboard forward. So many had died already, but Sami remained alive. Somehow, she was still breathing—still whole—and he intended to keep her that way. Alex kicked his legs, fighting the swells and the rain and the wind, turning himself into her motor. That felt good to him. It felt fine. He wanted to survive this, he truly did, but if he could just get Sami to shore, he didn't really care what happened to himself.

"If I don't make it—" he began.

"Shut up!"

"Listen to me. If I don't make it, don't ever let Tasha forget how much her daddy . . ." He faltered, unable to get the words out.

"I won't," Sami promised. "I swear, I won't. And the same goes for me."

Alex swam harder. Heart pumping, legs kicking, he started to make the kinds of promises that junkies and soldiers and shipwrecked sailors had always made, the desperate prayers to any deity within hailing distance, vowing to give his own life, or to worship God—anyone's god who would answer—for eternity, as long as Sami got out of this alive.

Then Sami started to scream.

The water itself seemed to fight him. He kept kicking but pulled himself up a bit onto the back of the surfboard, trying to look around. Trying to hear the words in the midst of her screams. Although, of course, he knew what she must be screaming about, and the moment he dragged himself up he caught a glimpse of the shark off to their left, slightly ahead and knifing through the lagoon on a diagonal course that would surely intercept them.

Alex wanted to unravel. A part of him had frayed so much from all the fear and horror of this day that it wanted to completely come apart. But he looked past Sami's head and saw how far they'd come while he'd put everything else out of his mind. Much farther than he'd expected. Farther, if he was being honest with himself, than he'd expected them to make it. Some of the sharks must still have been busy with Cat and Luisa and Nils and Patrick. They were all dead, he knew, and each of them had torn a piece of his heart out. Their blood would still be in the water. Whatever remained of their bodies—limbs and torsos—would still be in the lagoon. The sharks had been trained to eat human flesh and they must be doing that, even now. The blood would be there, in the water, still clouding around heads and legs, blossoming out of those wounds.

Buying us time, he thought.

But not this shark. Not the one arrowing toward them. Alex took one last glance at the shore—so close, now. Less than sixty yards, he figured.

"Whatever happens, keep paddling!" he shouted, and he bent his head to the task again, kicking his legs. Sami's motor, propelling her forward on that surfboard.

"No!" she shouted. "What are you doing? Turn around!" For a moment she started paddling off course.

"And go where?" Alex shouted, spitting saltwater, his throat parched. "Head for shore!"

Sami bent to her task just as he had. She'd never been religious—not really—but he heard her praying loudly now. The prayers turned into nothing but calling Jesus's name over and over. Alex felt his legs, wondered if he might be bleeding in the water. He felt the vulnerability of his belly and thighs and calves and feet, exposed and tender. Enraged by his own fear, he gritted his teeth and kicked harder.

Come and get me, he thought. It would give Sami time. If his blood spread out here, if the shark focused on tearing him apart, she might reach the shore without being attacked.

Then he felt it, right there. Beneath him. In front of them.

It rushed at the surface, struck the underside of Sami's surfboard. The rear of the board smashed Alex's forehead and he felt his grip release. The shark passed him so close that its thrashing body thudded against his chest. He closed his eyes, disoriented, the blow to his forehead enough to put his lights out for a second or two.

He blinked. "Sami!"

The surfboard rose and fell on a wave. Sami wasn't on it.

Alex heard her shout for him. He turned. Saw that she was all right, swimming for the board. Awash with relief for just an instant, he knew the shark would return in mere moments.

Again he blinked, but this time there was blood in his eyes. He tasted it on his lips. The surfboard had cut his forehead and he was bleeding. Bleeding into the water.

He almost stopped swimming. If he just gave up, let himself bleed, surely the shark would take him first. But fuck it, he wanted to live.

"Go, Sami! I'll race you!" he called, feeling closer to crazy than he ever had before.

She'd almost reached the surfboard. He thought they could go side by side, keep distance between them. He could swim for shore, try like hell to make it there alive, and if the shark came back it would still go after him first. It would. It had to. Alex lowered his face into the water even as he swam, swished his head back and forth, letting his blood mix with the sea.

His lungs burned. Every muscle in his neck and shoulders and back felt like it had suffered a thousand blows. The weariness hurt his bones, but the tautness of those muscles hurt so much more. He swam. He kicked with legs he could barely feel.

He lifted his head—and heard the screaming.

Turned . . . and saw Nalani. He'd thought the shrieking woman had been his wife. Instead, he saw his old friend clinging to half of the surfboard she'd gotten hold of. Even on the storm-darkened lagoon, with waves gone deep green and gray, her blood glistened a bright scarlet as it spread around her. Alex knew the second he saw that blood that Nalani's screams might as well have come from a phantom. She clung to that broken surfboard, snapped in half by the same shark— Alex thought—that had knocked Sami off her board, and she kept screaming.

Staring right at Alex.

He plunged ahead, swimming hard, heading for shore. There were two fins in the water near Nalani, circling around her, moving to finish the job. Just that glimpse had been enough for him to know what had happened and what would happen next. Part of her— some piece of her body invisible from the surface— had already been removed. A leg, maybe both.

Sickened by self-loathing, he tried to push Nalani's staring eyes from his thoughts. As he swam, Nalani's screams turned ragged and weak and then ceased entirely.

Ahead of him, Sami shouted for him to swim. Alex obeyed.

Nalani's gaze would stay with him forever, but God help him, he wanted to live.

CHAPTER 22

Alliyah lay against the coral and waited for the shark to finish her.

When Dev's hands grabbed her wrists, it startled her so much that she tried to pull away. He swore at her. Down on his knees—the coral cutting his skin, drawing blood—he hauled her out of the water. He'd never been the strongest man, too thin, too wiry, but he dragged her out and across his lap like a parent intending to spank a child. The soft skin of her belly, the taut stomach she'd worked so hard for, scraped and bled. Alliyah barely felt it.

"Oh, my God," Dev said. "Alli. Oh, my God."

He kept repeating it, like a sample in some irritating club jam. Alliyah knew her chest still rose and fell, which meant she was still breathing. Which meant she was still alive. Her eyes were open, but she found herself unable to focus. The wounds in her back still throbbed, but the stabbing pain there had subsided. *That must be a good sign,* she thought. Though she knew it might also be a very, very bad one.

"Alli," Dev said again.

She found herself on the verge of hating the nickname as much as she hated him.

"Am I bitten?" she asked. "It got me, didn't it?"

"Yeah. It did." His voice sounded almost as raspy and weak as her own. "The bite's not that bad, though. We can bind it. Help's coming."

The sting of the abrasions on her stomach hit her, then. She hissed through her teeth. *Delayed reaction,* she thought. If she'd had the energy, she would have laughed. Knife wounds in her back, fucking shark bite on her leg, and her biggest worry was the scrapes on her belly.

Dev bundled her into his arms and lifted her. Alliyah wouldn't have thought it possible, but he cradled her against his chest and carried her back the way he'd come. The wind buffeted them and he stumbled a little but kept going. With the merciless rain pouring down, Dev marched across the ridge. She didn't have the strength or the will to look around, but she knew he was carrying her to the place where the two of them had been hiding when the smugglers arrived, trying to save their own asses.

What she did notice, even with the numbness spreading through her and the weird, cottony swelling she felt inside her skull, was that this fragment of the atoll had gotten much smaller, even in these last few minutes. With the storm and the tide, there wasn't much left of it.

"Alli . . . ," Dev said, one last time.

When he put her down, he was gentle as could be. Alliyah rolled on her side and watched him as he went and sat a few feet away. Once upon a time, he'd been full of confidence, a swaggering and charismatic husband. Now he put his head in his hands and sat in the rain with the tide coming in. She wondered, as consciousness crashed in and then rolled away like the waves around them, if what she witnessed in that moment was exhaustion or grief or sorrow.

All of them, she realized. *And more.*

Alliyah had seen the parts of Dev that he'd always kept hidden. All her life she'd heard variations on that old cliché that you never really knew a person until times got hard. Now it had turned out to be true, but she thought it had another wrinkle. Alliyah believed that Dev hadn't really known himself until now, and that he didn't like what he'd learned.

She lay there and watched him until the first wave rolled up high enough to wash around her ankles, and then she closed her eyes.

The rain kept falling.

From somewhere nearby, Alliyah heard shouting, but there was nothing she could do to help. Nothing anyone could do.

The next wave that crashed over her came not from

the ocean, but from the darkness, and she let it carry her away.

Sami let the surfboard take her within twenty feet of the shore before her patience broke. She glanced over her shoulder, as she'd been doing over and over. One fin split the water off to her right, but in the storm and the waves there could be more—likely *were* more. Desperation drove her.

Alex had kept swimming off to her left. She'd caught sight of him many times, but now, with her pulse racing and her breath caught in her throat, with the waves lifting and plunging her and the rain and wind, she didn't see him.

Wild, awful thoughts ripped through her. She caught a glimpse of someone onshore ahead of her and a flare of hope burst within her. Watching the shark, she tried to time its approach, wondering if she could make it.

Sami couldn't wait. She slipped off the board, nearly left it behind but grabbed hold of it, slid it over the surface as she waded for shore. Hip deep now, she picked the board up, carried it under her arm, and started running, struggling against the surf. Emerging, letting herself believe.

The wave caught her, then. With the board under her arm, the wave knocked her down and she tumbled, smashed herself against the surfboard. She rolled, swallowing seawater, and slammed against the shore. The sandy bit of beach had long since been hidden by the tide. The ground here was hard. Sami cried out in pain, coughed up a bit of water—

But then the wave receded and she found herself on land, one arm draped over the surfboard that she thought had probably saved her life. A shudder went through her and for a few seconds all she could think about was the fact that she was alive. Her whole body ached and her left elbow felt swollen, but the rain pelted her face and her shoes squelched with water and she roared at the sky in triumph.

I'm alive.

"Sami."

Shielding her eyes from the rain, she looked up. Sami wanted to think it was Alex standing over her, but she knew her husband's voice—the way he said her name—and this wasn't him.

"Dev," she said.

Alliyah's husband stared at her. He stood with his arms crossed, almost hugging himself against the storm. His eyes were so wide she'd have thought he must be flying on one drug or another, but she had seen eyes like his before on people who hadn't touched anything pharmaceutical. Dev was in shock.

So are you, she thought.

But the buzz of her victory, her survival, still raced through her veins like a drug of its own. Careful on the rocks, she levered herself up and stood. Dev didn't offer her a hand, nor did he back up a step to give her room. He stared at her as if she were some sort of exotic bird whose presence he could not explain.

"Where's Alex?" she asked.

Dev frowned. The question confused him, and that banished Sami's feelings of triumph. She opened her mouth to ask again, then shook her head. Talking to this man would be pointless. The lights were on in Dev's skull, but nobody was home.

Shielding her eyes again, she glanced up and down the shore, and instantly spotted Alliyah. Sami cursed under her breath and rushed toward the woman, who lay curled on her side, almost fetal, a few feet from the edge of this fragment of atoll.

"Alliyah," she said, kneeling. "Alli?"

Sami swore again. Alliyah's breathing was shallow and her pulse was thin. Gently but swiftly, Sami examined the woman. It wasn't difficult, under the circumstances. Alliyah wore a thin blue tank top and a peach bikini. She had one sandal on her left foot, but the right was bare and scraped all to hell. It was the least of her injuries. The shark bite on her right calf drew Sami's attention first. The teeth marks were deep and ragged, bleeding, but not as badly as she'd have expected. The muscle and meat were still attached. The shark bite wouldn't kill her.

The wounds on her back would do that.

"She shouldn't even be here," Sami said, more to herself than Dev. Alex had told her that the smugglers had murdered Alliyah. Obviously that wasn't true, but how the woman had gotten here was a mystery.

Sami glanced along the atoll's ring toward the Coast Guard station. Even with the rain, fire still flickered inside its windows and thick smoke poured from inside the building. Had Dev gone over there and gotten her, managed to bring her back here before the channels between the fragments of the atoll—the volcano's fangs—had gotten too deep?

One look at Dev gave her an answer. Not a chance.

Sami shot to her feet again, wincing at scrapes and aches but blessing every one of them for reminding her she was still alive.

"Can you help her?" Dev asked, as if he'd just remembered Alliyah was there.

"I'll try," Sami said, knowing how it would end. "But I need to find Alex."

"He's not here," Dev replied. So sure.

Sami ignored him and started walking back the way she'd come. She glanced out at the water and saw a fin. Then a second and third. There might have been a fourth. They were swimming close to shore, lurking in the waves. *Fuck you,* she thought. *Nothing you can do now.*

This fragment of Orchid Atoll had shrunk to a rough patch about eighty feet long and twenty feet wide. Whatever remnants might have remained of their picnic—if this had been the location of that picnic—had been washed away, with the exception of a single green towel. She thought it had belonged to Luisa, but Luisa wouldn't be needing it anymore. The towel and the surfboard she'd washed up with were the only items in view, and there were certainly no other people. Not right here. But the atoll's ring kept going.

The rain turned the world gray. She'd walked about two-thirds of the way along the shore of this bit of land. Up ahead, she could see the gap between this part of the ring and the next. Waves crashed through it.

Alex was on the other side.

"Sami!" he shouted.

She ran, grateful that she hadn't kicked her shoes off in the water. Alex stood on the opposite side—fifty feet away. Maybe less.

"Baby, I thought you were—" she started.

"I'm not," he said quickly. "Not yet."

He started into the water. Sami saw the shark before Alex did, but only a second before. He threw himself backward, scrambled to his feet, and stared at the enormous back of the monster as it slid slowly through the gap between them.

Alex turned, just for a moment, and Sami realized immediately what he was looking at.

A wave crashed behind him and washed right over the top of the little island he was on. If the tide rose any higher, if the storm got any worse, the spot where he was standing would be underwater. The sprit where Dev, Sami, and Alliyah were wasn't just bigger, but slightly taller.

"You can't stay there!" Sami called to Alex.

As if in reply, the shark swam back through the gap. A sentry, making its rounds. Only this time, a second one passed it going in the other direction. It surfaced, one black eye tracking her. The shark swam toward the spot where Sami stood. A wave swelled beneath it and Sami backed away. In her head she knew it couldn't reach her, but in her gut the terror of sinking on the *Kid Galahad* and swimming to shore remained.

She glanced back at Dev, but he'd sat down beside Alliyah, knees drawn up under him, staring out at the lagoon. A wave rolled up the coral ridge and lifted the surfboard and a dreadful tremor went through her.

"Wait for me!" she shouted.

Sami stumbled into the water, leaping above the highest wave. In seconds she was up to her waist in the surf, lunging for the board as the sea tried to steal it away. A glance across the water made her heart stop. How many fins had she counted in that moment? Six or seven, at least, probably more. Not counting the ones patrolling the pass where Alex stood waiting for her.

She grabbed the surfboard and dragged it ashore.

The time for fear had ended.

Which didn't mean she had any desire to be stupid. She needed something more than the surfboard. That deep pass wouldn't get any narrower while she waited to see if the tide rose higher. She ran the surfboard over to Dev and dropped it onto the ground beside him.

"Don't let this get swept away."

She started past him, but he grabbed her wrist.

"Help her," Dev said. Still lost in shock, he glanced at Alliyah as if Sami needed reminding.

And maybe she did.

How much time did Alex have? She didn't know the answer, but she couldn't walk away from Dev and Alliyah without doing something. Working swiftly, she crouched and slipped Alliyah's tank top off. The woman's face contorted with pain and she groaned aloud.

"What are you—" Dev began.

"That's a good sign," Sami told him. And it might even have been true if they could have gotten her to a hospital right now, somewhere she could get an infusion to replace some of the blood she'd lost.

The bite on Alliyah's leg needed bandaging, but all they had was her tank top. Sami folded it longways.

"Roll her onto her stomach."

As if in slow motion, Dev complied. Sami pressed the soaked cloth against the two stab wounds, then looked up at him.

"You put your hands where mine are and you hold them here. Compression. She's lost a ton of blood. Maybe you can stop her from losing more."

"There's nothing else you can do?" Dev asked hopelessly.

Sami stood up. He quickly replaced her hands with his own, pressing down on his wife's wounds. Alliyah groaned again, and then Sami was gone. She hurried along the ridge to the edge of the fragment, staring at the Coast Guard station as she moved.

The gap on this side was narrower but still wide. She could make a good third of the distance with a leap. A quick glance showed no sign of sharks and she didn't want to give herself a moment to reconsider, so she backed up, got a running start, and hurled herself out over the channel. She plunged into the water. Her feet touched bottom and she pushed off, certain a shark must be waiting for her.

Then she was on the other side, crawling out. The ground was softer here, not as rough, and she set off running along the water's edge toward the burning Coast Guard station.

Sami hadn't told Alex what she planned to do

because she hadn't wanted him to talk her out of it, but less than two minutes after she'd reached the structure she knew it had been a waste of time. The windows were shattered. Fire burned inside, smoke pouring out, charring the outer walls. The open door revealed the scene within—not an inferno now, but a tunnel of flickering shadows with fire coating the ceiling. The doors on either side of the corridor just inside were burning.

Alex had told her the place was virtually empty, but she'd thought about the metal frames for the cots. Maybe she could break off a leg, use it as a weapon. She'd even considered the idea that she could bring back two, toss one across the waves to her husband.

"Stupid," she whispered to herself, backing away from the burning doorframe. "So stupid."

How much time had she wasted? How many waves had crashed over the spit of land where Alex waited? Sami hesitated another moment, wracking her brain, trying to find a way to save her husband that didn't involve him swimming so far unprotected.

She had nothing.

Sami started running back. To her right were the trees she'd already passed more than once. A cluster of koa trees drew her attention. Several were broken, half-fallen, knocked over by one storm or another over the past few years. Thinking anything was better than nothing to show for her efforts, Sami grabbed hold of a thick branch, put her foot on the trunk of one of those fallen trees, and wrenched upward. The wood gave with the crack, and suddenly she was running back the way she'd come with a long, leafless tree branch whose splintered end seemed a halfway decent spear. She had no illusions she could kill a shark with a length of wood, but she needed something—anything— that would at least serve as a distraction.

She'd wasted this time. She couldn't go back empty-handed.

Gripping her makeshift spear, Sami ran through the rain, hoping her husband would still be there.

CHAPTER 23

The little stretch of rock where Alex had dragged himself out of the water had been shrinking ever since. The tide kept rising, the water washing over the stone beneath his feet. He stood on the highest point, but his personal island didn't have much variation in elevation, and even in the troughs between waves he was mostly surrounded by water. The only thing keeping the sharks away was how shallow it was. Even in the gray of the storm, with the gloom of the rain, he could see through the rippling surf. Two steps away from him, the water was only a few inches deep. Four steps, it dropped to perhaps nine inches, and deeper the farther out he went. When a big wave crashed in, he had to crouch and tense himself against it every time to make sure he didn't get swept off his perch. That would be bad. Probably fatal.

The sharks were waiting. Alex told himself that was

insane, that the sharks had brains the size of walnuts or something and they couldn't possibly be smart enough to really be waiting for him, but he wondered how much of that was true. They were predators, after all. Predators that had learned to see humans as prey. The cut on Alex's forehead had bled into the water and they had followed him, nearly killed him. Only Nalani's death had distracted them long enough for him—and for Sami—to reach the rocky fangs of the atoll.

Now they circled. He'd counted at least eight or nine out in the lagoon, but there were three here paying special attention to him. They swam in a kind of pattern as if guarding their prey, waiting for a wave to knock him into the deeper water or for the storm surge to drive the tide even higher.

A wave crashed in. He crouched again, one knee on the ground. The wave smashed against him and he scrambled a bit, shifting his hands to catch himself. When the wave subsided, the tide seemed higher to him. It couldn't have risen with just that one wave, but now he noticed it.

Yes. Definitely still rising.

Still on one knee, crouched there with his hands on the rock, nearly half a foot of water rushing around his legs and forearms, he knew the end had come. He would have to swim for it again. The last time, he had barely made it. Now he had fifty or sixty feet to go—twenty yards. He could do that in thirty seconds if he got a running start and dove. Alex wouldn't be in the water long at all. He had to risk it.

Another wave crashed in. He waited as it swept over him, went down on both knees to hold on, and then he was up again, counting fins. One, two . . . where was the third one? Shit, he couldn't see it. Had the shark gone underwater? Even if he spotted it, how could he be certain there were only three nearby?

He couldn't.

But he couldn't wait.

Alex took a deep breath. He spotted another huge wave rolling in, and decided he wasn't going to wait, but when he glanced at the nearest fragment of the atoll he saw that Sami had returned. In the rain, he could barely make her out. She had that same surf-board—he saw that much—and she called out to him as she hurried toward him.

"No. Sami, wait!" he called.

Shit. The wave was nearly on him before he remembered it and knelt down, trying to dig his fingers into the rock to hold on. Alex held his breath. Water shot up his nose as he scrambled sideways, losing his grip. It lifted him, started to sweep him away. His heart thundered in panic as he reached down, scrabbling at the rock beneath the wave, and caught enough of a grip to slow himself until the wave subsided.

"Alex, come on!" Sami shouted, as if he'd been playing instead of trying to save himself. He'd have laughed if he'd been capable of it.

He sprang to his feet again. The wind gusted hard, but he fought against it, closed his eyes to the rain and the oncoming waves, and he stopped worrying about counting fins. One more wave like that and he'd be in the water anyway, and nowhere near the one piece of hard ground that might still save his life.

"Meet me halfway!" Sami called.

Then she dove. He'd seen her rushing toward the end of that spit of land, but now she had surrendered her safety for him. Alex had wanted to be ready, had wanted to get a good running, splashing start. But Sami had already gone into the water and they were out of time. He took three staggering steps and hurled himself forward, reaching his arms out toward the surfboard—toward his wife.

He plunged into the water just as another wave crashed over him. Alex ducked his head under, fought the powerful current beneath the wave, and rose up again. The surfboard had been dragged nearly sideways, but he saw Sami swimming toward him even as she tried to get the surfboard stretched out between them again.

"Get on, damn it!" he snapped.

She ignored him, and only then did he see the dark length of something in her hand. Something metal, he thought, before realizing it was nothing more than a broken branch. Fifteen feet apart, they swam toward each other. The surfboard filled six of those feet, and as the water began to rise with another oncoming wave Alex lunged and kicked and crossed half that distance, grabbing hold of the other end of the surfboard.

He had a moment to meet Sami's gaze, a moment for them both to feel the strength of that connection, and then the wave crashed over them. They had to kick and grip to keep the surfboard from being carried away, and when the wave had passed they were nearer to Sami's side, both swimming hard, trying to get back to yet another vanishing fragment of the atoll.

Twenty feet from the coral ridge. Fifteen feet. Alex caught up, the surfboard turning so that it was between them. He thought about letting go, but he had no idea if they'd need it, and he liked that for the moment it connected him to his wife. He thought about Sami, about what she'd done—how she'd gotten that branch, which she clearly intended as a weapon. The only trees were by the Coast Guard station. She'd gone back there, trying to find a way to save him. He hadn't brought her out here, it had been a joint decision for them to come, but he knew that she had done it for him. A free first-class Hawaiian vacation had its allure, but she had wanted him to put old resentments behind him. That was the real reason she'd been so eager to make the trip.

Ten feet from the coral ridge. He started swimming harder, kicking his feet, holding the surfboard with one hand.

When the shark surfaced behind him, he jerked to the right. It clamped its jaws down onto the surfboard instead of his arm. But it caught part of his left hand— the one holding the board—in that bite. Alex roared with pain. He tried to pull away, but his ruined hand had been caught in the shark's teeth, pinned against the board as the shark bit down, thrashing its body, trying to bite through the surfboard. He saw his blood stain the board, saw the water wash it away, saw it bloom around them. The moment stretched, the space of seconds seeming to expand to an eternity. Bone crunched and tendons tore and he felt it all. Pain turned to fury and ferocity and Alex used his other fist to pound on the shark's nose, then smash its dull black eye, tempted to try forcing its jaws open but—even in agony— knowing better.

Something gave in his hand, shark's teeth tearing, severing, breaking, and he threw his head back and screamed.

A wave came in, and Sami rode with it. She let the swell carry her up, pushing the board beneath her. Alex saw it happen, closed his eyes against the wave even as he roared again. When he opened his eyes, the shark had pulled away. The spear that Sami had made jutted from its left eye as it submerged, fin barely visible.

"Swim," Sami said. "Jesus Christ, Alex . . . swim!"

He stared at his blood in the water, and the gleaming, dark nub of flesh that floated for a moment just beneath the surface before the current swept it away and it began to sink. His left hand had been mangled. His third and fourth fingers were gone—one with his wedding ring—and he'd just seen one of those fingers sinking into the water. His hand throbbed. In the water, he saw pale bone in the ragged flesh and his blood trailed around him.

Then Sami had him by the arm. He met her eyes.

"Get out of the water, honey."

Alex gritted his teeth against the pain and he swam. It was only a few more feet, really. The shark would be back, or another would come. Sami wouldn't get out of the water unless he did, and that was what really got him moving, what drove him to swim in spite of how mesmerized he'd been by that floating nub of flesh and by the sight of his blood in the water. He couldn't let Sami stay here, couldn't let it get her the way it had gotten the others.

Then his right hand touched the coral, just beneath the water, and he scrambled up the ridge, pulling himself out. Sami climbed out right beside him. Numb with shock, Alex turned around and saw two fins passing in opposite directions, the surfboard rolling on the water between them as another wave crashed through the gap. A round edge of the board had been bitten clean through. It floated out of the gap—

Only it wasn't a gap anymore, was it? The fragment of the ring he'd been standing on had vanished completely. The next one along jutted out like some kind of monument, but it was well over a hundred yards farther around the ring.

Alex smelled his own blood. He inhaled deeply, letting it clear his head. The pain sang through the bones of his arm, throbbing deeply.

Sami took his wrist and lifted the hand.

"Hold this up," she said, turning his chin so that he was staring into her eyes. "I'll bind it. I can stop the bleeding."

Alex took a deep breath. Even the wind and rain hurt his ruined hand, but he managed a grimace that he'd intended as a smile.

"I have faith in you, Dr. Simmons," he said. "Also, I'd like to sit down now."

Sami smiled thinly, nodding, still visibly shaken herself. "Me too. But not just yet. Come with me."

Together they started walking across the thin coral ridge. At the far end, Alex saw Dev cradling Alliyah in his lap, but nearer than that a soaking-wet green towel lay on what seemed the highest part of the ridge. The towel was all that remained of their picnic earlier that day.

It seemed only right that if Alex was to manage to live until morning it would be that remnant of paradise that saved him.

Alliyah felt Dev there. She couldn't open her eyes, but she heard his voice. He whispered to her for a while, with the wind blowing. She could hear the waves and she wondered if it was still raining, because she couldn't feel the rain anymore.

Quietly, somehow so far away, she heard Dev singing softly to her. An old song, a lullaby. He'd often sung it to himself in the shower, and though he had always said it would be her decision whether they had children or not, she had known when he sang this lullaby that he wanted a child to hold.

She hated him.

For a while, she could feel his arms around her. Could feel his body warm beneath her. Knew that he cradled her. Felt a kiss upon her forehead.

She hated him.

He sang, and he whispered, and he told her everything would be all right, until at last she couldn't feel his arms on her anymore. Until, at last, she couldn't hear him anymore.

She loved him.

Dev looked down at Alliyah as he felt her body relax, felt all the pain and tension leave her. As her head began to loll backward, he propped her up, resettled her so that her head leaned against his chest. Her shallow, reedy breathing had stopped, but he started the lullaby over from the beginning, wondering if somewhere she might still be able to hear.

He hated her.

Dev pushed damp strands of hair out of her face and kissed her forehead, and then continued the song, quietly, holding her a bit more tightly now that he knew his embrace could not hurt her.

He hated her.

Dev had let her down. He'd betrayed her faith in him and his own in himself. Now, at the end, he'd been unable to save her or do anything to help, but at least he could do this. Alliyah deserved this much, at least. He could sit and wait with her through the storm and the long night, sit and wait for the tide to go out. Most of her friends had been lost in the lagoon, nothing left of them, but he could see to it that she made it home.

He loved her.

And he sang to her.

And the wind blew.

Sami didn't bother Dev. She saw it happen, sensed it from the way Alliyah's hands drooped at her sides and the way Dev held her more tightly. Sami and Alex were there, so at least Dev wasn't alone, but she wasn't going to disturb him.

"How's it look?" she asked Alex.

He held up his ruined hand. She had torn the green towel into broad strips, using one as a tourniquet to get the blood to stop flowing. Another she'd tied around the mangled hand. Already she'd had to replace that second strip with a third, but now the tourniquet seemed to be working. Alex held the hand up, resting it across his chest. Sami knew that a great deal depended on time, now. The towel had not been dry or clean. The risk of infection was much higher than she'd like. But the blood had started to crust where his missing fingers had been torn away. If she could release the tourniquet now and then to keep the hand from becoming necrotic, and if he didn't get an infection, she thought they would be okay. That they would make it until morning, or until the Coast Guard came to collect them, whichever happened first.

They would get home to Tasha.

If the tide didn't rise any higher.

If the storm didn't get any worse.

If the waves didn't knock them off the little bit of ridge that was all that remained of this fragment of the ring.

"You think you'll live?" she asked Alex, smiling.

"I think *we* will," he replied, his good arm around her.

They leaned against each other and they watched the lagoon. Watched the sharks.

It seemed to her that the rain had let up a little. That the wind had lessened. That the sharks had begun to lose interest.

Maybe, she thought. *Just* maybe.

It was her new favorite word.